山／海／經
CLASSIC OF MOUNTAINS AND SEAS

劉鋆——著

黃效文——攝影

黃效文
與探險學會

Wong How-Man
and 30 Years
of CERS

目錄 CONTENTS

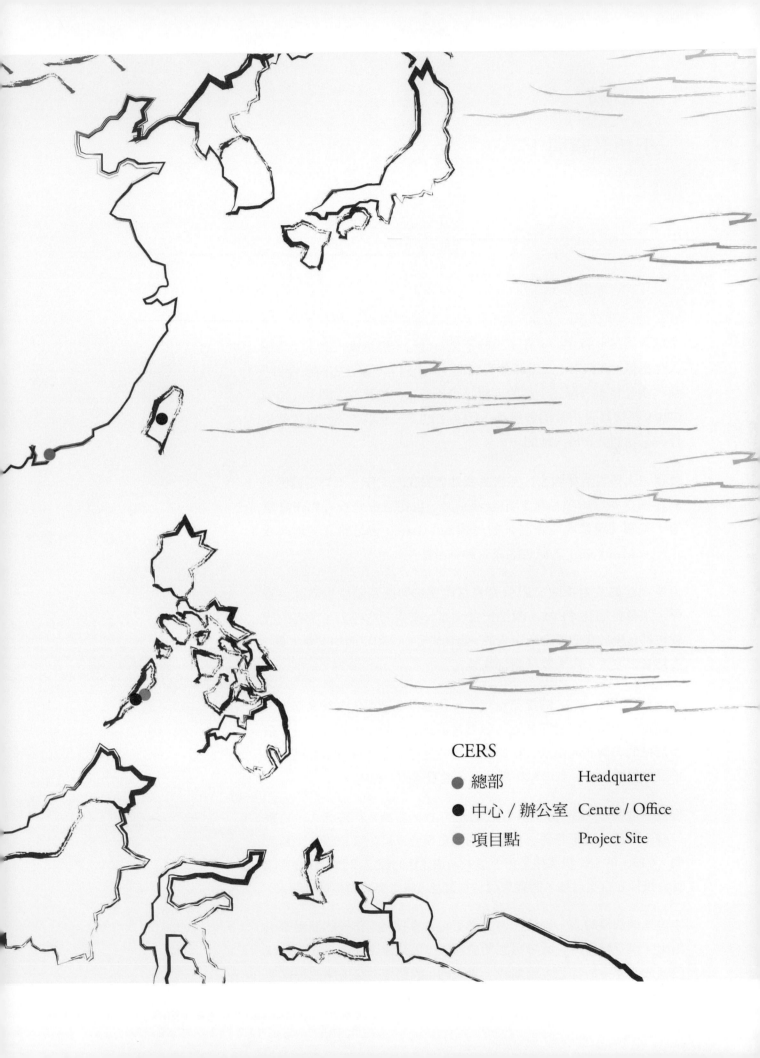

CERS

● 總部　　　　　Headquarter
● 中心 / 辦公室　Centre / Office
● 項目點　　　　Project Site

三十功名塵與土

子曰：「三十而立」。孔子說的不僅為自己，也為後人立下了這個人生指標：人到三十，就該頂天立地。三十歲，不論在古時或今日，都代表壯年；一個三十歲的人應該可以獨立，並昂首人間了。這對CERS同樣具有相當的象徵性，因為CERS三十年了，跨過這個里程碑，我們挺立於天地間。

每當有人稱我為探險家，並告訴我他們對我的工作，不管是攝影，寫作還是執行的項目感到印象深刻時，我總是會覺得有點不好意思。美國《國家地理雜誌》的總編 Bill Garrett 總是開玩笑地叫我「How Man Polo」，這也讓我有點不自在。

但是現在的我對探險家跟保育家這兩個殊榮感到驕傲也默認這身分。這都是因為CERS。我知道這全是大家共同的努力，所有的成就也都是屬於我們學會所有人的。我代表CERS和我們的工作人員，支持者跟友人，向大家感謝這殊榮。

是時候要回顧CERS的這三十年了，我思考著是不是由我執筆，來回顧這三十年。但是我知道，也非常清楚地意識到，我自己是有很多偏見的。倘若能由別人從有點距離的地方來觀察與書寫我們，似乎是比較恰當的，有一點距離但又不是很遠的旁觀者。

很自然地我想到作者劉鋆。過去十五年裡她認識我們許多人，也跟一些人熟識。我不想要一個單純的歷史學者或是紀實紀錄者來寫我們。CERS的工作跟風格是很浪漫的。描述性的陳述我們的探險和成就會很像在自吹自擂，對我來說也很無趣。我想要兼顧事實與個人。

劉鋆是個浪漫的人，她比任何人都更可以將我們工作裡的浪漫帶引出來。幾乎我們所有的項目都始於浪漫，因此灌注在項目裡的熱情已經成為學會的特色。就像我一直說的，我們是從心中開始每個項

At 30, fame and glory are but like dust and earth

Confucius said, " 三十而立 ", meaning "At 30, stand upright". That was in reference to himself, as well as to others, urging that, at mid-life, a man should become independent and stand upright in the world. So it is quite symbolic that CERS has reached its 30th year and crossed that milestone to stand upright.

I used to feel embarrassed when others called me an explorer and said how impressed they were with my work, be it photography, writing or project implementation. I always felt uncomfortable when National Geographic Editor Bill Garrett called me, jokingly, "How Man Polo".

Today however, I take such accolades with pride and acquiesce to the titles of both explorer and conservationist. This is because of CERS. I know that such acclaim is due to joint efforts, and that all subsequent accomplishments have been collective ones. I acknowledge such flattery on behalf of CERS and all our staff, supporters and friends.

When it was time to reflect on CERS' 30 years of existence, I pondered myself writing a book to reflect on these three decades. But I have always known, and am acutely aware of, my own prejudices, and it seems more appropriate for someone to assess us from a distance - but not too far a distance.

Daphane Liu came to mind as a natural choice for the author. She has known many of us, some intimately, for the last 15 years. I did not want someone who is simply a historian or documentarian to write about us. There is a lot of romance in CERS' work, and work style. A descriptive run-down of expeditions and project accomplishments

目，然後腦袋思考才加入規畫和解決辦法。或許浪漫不會永遠持續，熱情也會慢慢散去，但是我們的承諾、承擔與投入都會還在，這是我們的紀律和尊嚴。

我希望這本書紀錄學會這三十年來的成就，以及屬於我們的浪漫風格。稱我們自己為學會只是為了方便。對我來說這名詞很老套也很過時。CERS 是個家，一個大家庭，我們全體一起努力完成任務，而任務也會隨著新的時代與世代的來臨而改變。

宋朝名將岳飛曾說過「三十功名塵與土」。同樣的，我們不應該沉浸在過往的名聲和榮耀裡，我們應該看向未來，下一個三十年。

從前未曾有分厘，
乍看似乎沒道理，
三十年頭已過去，
還幸名字未掃除，
多年短跑西與東，
變成明天馬拉松。

would be like blowing our own trumpet, and indeed quite boring even for myself. I wanted an account that is both factual and personal.

Daphane is a romantic, and she, more than anyone else, should be able to bring out that romanticism in our work. Almost all our projects start with romance, thus the passion in their implementation that has become a hallmark of much of our work. As I always say, we start a project from the heart, before the brain comes in to find a way to make it work. While romance may not last forever, when the passion dissipates, the commitment is still there, a show of our discipline and honor.

I hope this book provides a record of achievements, as well as of the romance and style, of a 30-years young organization. Calling ourselves a Society is just for convenience. It is both a cliché and passé as far as I am concerned. CERS is a family, a very extended family, to all of us who have put effort into fulfilling its mission; a mission that is constantly changing as we move into a new age and a new generation.

The Song Dynasty patriot general Yue Fei wrote in his most famous prose saying, " 三十功名塵與土 " meaning "At thirty, fame and accomplishments are but dust and earth." So likewise, we should not be carried away by past fame and glory, but look to the future and the next thirty years.

In the beginning, it did not have two cents,
For a while it seemed to make no sense,
But for thirty years we have lasted,
Defying those who wished us busted,
Running a sprint three decades old,
Now the marathon is our goal.

他是個「探險家」，也是個作家跟攝影家。

他是 CERS 香港（中國）探險學會的創辦人。這個特別的非營利組織，致力於中國偏遠地區跟鄰近國家的探險，研究，保育跟教育工作。

一九八六年，在美國成立學會之前，黃效文就為當時服務的美國《國家地理雜誌》帶領了六次的探險，定位長江新源頭是他第一件為世人所知的成就。

他帶隊探索四大重要河川源頭（長江、黃河、湄公河、怒江）。是他以藝術的角度讓世界知道藏羚羊的危險處境並給予保護；是他深入藏區尋找並復育純種的藏獒犬；讓緬甸貓回到家鄉也是黃效文與 CERS。

海南島洪水村就這麼剛好讓他知道再過幾天傳統的茅屋即將被拆除，這意外中的難事是要介入，還是別裡它？

他知道如果不插手的話，海南黎族僅存的傳統茅屋以後只能在百科全書裡見到了，他開始張羅尋找資源和協助，花了二年修復了十五棟茅草屋。

這幾年 CERS 將觸角延伸到中國的鄰近國家，包括尼泊爾、寮國、印度、不丹、菲律賓，特別是緬甸。超過十年的時間，他將緬甸從北探索到南，在北部的撣邦進行幾個項目。二零一三年開始啟用一艘 106 呎的探險船，他的團隊將工作重心放在依洛瓦底江和欽敦江的上游，這兩條河是緬甸很重要的動脈。二零一五年 CERS 啟用一艘 70 呎的外伸支架艇在菲律賓的巴拉望從事海洋研究工作。

How Man Wong And CERS

He is an explorer, a writer, a photographer, also a conservationist.

He is the founder of CERS (China Exploration and Research Society). This unique non-profit organization dedicated itself to the exploration, research, conservation and education in remote parts of China and neighboring countries.

Prior to founding CERS in 1986 in the United States, he first entered China as a young journalist in 1974 and later worked for the National Geographic in the US, leading six major expeditions for the magazine. Finding a new source of the Yangtze River was one of his achievements that became known to the world.

He led four expeditions to define the source of major rivers (Yangtze, Yellow, Mekong, Salween). He gave voice to the endangered Tibetan Antelope; he entered deep into Tibet searched for the pure bred Tibetan Mastiff, to start a breeding program; he and CERS searched the world and brought pure bred Burmese cats back to Myanmar.

Hainan Hongshui Village indigenous Li minority's adobe-walled thatch-roofed houses were to be demolished within days; HM saw the opportunity just in time, pondered on it and came to its rescue. If it wasn't for him looking for resources and committed to preserve them, we could only see those precious houses in encyclopedia. At the end he saved and restored fifteen thatch-roofed houses within two years.

In more recent years CERS operated several centers and extended their work to covering China's neighboring countries, including Nepal,

三十年來，CERS 成功地主導多項保育項目，其中多個並製作成紀錄片。黃效文經常受邀到大學跟國際會議上為企業和特定人士演講。他曾被青年總裁組織 (Young President's Organization) 和世界總裁組織 (World President's Organization) 選為最佳演講。他曾多次在倫敦的「英國皇家地理學會」與其香港分會演講。他的探險與保育事業受到許多基金會，個人與企業的支持。

他很主觀也很極端，但他也珍惜他的失敗。
他只是本能地去搶救那些美好的事物。
從小他就知道「不行」不是一個選項。
他說，給我一個三歲小孩，我給你一個探險家。
他對世間萬物的好奇，讓他總是那麼活躍，一刻也停不下來。

他說，當我老了，真的走不動的時候，我就是一個講故事的人，把我所經歷的一切作為故事講給孩子們聽。

二零零二年黃效文被《時代雜誌》選為亞洲二十五位英雄其中的一員，稱他為「中國最有成就的在世探險家」。三十年裡，太多的殊榮與國際媒體報導聚集在這位探險家身上。

這樣的一位華人探險家，我們怎麼能不認識？

Laos, India, Bhutan, The Philippines, and in particular Myanmar. For over a decade, he has explored the full length of Myanmar from north to south, and implemented projects in northern Myanmar's Shan State. Since the launching in 2013 of his 106-foot exploration boat, his team focuses their work on the upper Irrawaddy and Chindwin River, two major arteries of Myanmar. In 2015, CERS also launched a 70-foot outrigger boat for marine work in Palawan of the Philippines.

Wong is often invited as keynote speaker at universities and international gatherings for corporations and select groups of audience. His lectures were chosen as Best of the YPO (Young Presidents' Organization) and of the WPO (World Presidents' Organization). He has delivered several lectures to the Royal Geographical Society in London and to the Hong Kong chapter annually. His work is supported by foundations, individuals and corporations.

He is subjective, single-minded, stubborn and at times extreme, hallmark of an explorer. Yet He values and learns from his failures.

His instinct guides him to save, to conserve what might be endangered. He simply wants to save those beautiful things for our future generations.

Since when he was little, he never took "no" for an answer.

He says show me a three years old, and I will show you an explorer.

He is an incredibly curious-minded person, always very energetic, always active.

黃效文自拍照 1972
Self-portrait 1972 while at college

He says "when I grow old, can't move as freely, then I will be a story teller, I will tell what I have experienced, my tall stories to little kids".

In 2002, Time Magazine honored Wong How Man among their 25 Asian Heroes, calling Wong "China's most accomplished living explorer". Over thirty years, he has won numerous awards and got the attention of various international media.

Such an accomplished explorer, why would we not want to learn more about him?

與景頗族孩童合照於克欽邦 1990
Among Jingpo/Kachin children 1990

若我是你的影子

若我是你的影子
跟隨你探險三十年
跟隨你上高原下江海
知道你的每一步是怎麼跨出的
也知道你停在哪裡
甚至在哪裡轉彎回頭
我會懂得你的故事
在每一個地圖上的經緯交叉點

若我是你的影子
我會知道你有多麼固執多蠻橫
你揮手趕走只會追隨但沒有目光的人
只堅信自己尋找好玩的直覺

在日出的太平洋岸清晨
或者高原帳篷裡冷冽的夜晚
我都得死心塌地的追隨著你
那我會懂得
一次的路過，就是十年的駐足
一秒眼神的關注
就是美好被保留下來的靈光
有些人一輩子關在山洞裡
有些人一睜眼就看到小花盛開
路途總是充滿了驚喜的感動
但我們不敢耽溺眼前的滿足
不曾停下向前探索的腳步

If I were your shadow

If I were your shadow, accompanying you for 30 years over the plateaus, rivers and seas, knowing every step of the way on your expedition and every place where you have stopped to admire nature or were forced to turn back, I would know all the stories about your expeditions over these years.

If I were your shadow, I would know how determined you were in achieving your mission goals and in sending off followers who have no insight and vision, and how confident you were that your instincts on how best to achieve these goals were right.

No matter where you were on mountain tops under the sun or in freezing cold tents at night, I followed you all through. Together we had experienced many delightful and unforgettable moments. We saw small beautiful flowers flourishing in the wilderness, solitary buddhist monks in remote mountain caves practicing meditation for life, etc. Though happy and excited to see all these, we never stopped long before moving on to our destination again.

You have said many people work hard to live but forget that they should also seek to live well. For you, living well is to live an explorer's life, because that makes your life happy and meaningful.

The expeditions you did over the past 30 years were like beautiful landscapes in a picture that a talented artist had painted. I saw that you were this artist ; you painted the maroon robed Tibetan monks, the white snow mountain tops and the white clouds against the blue

跟隨你探險三十年
你說 很多人努力生活 卻忘了要好好生活
你的探險就是生活
而這一切全都是為了好玩

三十年的人生是一張畫布
我見你拿起畫筆 畫下了紅色的寺廟僧人
白色的山峰雲朵
綠色的江洋河水
黃色的土地生靈
藍色的人情世故
多年之後 我們一起回首
這些竟是藏人的色彩
美的醜的 圓的方的 快的慢的
理解的 不理解的 流動的 停滯的
喜歡的 憂愁的 瞬間的 輕聲的
世間萬物 原來全都笑納到這五種色彩之中

此時此刻
我已是你的影子
我看見你將青春年華全留在了那裏
冰雪不融 青春的夢想也就永恆

sky. You painted the yellow and green river courses and grasslands, and wildlife in the wilderness and people in tranquil villages. A few years later, if we look at the picture again, we would realize that it is a masterpiece melting all things, all minds and feelings, into its beautiful colors.

I am your shadow now. I can see that you have devoted the best time in your life painting this picture. I have no doubt that your achievements and contributions will be long remembered.

＜ 緑・水 ＞ #Green・Water

在藏傳佛教中有一門獨特的宗教藝術「壇城沙畫」，Dul-tson-kyil-khor，藏語的意思是彩粉之曼陀羅。繁華世界，不過一掬彩沙，多日而成卻可瞬間散去。壇城中的北方以綠色表現，在佛教中綠色不空成就佛代表著北方。

綠，也是水。

Mandala pictures (Dul-tson-kyil-khor) made of colorful sands are a special form of art in Tibetan Buddhism. A subtle message that these pictures convey is that everything in our world is as impermanent as the sand images which form the picture. Green color in a mandela picture represents Buddha of the North. For the ordinary people, green stands for rivers and water.

因畏懼，順水而下；若為感恩，逆江溯源。

若要認真地從歷史或契機說起「香港中國探險學會」的成立，
就不得不回到 1985 年 HM 在美國國家地理雜誌支持下進行的
「長江溯源行」。那年，HM 重新界定了長江源頭。在此之前，
世人所認識的長江源頭是沱沱河源（通天河支流）的格拉丹東
雪山；然而，在 HM 的這次溯源後，長江的源頭被重新界定在
通天河的另一條支流「當曲」的源頭（發源於霞舍日阿巴山），
這個發現讓長江的長度增長了 6.5 公里。

「長江溯源」、「黃河溯源」這些項目聽起來無比浪漫，但執
行起來卻必須是科學與理性的，這完全符合 HM 喜愛極端的
個性。1985 年 HM 得到美國太空暨航空總署噴射推進實驗室
（NASA／JPL）的支持，從太空梭照片中成功判讀出長江的這
個源頭，然後經過縝密的規畫與無數的會議後才讓這個探險不
只是紙上談兵。這個計劃讓 HM 從一個浪漫的夢想者躍升為理
性的實踐家。我們不妨回過頭來看看 HM 的成長過程，當他在
美國威斯康辛大學念書時，同時修讀浪漫的「藝術」與追求真實
的「新聞」；他讓他孩童般的天真與好奇在藝術裡恣意生長，卻
也同時用著另一半的科學頭腦去平衡他嬉皮的浪漫情懷。

6.5 公里也許對這條全長 6300 公里的世界第三大河本身來說算
不了甚麼，當時也沒有馬上讓 HM 成為中國英雄，但這 6.5 公
里卻為這位華裔探險家未來之路打下的最堅固的基礎。

逆流上達三江源，探險學會也順水而下將項目發展至緬甸，甚
至容納百川的海洋。探險的方式也變得更全面，從四輪的探險
車到完全不用輪子的河船，唯一不變的是那個對世間萬物的「好
奇心」。

"Those who are frightened will proceed downstream to seek safety, only the grateful ones will go upstream to reach the river source."

CERS was founded in 1986 after an expedition to the source of the Yangtze River. The expedition, led by How Man and supported by the National Geographic Magazine, redefined the source of the River. Prior to the expedition, the River's source was erroneously taken as on the slope of the Geladandong Mountain, from which the Tuotuo He River (a tributary of the Yangtze River on the Tibetan Plateau) runs. The real source as found by How Man, was on the slope of the Xiasheriaba Mountain, from which another tributary of the Yangtze River on the Tibetan Plateau, the Dangqu River, runs. HM's discovery put 6.5 km more to the total length of the Yangtze River.

Going upstream along the Yangtze and the Yellow Rivers to their sources were romantic enough. But when one actually wants to do that, he needs to have a scientific and logical mind. Being romantic, logical and scientific, How Man was therefore most suitable for these tasks. In 1985, with the help of NASA, How Man scrutinized photographs taken of the Tibetan Plateau by the Space Shuttle and came to the conclusion that people in the past might have erroneously determined the source of the Yangtze River. Subsequent debates, discussions and researches by him and his explorer friends all concurred that his postulation was highly likely to be correct. So after the necessary preparations an expedition was organized. How Man was a romantic dreamer when he was young. He was also pragmatic too. So when he went to the University of Wisconsin to study, he took art and journalism as his major subjects.

The length of the Yangtze River is 6,300 km. Adding 6.5 km to this length is really not something very important in some people's eyes. And How Man was not made a hero because of his discovery. The expedition was however very important to HM, because it laid down a firm foundation for him to build his career as an explorer.

Expeditions which How Man subsequently did include those to the three rivers source region, along the Irrawaddy River in Myanmar and in the seas into which these rivers flow.

三探長江源頭・掬飲長江水

Thrice Expeditions to the source of the Yangtze River

當個探險家最棒的是「總是期待驚喜」

As an explorer, I always expect surprises.

---How Man

- 19 名探險隊員，包括醫生、生物學、地理學、人類學及太空科學的各類專家，與來自英國的 Land Rover 專業維修人員。
- 以在阿多鄉衛生院任職的茶高為首，帶領 6 名藏族嚮導。
- 26 匹馬，9 頭氂牛，7 天的糧食。

「1985 年探險前，我研究了 1984 年太空梭上傳回的大底片影像，當時這條支流不巧被雲層所遮掩。對於六千四百公里的河流來說，一公里不算甚麼；然而在河源上游比較兩個源頭時，長度相差一公里的話，意義就格外重大了。」這個在電腦螢幕上看來也許不到一公分的差距，卻讓 HM 發動了第三次長江溯源。他的第二次長江溯源是在 1995 年。

與二十年前的不同是，這次的出發地是 CERS 的雲南中甸中心；不變的依然是高原上的遼闊景致與突如其來的驚心大雪。每次的出發，探險隊並不會只有一個目標，只做一件事情。這次的終極雖然是要再次尋找長江新源頭，然而很多高原上的項目都在這次的路程上繼續著。協助土木寺重建藏醫學院的評估、發放可自行調整度數的眼鏡給偏遠地區的藏族、甚至意外地解救了兩隻幼隼而讓整個探險隊心情大好。這些在探險路上所發生的事情，不禁令人聯想到從自然取用並給予回饋的概念。青藏高原與天相接，風光縱然美好，但也總是會不經意地就丟出難題來試探企圖接近的人類，但只要謙卑地知道人類在大自然前有多麼的渺小，並懂得敬畏，高原也可以成為祝福之地。

探索新源頭的那日清晨，東南的雪山格外耀眼，地面上的一層濃霜也因朝暉而閃爍著童話故事般的金色光點，探險隊伍輕裝騎馬進入加色格拉山麓並沿著多朝能上溯。

* **The 19 members CERS expedition team included a doctor, a biologist, a geologist, an anthropologist, space scientists and an engineer from Land Rover.**

* **The 6 members Sherpa team was led by Chagao, a staff member of the Aerduo County Clinic.**

* **Logistics : 26 horses, 9 yaks and 7 day's water and ration.**

" Before taking on the 1985 expedition, I studied the photographs of the source region of the Yangtze River taken by the Space Shuttle. The entire length of this tributary was not shown on the photograph because of a piece of cloud above it. The distance between these two points is about 1 km, which might sound insignificant compared with the total length of the River, which is 6,400 km. But when they are two sources of the River, that makes a difference." The two points as appear on the computer screen was less than 1 cm apart, but that's more than enough for How Man to decide to launch a third expedition to the source of the Yangtze River. How Man's second expedition to the source was in 1995.

The third expedition was started from CERS' Centre in Zhongdian, Yunnan. Like previous expeditions on the plateau, these were strikingly beautiful landscapes, and there were snow storms that God has sent down to test How Man and his team's will. On the way, the team took the opportunity to continue some of its previously launched projects. These included distributing adjustable focus eye glasses to Tibetans in remote corners on the plateau, and helping the Tumu Monastery design and plan its work for rebuilding its school of Tibetan medicine.

「不同於若霞能的源頭，那是從地底湧出的泉眼；多朝能與格拉丹
冬的源頭類似，都是雪山融雪！」HM 恍然大悟的說著。是的，即
使再先進的科技也無法分辨出源頭是泉眼還是融雪，一切都必須自
己到達此地親眼為憑，而這，也就是探險的重要意義不是嗎？

- 北緯 32°36"14'
- 東經 94°30"44'
- 海拔 5710 公尺
- 2005 年 6 月 15 日下午 1 點 15 分

「就是這裡了！」HM 向空中拋灑了五彩風馬旗，拿著一片經幡鋪
在源頭處。他選了一池雪穴，下有雪水流經，代表源頭，並在雪地
跪下，以雙手捧起雪水，一飲長江水。

長江流域哺育超過四億人口，也是醞釀中華文化的母河之一；在
二十一世紀初，CERS 仍然能為地球上如此重要的地理特徵做出這
樣的貢獻，真的很棒！

The team marched along the Duochao Creek towards its source on
a valley slope of Mount Jashigela under the golden rays from the
morning sun. Reaching the source, How Man discovered that, unlike
the source of the Ria Sha Neng Creek which is a fountain, it is a piece
of wetland formed by melting snow. He knelt down scooped and drank
a palmful of water from the source. A prayer flag was land on the
ground and colorful prayer leafs were thrown up the sky.

* **32° 36' 14" N**
* **94° 30' 44" E**
* **Elevation 5,710 m**
* **Date : 15 June 2005. Time : 1315 hours**

Down this source flows the great Yangtze River, which nurture more
than four hundred million people in China. CERS is glad to have
contributed to people's knowledge about its sources.

湄公河發源地‧瀾滄江源頭‧
水是冰的卻暖了心

Source of the Mekong River
Icy cold water but heart warming

影子問：「藏人心中的瀾滄江源頭，跟衛星圖片上的源頭不是同一個地方呢？怎麼辦？」

HM 說：「這兩個發源地都很重要，都能夠振奮人心，彼此相輔相成，所以我們要把雙腳踏上這兩個源頭，一個也不能少！」

與長江、黃河一樣，湄公河上游的瀾滄江也同樣發源於札曲的高原濕地，但湄公河所代表的意義跟長江很不一樣。長江從源頭、流域全在中國境內，是一條完完全全的中國河流；湄公河全長四千九百零九公里，滋養著六千萬以上的人口，雖然不及長江所哺育的四億人口，但它流經亞洲六國（中國、寮國、緬甸、泰國、柬埔寨和越南），且河川地貌多元而豐富，是一條重要的國際大河。相對於中國的忽視，國外的探險團體對這一條「亞洲的萊茵河」卻有著更多的關注。因此為湄公河覓源，似乎更有跨越國與國，民族與民族的深刻意義。

為了這趟湄公河源頭探勘之行，CERS 從 2006 年就開始深入寮國境內的湄公河流域，而蜿蜒於泰國與緬甸邊境的熱帶叢林河段，CERS 也早就探訪過了。很多時候，花在準備上的時間要比行動階段更繁複與長久。

探險隊先繞道去看了藏人心中的瀾滄江源頭，那是一塊隆起的土地，上有一組水泉，流水汩汩，多少有些神秘性，它代表的不只是傳統更是信仰。30 年來的每一次探險，最仰望的還是老天的眷顧。這次，老天施了魔法般地在隊伍往源頭推進時停止了風雪，並露出一小塊藍天跟隨著 CERS。騎馬九十分鐘後，來到五千一百公尺高的果宗木茶山脊，刻有「瀾滄江源」的水泥石碑在此，這是 1999 年由中日合組的科考團所立。但 CERS 當然繼續跟隨科學家馬丁·路賽克 Martin Ruzek 手上的 GPS，朝著有科學證據的源頭前去。

The shadow asked: "What the satellite picture shows as the source of the Salween River (the section of the Mekong River in China) is not considered as correct by the Tibetan. They believe a different source elsewhere is the River's true source. What's your view on that How Man?"

HM replied, "Both sources are important and worth investigation. So we will go to both locations to see for ourselves."

Like the Yangtze and Yellow Rivers, the source of the Salween River is also located on the Tibetan plateau, in a place called the Zaqu wetland. The former two rivers run in China all the way. The Mekong River, however, runs through China and five other Asian countries (Laos, Myanmar, Thailand, Cambodia and Vietnam). Though the population this 4,909 km river nourishes is not as big as the Yangtze River, it is nonetheless very important due to the fact that it is an international river encompassing many different cultures.

To prepare for the expeditions to the source of the Mekong River, CERS first went through the section of the river in Laos in 2006. And before that, CERS had covered the section that twists between the Thailand and Myanmar border.

The expedition to the river source was conducted in 2007. CERS' expedition team first proceeded to the source which the Tibetan regard as the river's correct source. It is a piece of raise wetland. The weather was rather unsettled with occasional snow storms in the general area of the source. However the team was very fortunate in that, in its last 90 minute journey to the source on horse back, a small piece of blue sky was all along above it. This source, situated on the slope of Mount

· 北緯 33° 42" 38.8'
· 東經 94° 41" 45.4'
· 海拔 5175 公尺
· 2007 年 5 月 13 日 12 點 45 分

經緯度是科學的，時辰則帶有個人性。在那個時刻，汲飲一條世界
大河的源頭水既真實又神秘；這一掬水在科學上或精神上都是無比
潔淨的。執意到河水源頭的這個行為，除了彰顯人類在地理學上追
根溯源的探險精神外，更伴隨著一些難以言喻的情感心理。當科學
與心靈在如此聖潔的地方相遇，對 HM 而言，後者其實是更深刻的，
但是對於那些無法親自踏上江河源頭的多數人來說，科學的事實更
有其重要的意義。二十年前當 HM 第一次嘗到長江源頭的雪水時，
他寫下了一句話：水是冰的，但溫暖我的心。在湄公河上游、瀾滄
江源頭，他又體驗到了相同的感受。

Guozongmucha and had an elevation of 5,100 m, was marked with a concrete tablet which reads "Source of Salween River". The tablet was erected in 1999 by a team of explorers comprising Chinese and Japanese.

After this the CERS team then proceeded to the other source, which all scientific data indicate that it is the real source. With the help of Martin Ruzek's GPS the CERS team successfully located and arrived this source.

* **Position : 33° 42" 38.8' N; 94° 41" 45.4' E**
* **Elevation : 5,175 m**
* **Date : 13 May 2007. Time : 1245 hours**

A strong urge to discover the truth and an explorer's perseverance have enabled How Man, time and again, to succeed in his expedition goals. The wind was chilly, and the water he drank from the source was icy cold. His heart was however warm, and he was experiencing the same joy he felt twenty years ago when he first reached the source of the Yangtze River.

黃河新源頭・遠上白雲間

New Source of the Yellow River
Faraway among the White Clouds

- 18 名探險隊員成功抵達
- 21 天的高海拔歷程，徒步行走世界屋脊 50 餘公里

這一趟的溯源又有了全新體驗。不知道是不是因為詩人李白的「黃河之水天上來」，明明依賴著的是馬丁・路賽克的衛星圖像與 GPS，但心中的那個黃河源頭卻一直是在地平線最遠處的雲朵之間。又是一次詩意與科學的戰爭。

二十年前進藏時，探險學會的車隊總是夾雜在一輛輛超載的解放牌車陣中；現在因為青藏鐵路的開通，公路明顯地順暢了，危險超車的情況也少了很多。翻過 4767 公尺的崑崙山口，過去幾年保護藏羚羊回憶頓時湧上隊員的心頭。沿途經過的區域都是保護動物的出沒地，對 CERS 來說再熟悉不過了。這十幾年的時間，透過類似 CERS 這樣的 NGO 的宣導以及當地人的自省，大家開始有了保護動物的意識，就以野犛牛來說，從當時觀測的二十多隻，到現在已經有了一百多隻了。只是，便利文明的入侵，連高原上的藏民都無可抵擋；就像帶有色素的果汁飲料開始取代孩童碗裡的酥油茶那樣，一路上摩托車愈來愈多，就連平坦地區也出現了牧民以摩托車趕羊群的情況，真是令人驚訝。

一夜風雪，抵達黃河源頭的那日清晨，帳篷四周一片銀白，探險隊在細雪中朝著天邊前進，而這個心中的天邊其實就是巴顏喀喇山脈，探險隊翻越的這個陵線是長江與黃河的分水嶺。三個小時的徒步之後，HM 找到一個明顯的小水道，在眾人的見證下，將之標明為黃河的源頭，也就是黃河之水天上來的那個「天上」。

天上的座標是：
- 北緯 34° 29" 31.1'
- 東經 96° 20" 24.6'
- 海拔 4878 公尺
- 2008 年 6 月 29 日 12 時 15 分

*18 team members successfully reached the source.

*21 days on the plateau; walking over 50 km on foot on roof of the
 world.

In one of his poems, famous Chinese Tang Dynasty poet Li Bai said
the Yellow River is a river that flows down from the sky. How Man
knows that this is poetic exaggeration, and that the River's source can
be determined scientifically by satellite pictures and Martin Ruzek's
GPS instrument. He and his team marched on towards the location of
the source, which seems always lies beyond the horizon, according to
readings on the GPS instrument.

20 years ago when CERS' caravan went onto the Tibetan plateau, the
roads were dusty and the Liberation trucks running on these roads were
all overloaded with cargo. Nowadays these roads are much better and
safe and scenes of cars and trucks dangerously overtaking others are no
longer common sights. When passing through the Kunlun Mountain
Pass, How Man and his team members recalled the years they spent in
the vicinity to help protect the Tibetan antelopes. They remembered
the landscape and the wildlife they spotted were still vivid in their
memory. Over the years, local people on the plateau have gradually
become aware of the importance for them to protect nature and the
wildlife in it. In the past when such awareness was weak, sighting
of wild yaks was rare. The largest herd of wild yaks CERS had ever
spotted was only about 20. But now herds comprising as many as 100
can be seen on the plateau. Improvement in roads and modernization
have also changed people's style of living on the plateau. More and
more local people are drinking pre-packed fruit drinks instead of the
traditional yak butter tea, and most herdsmen are riding motor bikes,

中國地圖和世界地圖都將從此改寫了！黃河，中國的第二大河，這麼重要的一條河川，竟然在人類都上了月球將近 40 年後，還能被改寫，這個源頭比先前所知道竟然長了 15 公里。HM 向當地牧民們確定了這個源頭的名稱：發源於巴顏喀喇山脈的廣東札仁山，這條小支流被當地牧民稱為「札隆插呼曲」，它一路流向拉哈湧，與卡日曲、瑪曲匯流後進入扎陵湖形成黃河。

黃河之水由這個天上流向人間，與長江、瀾滄江一起孕育著兩種重要的文明：藏族文化與中華文化。至此，CERS 已經成功的探索了三江源頭。HM 按例將五彩色風馬旗懸於源頭上方，也同時向天空飄灑一落落的紙龍達，藏人相信風神可以接收這些訊息並帶給大家好運與祝福。HM 跪下掬飲黃河水，表達的不僅是 CERS 成就了這個歷史，更是感恩上蒼在 CERS 每一次的高原探險上所給予的包容與祝福。

「為甚麼要去找河流的源頭呢？現在的科技已經這麼進步了，在家裡 google 一下，那個源點就馬上可以跑了出來，不用幾秒的功夫，也不用這麼辛苦。」

「人類知道月球幾千年了，但是當太空人雙腳踏上月球的那一刻，可是一個劃時代的大事呢。同樣地，當我們站在河川的源頭時，他可能是我 HM 的一小步，但誰又可以說那不是人類的一大步呢？」

instead of horses, to drive their livestock to the grazing ground.

The morning the CERS team reached the source area, the place was covered with snow from the previous night. Snowing had not stopped yet, the team marched on towards the source along a ridge of Mount Bayankhar and came to a pass on the ridge. This is the watershed for the Yangtze and Yellow Rivers. After walking for three more hours, the team found the source ----- a piece of wetland from which a small water course originates and flows downward. Location, date and time as follows:

*34° 29" 31.1' N
*96° 20" 24.6' E
*Elevation 4,878 m
*June 29, 2008; 1215 hours

CERS' discovery of this source has added 15 more kilometers to the total length of the Yellow River. CERS' enquiries with the local herdsmen people revealed that the small water course is a tributary of the Jarong Qahu River, which in turn is a tributary of the Ka-ri Qu and Ma Qu Rivers. The Ka-ri Qu and Ma Qu Rivers then flow down the Zaling Lake to form the Yellow River.

The Yellow River and the Yangtze and Salween Rivers are three great rivers that nourish the Tibetan and Han cultures. CERS has by now successfully reached all their sources. In accordance with usual practice, How Man placed a prayer flag above the source and flied prayer papers into the sky. He then knelt down to scoop and drink water from the source. These ceremonies were meant as gestures of gratitude to heaven for all the care and blessings it has extended to the

society during its journey to the source.

"Why bother to take all these hardship and troubles ? Is it not true that a click on the Google map will get you all the information about the location of the source ? "one would ask. "That is very different" How Man replied, "just like knowing that there is a planet called the moon and actually stepping foot on it !"

與死亡擦肩的怒江探源

Expedition to the Source of Nu Jiang River
Narrowly Escaping Death

我珍惜我的失敗，我很主觀！

I value my failures. but I am very subjective.

---How Man

· 北緯 32°43"07'
· 東經 92°13"46.2'
· 海拔 5374 公尺
· 2011 年 6 月 14 日 15 時 1 分 30 秒

「這一切就像昨天才發生的，然而我休養剛滿一個星期，才能開始記述。」

這是一個所有人都不願意再次經歷的探險，但卻又最常被提起。HM 在他的探險筆記上這樣的開始這個探源之行。

六月，夏天，花朵綻放，旱獺、兔鼠成群，高原的生命欣欣向榮。選擇在這個季節踏上準備數月的探源就是為了避開高原惡劣的天候，沒想到，就在這明亮的夏日面具之後，大自然著實給了探險家一個陰暗恐怖的試煉。

成功地探過長江、黃河與瀾滄江源頭後，怒江源當然就成為 CERS 探險名單上的首位。怒江源頭位於海拔五千三百多公尺的唐古喇山南麓，水源來自高山冰河。當地藏人稱源頭的小溪流為阿隆，往下叫嘎東曲，然後是卡獲曲；經一一八班道注入安多的措那（黑湖）後，經雲南流向緬甸，改稱薩爾溫江，由毛淡棉注入安達曼海。怒江總長約三千五百六十二公里，流域面積二十六萬六千零三十七平方公里。整個二十世紀，探險家和科學家都沒有找到它的源頭，雖然曾經有過幾次的嘗試。

早在 1930 年間，英國的兩位探險家 Kaulback 和 Hanbury 就組隊並花了一年的時間企圖找到怒江源頭，然而惡劣的天候讓他們差點送命，不得不放棄。HM 帶著這兩位探險家的書籍前往源頭，希望能夠完成他們的使命，也是一種致敬。美國航太總署科學家 Martin Ruzek 利用高解析度的不同太空影像來測量水源區，幫忙界定了上

* Latitude 32° 43" 07' N
* Longitude 92° 13" 46.2' E
* Altitude 5,374m above sea level
* 1501 hours, 14 June 2011

"It seems like that all these happened just yesterday. I needed to rest for one whole week afterwards." How Man wrote in his expedition diary. No one in the CERS wanted to experience the same situation again, but everyone has been talking about it every now and then.

June and summer on the plateau are prosperous and lovely times. The place is full of sunshine, wild flowers, marmots and wild rabbits, and weather is usually mild and temperate. CERS therefore chose to do that expedition in June. However things did not turn out as smoothly as How Man had expected. The plateau wanted to put How Man and his expedition team to a test.

Having previously reached the sources of the Yangtze, Yellow and Lancang Rivers, CERS now turned its attention to the source of the Nu Jiang River, which lies on the southern slope of the 5,300m of Tanggula Mountain. There is a glacier at this location. Melting water flowing out from this glacier turns into a small stream and runs downward to form the uppermost stretch of the Nu Jiang River. This small stream is called the A-long River by the local people. Running downwards, the A-long River is joined by other, shorter tributaries (the Gadong and the Kahuo Rivers) to flow into the Cuona Lake in Anduo and becomes the Nu Jiang River. The Nu Jiang River continues its course in Yunnan and then flows into Myanmar. From this point onwards, the River is referred to as the Salween River by westerners.

游地區的許多支流。當然 Martin 所發現的怒江源頭得靠著 CERS 的實地考察才能給予證實。

單從地圖來看，怒江源落於西藏自治區內的唐古喇山脈，離青藏公路的唐古喇山口直線距離應在三十公里內，真是簡單。所有的隊員也都認為這將是一趟愉悅的溯源之旅；然而，面對大自然，人類最好懂得謙卑，這次與死亡擦肩的經歷是在抵達源頭、欣喜地完成任務後，在回程所遭遇的。

十九名隊員、五部越野車、一大堆器材、工具、食物在敦煌會合，六月十日出發。大隊人馬穿過祁連山、柴達木盆地、越過崑崙山向西藏高原前進。六月十一日晚在海拔四千七百八十五公尺的雁石坪紮營，高度嚇人的唐古喇山就在頭頂。當晚就有幾個隊員開始出現了高山反應。六月十二日越過海拔五千三百多公尺的唐古喇山隘口南行約二十公里後離開公路。草原上冬季的堅硬路跡，到了夏天就成了沼澤和軟泥；於是越野車相繼陷入動彈不得，半天的時間就在陷車、挖車與拉車中，大夥耗盡力氣。關於探險，很多時候，當我們在觀看影片或閱讀書籍時，總會把「結果、成就」看得太重，只記得贏得喝采的那個時刻；然而，在整個探險之路上，那個「風光的時刻」其實真的只是片刻而已。那天晚上，HM 決定在一棟牧民的房子附近設立基地營，距離源頭的直線距離是十七公里，海拔五千零六十公尺。

六月十三日，由於前一日的軟泥路況，CERS 決定向牧民租借馬匹前往源頭。只是高原上摩托車取代馬匹已是不爭的事實，所以也費了一番功夫才找到肯出借的馬匹，但其中不少根本只是「駑馬」，早就不是可以跟著騎士闖蕩天涯的那種，事後證明，這也是回程隊員之所以會落入險境的其中一個因素。

六月十四日，整隊出發前往怒江源頭。一早天氣好極了，藍天在上，

The Salween River flows on and finally exits to the Andaman Sea. The whole length of the River is 3,562 km and its basin areas is 266,037 km². For the entire 20th Century, explorers and scientists had been trying to determine the River's source but to no avail.

In 1930, an exploration team led by Kaulback and Hanbury spent one year trying to locate the River's source. Their attempt did not succeed because of bad weather (which almost killed them). How Man had read their books about this expedition with interest. He also brought them along in his expedition to the source. He hoped he could reach the source to finish their unfinished task and he believed that that is the best way to show his respect to the pioneers.

Before starting the expedition, NASA scientist, Martin Ruzek had carefully studied high definition satellite photographs of the River's source area. After these studies, the location of the River's source was found. What was left was to actually go there to confirm the finding.

From the map, the straight line distance between the River's source to the highest point on the Qinghai-Tibetan Highway (the Tanggula Pass) was about a mere 30km. "Easy job, going to be like a leisure walk," How Man and his CERS team thought. They would later realize that, when dealing with mother nature, people should always be humble. They succeeded in searching the source, but on their return, they went into trouble and narrowly escaped death.

The 19 member expedition team started their journey in five Land Rover on 10 June in Dunhuang after getting all supplies, equipment ready. The caravan passed through the Qilian Mountain, the Caidamu Basin, the Kunlun Mountain and moved towards the Tibetan plateau.

所有人都興致昂揚。這個探源之行計畫是一日來回，所以大家都只帶著水和點心，類似 power bar 和糖果。經過七個小時的「馬上」時間，一行人終於抵達一座寬闊的山谷，開始沿著小溪前行，直到距離冰河源頭差不多五百公尺時，馬匹無法再走因為地面布滿大圓石與碎石塊，因此大家下馬改為步行。小心翼翼地徒步前進，有時還必須橫著跨步，當爬過最後一道像是小啞口的山脊時，隊員們知道，怒江源頭就在前頭。

「最後二百公尺特別令人欣喜，我一陣風般地走完，此刻的快意彷彿令我腋下生出翅膀，拖著我前行……」這是多麼美妙的描述，在 HM 就要碰觸怒江源頭的那一刻。

畢蔚林博士拿出全球衛星定位系統，Christ 的攝影機也在不停地轉動，CERS 就這樣將世界最美的座標記錄下來，那一刻在所有隊員的心中，沒有更美的地方了。一如以往長江、黃河與湄公河的探源達陣，HM 跪下，從冰上挖開的洞裡，汲水而飲。隊員分享了一罐可口可樂和一瓶 Moet & Chandon 以示慶賀。

一小時之後，回基地營的路上，CERS 遭遇了高原在夏季最惡劣的暴風雪。HM 與隊友沒有回到基地營，若不是有牧民的小屋提供避難，他們也就只能暴露風雪當中，聽天由命。另外兩名隊友甚至和大家走散，在幾乎失溫的狀態下好不容易才躲進牧民帳篷，得以全身而退。這是一段完全彰顯在大自然前人類渺小的經歷，隊員們的生存不僅得於高原牧民之助，更是老天的仁慈。

預期輕鬆的行程竟然成為一趟玩命之旅，人類的計畫再細膩，也抵不過大自然的一瞬之怒。難怪 HM 總說，在大自然裡，最能使人謙卑。

On the night of June 11, the team reached Yanshipin and camped there. The altitude here was 4,785 m and several team members started to have altitude sickness. On June 12, about 20km after the Tanggula Pass, the caravan diverted from the Qinghai-Tibetan Highway and went along a dirt truck in the wilderness. As the team went deeper and deeper into the wilderness, it ran into a big piece of marshland. All the Land Rover sank into the soft mud. Team members spent great effort to try to pull them out but failed. All were very exhausted and it was getting dark. How Man decided to set up tents next to a herdsman's shed and spend the night there. The altitude here was 5,060m and its straight line distance to the source was 17 km.

As it was not possible to proceed further by car, How Man decided to go on horseback. On June 13, How Man went to some local herdsmen to ask if they could rent some horses to the expedition team. This wasn't an easy task because fewer and fewer herdsman people kept horses these days. Most people were using motor bikes instead to herd their livestock. In the end, however, they gathered some horses and rented them to the team. Some of these horses were small and weak, but nonetheless the team had to accept them because these were the only horses the herdsman could find for them.

In the morning of June 14, the team set off to the source on horseback, weather was great with bright sunshine and clear blue sky, and team members were happy and high-spirited. As the distance to go was not long, only a day's journey to and back, all carried light (just some drinking water and snacks like power bar). After 7 hours on horseback, they arrived an open valley and saw a small stream. They proceeded upstream towards the source, which as situated near the edge of a

glacier. When the team searched a point about ½ km from the source, they had to dismount and walk as the way ahead was full of big rocks and boulders and not passable on horseback. They walked on carefully and then, after climbing over a small mountain pass, they saw the source.

"Walking the last 200m to the source was so delightful. I felt like having wings and had searched the source by gliding." How Man recalled.

At the source, Dr William Bleisch took readings from his GPS equipment. Chris was busy recording the event with his camera. How Man knelt down, scooped a palmful of water from the source and drank it, like he did in the past when he reached the sources of the Yangtze, Yellow and Mekong Rivers. All were submerged in a joyous mood. To celebrate their achievement, a can of Coke and a bottle of Moet & Chandon were opened and shared among team members.

The team stayed at the source for about one hour before starting their journey back. On the return trip, weather had turned suddenly, a blinding snow storm came down on the team. They lost their way back and if it wasn't that they were lucky to find a herdsman's tent nearby to take refuge, they would have been killed by the bad weather. Two team members even lost contact with the main party for several hours. When they finally managed to get to the refuge tent to join the main party, they were in very bad shape because of hypothermia. After calming down in the tent, all were grateful that they were still alive. They had also learned a good lesson: human being is totally helpless when confronting the nature, so they need to be humble and not try to go against its will.

緬甸河船

The HM Explorer

好玩很重要，浪漫與理性的中間叫「好玩」

In between romantisicm and rationality is a process called "fun".

---How Man

伊洛瓦底江，在上個世紀乘載著太多的生命與故事。河水濯濯，漲潮時，水淹土，土化作河水，土水交融，成一黃色水脈。綠川雖不綠，水邊黃土卻因覆草而青綠，而滋養萬物，滋養緬甸一百三十多個民族。HM 相信，除了 Pagoda 佛塔和稻田，還有其他的很多東西可以代表緬甸，標誌緬甸的。如果因為 CERS 的觸角延伸，而能為當地保留或創造甚麼的話，那麼 HM 絕對是要跑在前面的。加上對於新鮮感的追尋，HM 這幾年逐漸將 CERS 的重心從青藏高原向外移動，鎖國多年的緬甸，正符合他心中值得探險的地域。

伊洛瓦底江最大的支流欽敦江，又名更的宛江（Chindwin River）在二次世界大戰時尤為出名。主要是因為孫立人將軍領導的中國遠征軍曾在仁安羌一役中以寡擊眾，以不滿一千的兵力擊退十倍的日軍，然後救出了十倍的英軍，並且躲過日軍的追擊，以竹排渡過寬五百公尺的更的宛江，成功保留主力轉入印度。遼闊的更的宛江是一道難以跨越的天然鴻溝，包含中國遠征軍在內的盟軍和日軍，大家都在此付出了慘痛的代價。悲傷的詩歌流淌在這黃濁的河水與陸上的叢林裡：

節〈森林之魅—祭胡康河上的白骨之祭歌〉
註：胡康河穀為欽敦江上游地區，1943 年中國遠征軍與日軍曾在此激戰

在陰暗的樹下 在急流的水邊
逝去的六月和七月 在無人的山間
你們的身體還掙扎地想要回返
而無名的野花已在頭上開滿……

靜靜的 在那被遺忘的山坡上
還下著密雨 還吹著細風
沒有人知道歷史曾在此走過
留下了英靈化入樹幹而滋生
　　　　　　　—穆旦 1945 年九月

The Irrawaddy River nourishes some 130 races and peoples in Myanmar. Along the river bank, HM saw many pagodas and paddy fields."Apart from those pagodas and paddy fields, there must also be other things that people will see as symbols of Myanmar," How Man thought. Always wanting to search and discover new things, HM started to turn his attention from the Tibetan plateau to Myanmar, a country little known by the outside world because of its isolation from the international community.

The Irrawaddy River's largest tributary is the Chindwin River. Chindwin was famous in WWII because of a battle against the invading Japanese forces. A dispatch force of Chinese soldiers led by General Sun Liren miracally defeated a regiment of Japanese soldiers ten times its size and successfully saved a similarly large regiment of besieged British troops from being annihilated by the Japanese. The British soldiers were then able to safely retreat into India, crossing the Chindwin River by bamboo rafts. Many lives were lost in the battle :

"Underneath the trees and on the river bank,
You lie silently and motionless,
Your souls wanting to crawl,
Over the hills and mountains full of wild flowers,
To return to your homelands.
Rain drizzle on these hills and mountains and
Soft breezes brush the flowers and grasses on them.
Your flesh and blood have nourished them,
And your heroic acts will be remembered."

A poem composed by Mudan in September 1945

2013 年，CERS 打造的探險家號（HM Explorer）正式下水，開始伊洛瓦底江與支流沿岸的文化考察與水文紀錄。探險家號船身長三十公尺，寬五公尺，以柚木分築成兩層船艙，並巧妙的隔出了六個艙房與一個餐廳，船頂上有開會的區域與工作台。另外還有三艘橡皮艇與八輛自行車，橡皮艇可以載隊員到河輪無法進入的支流探勘，自行車則便於拜訪鄰近的村落。

就像文學家們心中那艘〈開往中國的慢船〉一樣，HM Explorer 以時速每小時約 13 公里的速度沿著欽敦江向上游航行，神秘的北方緬甸。許多不知名小村子開始有了 CERS 的足跡，從製作陶罐的幾十戶小村子，到仍舊用著傳統木造織布機的世外桃花源，或是村子裡的傳統市場，CERS 想的是如何為這些珍貴的傳統文化注入新的價值。「add value」是 HM 很重要的工作哲學，因此項目的實際內容跟選擇項目本身一樣的重要。若是無法為這個地方加分，就乾脆不要做。

HM 喜歡這麼說緬甸：「有路可到的地方，大概落後文明世界五十年；沒路可到的地方，落後一百年。」這艘 HM Explorer 帶著探險隊伍跨越時空，回首記錄與研究那些尚未被文明改變或摧毀的原始緬甸風貌，自然的與人文的。終於，探險家可以又再趕到改變之前了。

從一雙夾腳拖鞋和一件桶裙（longyi），HM 融入緬甸當地生活，沒有客人的時候他甚至可以光著上身閱讀和工作。小時候的 HM 騎著兩輪的自行車從香港半山衝向灣仔碼頭上學去。開始探險之路後，他的四輪傳動 Land Rover 帶著他上到青藏高原經幡飄揚之處；此刻，他的探險工具成了不用輪子也能前進的三十公尺長河船。

大河上的航行是一個孤獨的旅程，隔著水，彷彿就與世界隔絕了。伊洛瓦底江邊的佛塔一座接著一座，「你若不親身經歷，你不會知道日出前的一個小時會有多特別」HM 對著我這個沒有陽光就不會

In 2013, CERS constructed and launched a river boat "HM Explorer". Designated for cultural and heritage research along the Irrawaddy River, the teak wood boat is 30 m long and 5 m wide. It has two decks, six cabins, one canteen and a roof working/meeting platform. Three inflatable boats and eight bicycles are stowed on board as means of transport to shallow water places and villages along the river bank.

Like "on a slow boat to China", navigating upstream at a speed of 13 km per hour, HM Explorer has since visited many villages along the river. These ranged from small villages with a dozen or so households, to places where people are still using traditional materials and methods to produce earth pots and containers, or are still using the long obsolete hand driven wooden weaving machines to produce cloth. To How Man, these were heritage from the past and he was glad that he would still see them today. He was also considering ways to help these villagers add value to their industries.

HM said places in Myanmar were behind the world in almost everything by fifty to hundred years, depending on their accessibility. The HM Explorer was therefore like traveling back in time, allowing CERS to see and experience matters and things that have long disappeared in the outside world.

HM was quick to adapt to Burmese style of living. While on the HM Explorer, he often wore only slippers and the traditional "longyi" (kind of skirt) which the Burmese wear, leaving his upper body naked. After a day's work, he would enjoy reading on the desk. He remembered his school days in Hong Kong, riding an old bicycle to Wanchai to get to school. After becoming an explorer, his means of transport have

出現的影子說。而我卻清楚知道，2006 年那幾個對美毫無保留的伊洛瓦底江上日出，早就徹底擄獲了 HM 的探險之心。

<Jungle Salt> 裡 說 "you can take a man out of a jungle, but if he is born to it, you cannot take the jungle out of a man." 好奇、冒險和不聽話是流淌在 HM 血液裡的，因此我們完全不用擔心他有一天會失去這些特質；一如我們的血型，是不會因為愛或不愛或經歷世事風霜而轉變為另一種的。

diversified : bicycles, horses, Land Rovers, and the present 30 m river
boat.

A boat journey on the river is a lonely one. How Man appeared to
have been isolated from the world. Silently the boat passed pagoda
by pagoda along the river. With a calm voice, How Man said to
his shadow "If you haven't experienced this, you never know how
different it is before and after sun rise on the river." As HM's shadow,
I know the sun rises and mornings on the Irrawaddy River in 2006
have completely captured his soul and mind.

A passage in the "Jungle Salt" said " you can take a man out of a
jungle, but if he is born to it, you cannot take the jungle out of him."
Similarly, for a person with such keen interest to discover things and
venture into the unknown like How Man, these is no doubt that all the
qualities that make one become an explorer have embedded deep in his
character. No one can take these out of him.

茵萊湖與緬甸貓復育

Inle Lake & Burmese Cats

給我一個 3 歲的孩子，我給你一個探險家

Show me a three years old child, and I will show you an explorer.

---How Man

初夏的湖水有點枯竭，湖面上本來自由漂浮的綠色小島遠望都成了陸地。雨季來臨之前船伕還要負起挖深河道的工作，把一船一船的河底淤泥堆積岸邊，這樣才能確保河上的每一條小船都能快速安全的到達他們的目的地。過度的開墾使得茵萊湖的面積迅速萎縮，在傳統和現代的汰換過程中，茵萊湖所孕育的傳統文化也面臨危機。

為了讓更多當地人與外來遊客可以更深入地認識緬甸，CERS 特別將「緬甸貓」與「水文生態研究」這兩個項目與茵萊湖上的 Inthar Heritage House 合作。HM 將原本已經在緬甸消失了的緬甸貓，從澳洲、英國找到香港復育，經過三年的努力重新引回緬甸。現在，那成功復育的四十多隻緬甸貓儼然成為 IHH 的吉祥物了，幾乎所有的參觀者或住宿旅客都會花最多的時間去認識與陪伴那些超乎想像與人親近到黏人地步的緬甸貓們。最近，連緬甸總統也來這裡參觀緬甸貓的復育工作。

CERS 在茵萊湖的基地位在河道與河道中的綠草地上，乾季時看到的是草地，還有稻田，雨季來臨時，低處當然就成一小片汪洋。大風吹或有船經過時，都能感覺房子在搖動，但這種高腳建築卻是這個區域最傳統且安全的建築。學會附近的高腳房子裡很多織布的工作坊，時不時傳來傳統織布機的答答聲。此刻，夾雜織布機柱聲裡的是 CERS 的工作人員用著她們熟悉的緬甸母語熱烈地討論全新項目。

三個年輕的緬甸女孩，其中兩人擁有碩士學位，正一言一語地激盪著彼此腦力，看看如何把 CERS 為自己家鄉所做的項目轉化成一本有趣的漫畫書，好讓更多人知道自己家鄉的珍貴事物正在被保留下來。HM 不介意從頭教起沒有經驗的年輕人，反而，他要凝聚當地人的活力與向心力。但他會嚴屬要求他們展現出沒有模式可依循的創造力，因為他本人，就是這樣的不受限；如果這是一個好的溝通媒介，那麼就可以是 CERS 的項目，決不會因為沒做過就不做。你很難在他不同的探險項目中看到相同的筆觸，唯一的線索就是那種

The water level was a bit low in Inle Lake in early summer. What used
to be an island in the lake had now become a small mound on the dry
river bed. Workers were busy dredging the river bed and depositing the
dredged mud onto the river bank. This would ensure, when the rainy
season comes, the river is navigable again. In recent years, the size of
the lake was shrinking due to reclamation to produce more farm land
by the local people. Traditional things were also gradually dying out
because of the intrusion of modernization.

To help local people preserve things that are indigenous to Myanmar
and also to help visitors and tourists better understand the nation,
CERS had launched two projects (one concerning the pure bred
Burmese cats and the other water ecology) in conjunction with the
Inthar Heritage House (IHH), an constitution that is situated on the
Inle Lake. The pure bred Burmese cats had extinct in Myanmar for
quite some time, to bring them back to Myanmar HM first acquired
a number of these pure bred felines in pet shops in England and
Australia and bred and reared them in Hong Kong. The pure breds
were then flown to IHH and kept there. There are now more than 40
of them. As they are playful and active, teasing and stroking them have
become visitors' and tourists' most enjoyable past time at Inle Lake.
Even Myanmar's president recently came here to visit.

The CERS/IHH base in Inle Lake is situated in a house supported by
poles above the water (or ground in dry season). When boats pass by
or when there is wind, you can feel the house sways a little bit. But
don't let this frighten you: this type of traditional houses have been
proven to be the most safe in the area. In the neighbouring houses
there are many weaving workshops. Amid the weaving sounds the three
local CERS staff members would discuss and debate in their mother

推到極端卻又力圖平衡的冒險精神吧。

從緬甸貓的復育開始，到伊洛瓦底江的河豚水文生態研究，以及緬甸幾種傳統手工藝的保護與再生（像是 Nang House 裡蓮藕絲製品；CERS 的 Bamboo House 裡的傳統竹藝製品等等），都是 CERS 希望能成為緬甸文化中足以讓世人所知的美好。

CERS 在緬甸已經有十年的積極投入了，很多人會問這裡的項目是否已經「完成」了，其實對 HM 來說，這些項目才沒有所謂「完成或結束」的那天，因為在深耕緬甸十年後，新的項目「漫畫伊洛瓦底江」才正要開始起步呢，HM 的執著加上當地年輕人的熱血，令 CERS 在緬甸的項目頓時年輕活躍了起來。

探險家的雙眼究竟會不會有失焦或模糊的時候呢？身為他的影子，我很希望能走到他前方看看，但是三十年了，HM 始終走得又快又急，我也只能好好跟著，因為他根本不休息，靠岸也只是為了尋找另一個好玩的目的地而已。探險家的雙眼總是聚焦在下一個目標，這就是他，就是 CERS。

language on how best to perform their assignments.

There are three young Burmese girls. Two of them hold a Master Degree. Their brain storming discussion was about producing an interesting cartoon book to arouse their fellow country men's awareness on protection and preservation of precious traditions. How Man likes using young persons and doesn't mind teaching them how to work from the very beginning. What he wants from them is that they should have creativity, team spirit and determination to accomplish the goal. And these are the very qualities that he and other successful explorers possess.

The pure bred Burmese cats and the water ecology (including study of the river dolphin) projects, and the projects to resurrect/preserve some traditional local Burmese industries (e.g. products made from lotus roots silk, bamboo products), are the areas of work CERS has embarked. CERS hopes that these works would help people in the outside world better understand and appreciate Burmese culture and traditions.

CERS has begun worked in Myanmar for more than ten years now. For How Man, these works will continue in future in order to arouse and sustain the local people's awareness to preserve and protect their traditions and culture. A new project on compiling the cartoon book about the Irrawaddy River has also just begun, drawing new bloods from the local community.

As How Man's shadow, I have been following him all along. He seems never wanting to stop to rest, and is always in search of a new assignment.

從流放到度假．
海南洪水村黎族保護項目

Project in Hong Shui Village,
Hainan Island

就像好萊塢電影《緊急救援》或《即刻任務》那樣，對於洪水村內黎族房舍的保護，一刻也不能耽誤。HM 第一次誤打誤撞地見到這個村子的時間是 2007 年三月三日，而這個村子的拆遷執行日是在 2007 年三月十五日，他只有不到兩個星期的時間來留下這個村子。HM 很清楚這是最後一座這樣的村子了。於是他四處奔走透過層層關係，終於暫時拖住了改建方案的實施。那個三月底，他也迅速地向當地縣政府提出了可以挽救多達二十棟傳統房舍的計畫，終於，政府被說服了，願意採替代方案，將村民遷往另一塊鄰接的土地。

洪水村隱身於海南島西部昌江縣的霸王嶺山腳，一棟棟茅草為頂的房子，位於水田邊，聚落成村，且有椰子樹錯落其間，完全是以一個時空膠囊的狀態，讓黎族的生活樣貌停滯在至少五十年前。從三亞或海口開車兩個小時可到縣城，從縣城需要另外兩個小時才能到達洪水村。因為地處偏遠與交通的不便利，甚至在十多年前這裡都還是瘧疾疫區；許多年長婦女臉上都還有刺青。在大多數黎族人已經融入漢族社會的今日來說，這樣的村子當然十分珍貴。這也必須拜洪水村地處偏遠所賜，因此才會被不顧一切向前衝的時代巨輪遺落在後。不僅房舍仍保持著傳統的茅草屋頂，洪水村地區也擁有十分多元的生態，僅剩的十幾隻黑冠長臂猿在霸王嶺一帶活動，品種豐富的日間與夜間飛蟲、甲殼蟲，甚至尺寸較大的壁虎和蜈蚣，整體來說這種多元的現象是大自然夠原始與未受汙染的指標。

儘管探險學會擁有的人力與財力都有限，但是很明顯地，人口一百二十萬的黎族傳統與建築型態絕對需要被保留。這是一個道地的、無瑕的傳統房舍，而不是那些以觀光為目的，徒有門面的歷史村。原本是海南島或中央政府的工作，再一次，又掉進了 CERS 這個非營利的小組織的手上。這又回到 HM 的個性，如果算得太多就根本不可能開始這個項目，重點是要拯救海南原住民黎族的傳統村莊，加上情況急迫，必須且戰且走。其實，早在 1980 年代初期，

Hong Shui Village was a traditional Li people (a minority people on Hainan Island) village. Situated at the bottom of the Bawangling in Changjiang County on the west of Hainan Island, it was remote and difficult to access. Like isolated from the outside world, the way and style of living, and all things in this village were pretty the same as it was 50 years ago. When HM first learnt of this village and went there on March 3, 2007, the local authorities were in the process of moving out all the villagers to a new settlement and pull down the entire village.

Because of poor medical conditions, the village was proliferated with malaria a decade ago. The older females in the village still had tattoos on their faces when HM first arrived there. As more and more Li people have integrated themselves into the Han community, things indigenous to the Li race were gradually disappearing in the village. Houses in the village were the tradition Li style thatch-roofed huts with walls constructed of mud bricks. Behind the village was the Bawangling, where a dozen or so black headed gibbons could sometimes be seen. In the nearby brush areas, insects, beetles, centipedes and geckos were plentiful, indicating that the environment surrounding the village was largely uncontaminated.

In Chinese history, Hainan Island is traditionally very undeveloped. In the old days, exile prisoners were sent there. Emperors also liked to demote officers they don't like to work as magistron on the island, as a mean of punishment. When How Man first stepped foot on Hainan Island in the early eighties, he saw many traditional Li villages. These were villages comprising purely the traditional Li style huts thatch-roofed and walls built with mud bricks. In later years, with a blind

HM 就已經造訪過海南的黎族村落，那時的村莊都還保有原始的風貌，才不過二十幾年的「現代化光陰」，就讓幾乎所有的傳統房舍面目全非－這些水泥牆加鐵皮屋頂的新房舍，沿著道路的兩側一棟接一棟，整個村子看起來跟收容難民的招待所差不多，連生活都顯得單調無趣。

然而，能夠成功說服當地政府接收 CERS 的保護計畫，靈活運用媒體也是其中的關鍵。新加坡的《新海峽時報》在 CERS 抵達洪水村的一個月內就報導了這個重要的文化遺產所面臨的威脅；然後是台灣雜誌的跟進，以長文做大篇幅故事；《亞洲華爾街日報》也用了三整頁做了報導；洪水村的紀錄片也快速製作完成；就連香港無線電視台的一組人員也跟著 CERS 的腳步進入洪水村。繼藏羚羊的項目後，CERS 又再一次的結合了眾人的力量來打贏這場仗。

兩年的時間，除了有項目計畫的負責人常駐以外，HM 跑了六趟，其中一次甚至帶著十七個人的大隊伍前來，裡面有各類型的專家，每個人都貢獻了一己之力。這個項目的進行分成三個階段，首先取得管理權的九棟房舍，其中六棟改成居住的房舍以及餐廳、工作間。第二階段則將三間房舍改為一個高級別墅和雙間套房，透過台灣設計師黃毓芳的設計，讓人們看見維持傳統的房舍特色也可以成為一棟棟獨特且有價值的黎族家屋。第三階段則是博物館與展示廳的修建前後共十五棟房子。關於中國少數民族及民族地理圖書，CERS 可是主要的收藏者，光是關於海南島的就有超過一百五十件書籍、文稿、論文，這整套複本都將藏於洪水村。這些茅草為頂、土磚為牆的簡樸的小屋讓人置身真實的場景，體驗真正的少數民族 -- 黎族的文化。未來的學者和科學家會明白，無論在軟體或硬體上，CERS 所做的都在學術研究上提供了很高的價值。對於那些黎族的下一代來說，CERS 希望他們不僅能夠享受到經濟進步、教育提高的福利，過去的歷史則會讓他們知道自己這個種族的完整性與文化的認同。

quest for "modernization", more and more people in these villages pulled down their traditional style huts and built concrete walled, zinc roofed houses, making their villages as unsightly as refugee camps. Fewer and fewer traditional Li villages could be seen. How Man was quite sad about that.

As soon as he learnt of the Hong Shui village and that this was about the only Li style village left, How Man immediately went there to plead the local authority not to pull it down. That was on March 3, 2007 and the target date for pulling down the village was March 15, 2007. How Man also asked those of his Mainland friends who might have an influence to help him. In parallel with these internal works, he also succeeded in getting some outside media to help him. His plea to preserve the vanishing heritage was reported by the Asian Wall Street Journal, Singapore's "New Strait Times", Hong Kong's Television Broadcasting Limited and several magazines in Taiwan.

These efforts paid. The local authorities were successfully persuaded to amend its plan to allow for some 20 tradition Li style houses to remain in the village. They also approved a CERS proposed project on restoring and fitting onto these houses and on how they should be used and managed.

In the following two years, for the purpose of the project, How Man and his CERS staff went to the village on six occasions to help and oversee the work. A CERS staff member was also stationed there to ensure smooth progress of the project. On one of the occasions, How Man took 17 professionals along, among them were architects and experts in other field, to survey the place and the houses to lay down specifications and procedures for the restoration and fitting out works.

很多時候，立意的良善並不能保證結果一定是好的，洪水村的項目從此刻來看確實有很大的問題。在熱帶的天氣狀況下，若是沒有長期的看顧與人員的居住使用，這些傳統天然建材的茅草屋是很容易就損壞的；加上並沒有找到合適的人來做商業性的經營管理，這批傳統房舍並沒有起到 CERS 當初所設想的作用。項目負責人王健花了整整七個月的時間在這裡，一個人，一部車，滿是遺憾的說：「如果再找不到適合的人來經營管理，或許就回到最初的想法，將這些修繕好的房子交給當地鄉政府來處理了……」。

這個項目給了探險學會一個很好的思考，跨度大的文化的保存與再生需要更全面的計畫和組織，滿腔熱血是行動的必需，但也要為「再生」與「永續」做更冷靜的全盤規劃才是。

在歷史上，這個名為「不歸島」的流放之地，顯然已經成為當代中國達官貴人（甚至一般民眾）的度假天堂了。不管是唐朝的李德裕甚至文人蘇東坡，若地下有知，一定又會大嘆生不逢時了！

Among these experts was famous Taiwanese architect Hwang Eufung. The project was in three phases. The first one was to restore six houses and fit them out to contain dwelling, dinning and working spaces in the interior, retaining the Li traditional style and fashion. The second phase was to restore those houses and to fit out their interior into a bungalow style double room accommodation. This was meant to demonstrate to people that primitive looking, old fashion, traditional houses can have a comfortable interior. In the last phase, fifteen houses were restored to become libraries and exhibition rooms. The books and exhibits were all provided by CERS and they were all about subjects and matters concerning the Li people or the Hainan Island. CERS hopes that the work it has done in Hong Shui village would provide a good basis for future scholars and researchers who want to know more about the Li people, their culture and traditions. For the Li people, CERS hopes that its work would prompt them to treasure and identify with their own culture and traditions.

Despite CERS' good intentions, a problem is now facing the project. Under tropical, humid conditions and without people constantly living in or caring for these houses, which are made up of primitive materials like thatch and mud, they will become worn out or damaged easily. CERS' resident staff in the village Wang Jian was all by himself for seven months looking after these restored but empty houses. So far neither he nor How Man had been able to find someone willing to manage and run the village as a show piece of the Li people culture. "If this situation continues, we will need to adopt our contingency plan of letting the local authorities to manage and run the village" he said.

Palawan – HM Explorer II

CERS 像一席自助餐，每個人都能以自己喜好
選擇其中項目。

**CERS is like a buffet table, you can choose
what interest you.**

---How Man

過去的 30 年，「水」總在探險之路上扮演著將 HM 浮抬起的那個
角色；現在，CERS 開始將項目觸角從高原陸地的大江大河伸進廣
納百川的海洋了。

巴拉望的探險 2 號 （HM Explorer II ）已經在 2015 年五月成功下
水。很快地，巴拉望外海一千七百個島嶼間的珊瑚礁、熱帶魚、海
龜、鳥巢、洞穴等等都將走進 CERS 的海洋研究之內。為何是巴拉
望呢？應該不只是海水漂亮夕陽美好這樣的理由而已吧。也許就像
海洋探險家庫斯托在他的探險生涯接近尾聲時說的，巴拉望提供海
洋生物學家種種海中生物與生態系統，是最好的研究地點之一。在
它的海水仍舊清澈，海風沒有汙染之前，很慶幸 CERS 就採取了行
動。30 年的探險之路，讓我們也把心情從高原轉換到海邊，且拭目
以待 CERS 萬花筒般的探險驚喜。

For the past 30 years, How Man's exploration trips had always got something to do with water, like finding sources of the big rivers on the Tibetan plateau. In recent years, How Man's attention has turned away from the plateau to some where else. But it is still about water. This time it's the crystal clear sea water in Palawan, Philippines.

Palawan is a large piece of water in the Philippines that has some 1,700 islands, sea cliffs and sand and coral reefs. In this piece of water, there are numerous sea caves, green turtles and many kinds of fish, birds, and bird's nests. According to ocean explorer Jacques-Yves Cousteau, this piece of water is one of the best places to conduct research on ocean ecology. CERS is set to conduct study and research there before the place get polluted and, for this purpose, has acquired a sea vessel the HM Explorer II in May 2015. Let's wait to see what delights and amazements the CERS will bring us.

溯源的探險在抵達源頭的那一刻確實很浪漫，但路程的艱辛與考驗才最令人刻骨難忘。　上／中：黃河源 2008　　下：瀾滄江源之行 2007

The moment reaching the source of the Yangtze River felt romantic. The hardship of the journey was most memorable.

Above: Yellow River Source 2008

Bellow: Lancang River Source 2007

三十年來探險隊員以天地為家，更懂得以謙卑的心與自然
共存。阿爾金山。

When dealing with mother nature, people should always be
humble. Mt. Arjin

探險路上的驚奇是，你不知道藏在藍天白雲後的會是甚麼。
三十年的學習：再好的越野車都會陷入於青藏高原的泥巴裡。
左：長江探源路上 2005　上／中：藏北高原 1993
下：阿爾金山 2010

Learning from the exploration is you will never know what hides behind a blue sky. After thirty years of learning: Even the finest off-road jeep is mired in the mud on Qinghai-Tibet Plateau

Left: Yangtze River Source Expedition 2005

Top/middle right: Northern Tibetan Plateau 1993

Bottom right: Mt. Arjin 2010

在冰原，在雪地，前進湄公河源頭依靠雙腳、馬匹、
犛牛、思念與意志力。 左：基地營

Base camp, riding and hiking to Mekong source.

菲律賓巴拉望的海上探險研究船 HM Explorer II
HM Explorer II, exploration and research boat in Palawan, Philippines.

（左上）茵萊湖上緬甸貓的第一個家。
(left top) Burmese Cat's first home in Myanmar. Inle Lake.

（左中）茵萊湖上的傳統竹編屋，生活、工作幾乎全部可以在一個屋子裡。
(middle left) Inle Lake bamboo house. A place for work and everyday living.

（上排中）茵萊湖的夕陽時分，湖中島，水上屋，寧靜的緬甸水鄉。
(middle top) Sunset at Inle Lake. Island in the lake, water bungalow, serene county in Myanmar.

（上排右）以茅草蓋頂的海南島洪水村的原始聚落，像是存活在百年前的時光膠囊中。
(right top) Village sealed in time capsule. Hainan Hongshui village, thatch-roof houses.

緬甸探險河船 HM Explorer I 停靠在小村渡口，一早就有當地居民頭頂食物趕往市集。

HM Explorer I docked at a village in Myanmar. Early in the morning villagers were heading to the market carrying goods on top of their heads.

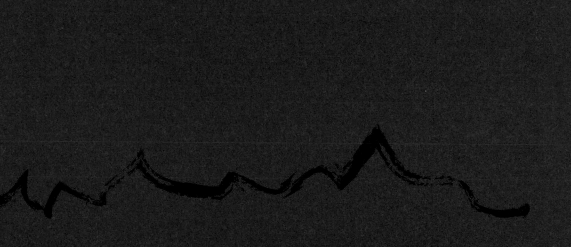

〈紅・火〉 #Red・Fire

在藏族的宗教與藝術世界中，代表紅色的西方極樂世界坐鎮的是阿彌陀佛。早期在印度，紅色是最不起眼與低廉的顏色，因此出家人以此為衣著色，以示不受世俗干擾，超脫外表，只求精神的完美。

In Tibetan art and religion, red color is the symbol of Amitabha, buddha of the Western Pure Land. In ancient India, red color was considered cheap and unpopular. Monks wore red robes to show that they want to distant themselves from secular ties and affairs, and that their pursuit is for purification of spirit and mind.

用斧頭把烏雲劈開吧
騎白馬的婆婆來了
騎黑馬的婆婆也來了
太陽快點照過來吧
讓騎黑馬的婆婆快點走吧
——藏族童謠

清晨薄霧，像白色絲帶一樣隔斷山腰。中甸迪慶機場四周的山
頭依然覆雪。跟每一年的每一天一樣，神山給予藏族人保佑，
CERS 也剛剛結束了這次的達摩祖師洞行程。此刻是 2016 年五
月十日，距離 HM 第一次踏上這塊應許之地已經有三十年了。
這三十年間烏雲曾經密布，HM 也曾像個天真的小孩般，拿著
斧頭奮力劈開空中的陰霾。當年陰霾不知飄向何方，但舒展婀
娜的彩虹確實在他的照片裡出現過好幾次。

CERS 在藏區的三十年探險中，與宗教有著像火與薪柴那般密切
的關係。更與僧人和阿尼們一起創造了許多奇妙的故事。

那一年，一個在冰川旁閉關二十五年、赤足、披著長捲髮的喇
嘛多加，對著白雅仁波切說，HM 是佛教寧瑪派創始人蓮花生
大師的第二十五個大弟子。雖然當時的 HM 因為思及自己多采
多姿的俗世生活而一笑置之，但以這樣一個並未皈依任何教派
的俗人來說，HM 與高原上的寺廟、僧人的種種緣分確實是神
祕難言的。

因為修復壁畫，使得雲南唯一一座藏族尼姑寺裡的八十七個尼
姑從此改變命運；因為尋找長江源頭，路經並協助達賴七世出
生地房頂漏水的修繕，因此與扎西仁波切結緣；因為扎西仁波

"Axe open the dark cloud and out runs two old women, one riding a white horse and the other a black one. Pray the sun will come out too so that the old woman on black horse dare not come down on us" --- A Tibetan children's folk rhyme.

The thin morning mist was like a white ribbon on the mountain slope. The mountains off the Diqing airport were still covered with shining white snow. These mountains were considered dwelling places of the gods who give protection and blessings to the local Tibetan people. This was the morning of May 10, 2016, just after CERS had made an expedition to the Damozong Cave. Thirty years ago HM came here and, like the innocent kids in the folk rhyme, diligently axed open dark clouds of difficulties and established CERS. Now the dark clouds are gone and sunshine and rainbow have taken over, as can be seen in many of the photographs he has taken. There were many fascinating stories about CERS' encounters with Tibetan buddhist monasteries over the past 30 years.

One year, a bare footed and long haired lama Duojia, who had just finished doing solitary meditation on a remote glacier for 25 years, told a fellow lama, Rinpoche Baiya, that he had no doubt that HM was the 25th reincarnation of a principal disciple of the Holy Monk Padmasambhava, founder of the Nyingma Sect of Tibetan buddhism. HM brushed off the proclamation with a smile. He was not a buddhist and was still very much attached to secular live. Maybe, unknown to him in his precious lives, HM was really somehow connected with the Holy Monk or certain monasteries in Tibet.

切與 CERS 成為好友，他因而協助了 CERS 藏區的許多項目，像是純種藏獒的尋找。協助土木寺修建後山的擋土牆也是一個珍惜緣分的好例子。

藏區的三十年裡因為路過而結的緣分，如同瑪尼堆上飄揚的經幡，早已無法細數，也無法知悉這些緣分飄揚到了哪個角落、影響了哪次和哪些人的相遇又或者哪個項目的完成。有些人因為項目而結識，又因這些人的結識而推動了另外的項目，善因善果循環生息，是佛陀給予 CERS 最良善美好的回應。

在五彩風馬旗飄揚的青藏高原上，或許一般人的眼裡只有藏傳佛教的身影，然而，HM 卻找到了 1952 年最後一個離開那塊土地的天主教傳教士－沙智勇神父。為了清楚 1949 年新中國成立前天主教在藏區的狀況，HM 溯著沙神父的足跡從台灣天祥一路到了瑞士的大聖伯納教堂。沙神父娓娓細數的故事不僅讓 HM 紀錄了那段歷史，更讓兩人成為跨越世紀、種族、文化、與信仰的忘年之交。

CERS had helped the only Tibetan buddhist nunnery in Yunnan mend
and recover its precious wall paintings. Completion of the work had
resulted in protection of the nunnery's future and great improvements
in the nuns' living conditions. While on the way to discover the
true source of the Yangtze River, the Society met Rinpoche Tashi.
He became the Society's good friend after it helped fix and repair
the leakage on the roof of house where the 7th Dalai Lama was born.
He also helped the Society launch many projects in various Tibetan
communities. Examples included researching for the pure bred Tibetan
mastiffs and construction of a containing wall to prevent mud slide
behind the Tumu Monastery. These projects in turn resulted in the
Society getting to know more ethnic Tibetans and becoming their
friend, and gradually getting more and more people to understand
and appreciate the Society's values and goals. The Buddha had said,
by sowing seeds of kindness and love, fruits bearing a higher level of
kindness and love would be harvested. This was a motto that HM and
the Society always bear in mind.

達摩祖師洞

Master Damozong Cave

下一次如果有人問「你看過這個嗎？」
你應該回答：「還沒！」

Next time when someone asks you "have you seen this?", you should answer "Not yet!".

---How Man

掛經幡、念經、煨桑，這個由 CERS 修復過後的達摩祖師洞旁的閉關室 2016 年五月正式啟用。來自台灣星雲大師的毛筆大字「禪」被安靜慎重地掛在閉關室的牆上。跟著扎西仁波切和 HM 的規律腳步，一行人開始了今年薩珈達瓦節（SAKADAWA）的轉山。雖然只是藏人轉山中的「小轉」，但達摩祖師洞這個項目在所有人的預期之外出現；也在所有人的預期之外就有了成績，這讓達摩祖師的本命年，猴年，的薩珈達瓦節（SAKADAWA）別具意義。

我們也許很難把這個項目跟長江探源或者黑頸鶴的保育相比較，時間、精力、費用都無法相比；但小，並不一定不重要，HM 喜歡「在大裡找小」做些畫龍點睛的項目，這個短而快速的項目也完全印證了 HM 的那句話「算得太多就做不成事」。

類似的項目還有西藏邊壩的東普增登寺，這個寺廟位於西藏東部，有雪山、冰川相伴，天堂似的地方。只是 2014 那一年，這個寺廟的閉關室卻只是三間破敗的傳統藏式房舍，連屋頂都只是以泥漿澆在乾草枯枝上而成。不到幾個小時，沒有多餘的形式與廢話，CERS 現場立約並拿出現金協助修繕保存這三間房舍。幾個修繕的原則也清楚明確：不用水泥，保留土牆、土磚，原本已經在壁上的圖畫紋飾盡量維持原貌。CERS 在青藏高原上的很多項目都是一期一會的因緣，難怪 HM 總喜歡說，做好事也是需要機緣和運氣的。

這些因緣際會型的項目多半決定得很匆促，但，絕不草率。能夠快速準確的做這樣的判斷，除了跟 HM 急躁不願等待的個性有關以外，很重要的一點來自於他大量閱讀、大量吸取相關知識的習慣。他的博學與見聞總是讓人驚訝，但他卻也能誠實地承認自己並非一般人眼中的「好學生」。他喜歡比較考是非題時的 0 分與 100 分，他說 "I learn, but I don't study"，不管這是不是他年輕時叛逆的藉口，畢竟以結果論英雄，這個得過《時代雜誌》亞洲英雄頭銜的 HM，完全可以把這個觀念作為他成功人生的哲學之一，不是嗎？

The cave chamber where Master Damo practiced meditation was refurbished by the CERS. In May 2016, refurbishment work was completed and a ceremony marking the occasion was held. Prayer flags were raised and incense burnt. A piece of calligraphic work (bearing the Chinese character "Zen" by Taiwan's Master Buddhist Monk Hsing Yun was solemnly put up to the chamber wall. Slowly and step by step, HM and Rinpoche Tashi then led all those attending the ceremony to walk round the hill where the cave was situated, starting the year's Sakadawa circumambulation event. Master Damo was born in the year of the monkey and 2016 is also a year of the monkey. This, together with the fact that the CERS has successfully completed the Damozong Cave project, have given the ceremony a special meaning.

Although the efforts, time and funding which the CERS has spent for this project were small compared with that for finding the origin source of the Yangtze River, or that for protection the Black-necked Crane, it doesn't mean that it is not important. HM always believes small can be beautiful. He said if one only looks for grand and magnificent things, he will miss many things really worth doing, as these are often not shinny or so eye catching.

Another similar project was done in the Dongpu Tsengteng Monastery in eastern Tibet. The monastery was located in a heaven-like place, surrounded by snow capped mountains and a glacier. In 2014, CERS passed by and noticed that the monastery's chambers for solitary meditation (three Tibetan style sheds) were in a very ruined and dilapidated state. Their straw and mud roofs were leaking seriously. Without further ado, the Society immediately signed up to pay for the repair and renovation of these chambers. The only condition the

Society imposed was that traditional building materials should be used and that the original decorative patterns and fit-outs on the chamber walls should as far as possible be preserved. Many of CERS' projects were initiated by coincidences like this and HM welcomes these encounters, since they give the Society the opportunity to promote its course.

Although decisions to render help in these cases were often made within a short span of time, they were not made recklessly. HM is a man who hates sluggishness in performing any task so he always likes to act promptly. His extensive reading makes him a very knowledgeable person which helps him greatly in making correct plans and decisions. Although well read and knowledgeable, HM said when he was young he was not good at school." I learn, but I don' t study" was a motto he likes to use to describe himself. Elected as one of Asia' s heroes by the Time Magazine, was his success due to this motto ?

東竹林尼姑寺

Dongjulin Nunnery

能坐在八十七個藏族阿尼中來個大合照，這可真不是一般人可以做得到的。阿尼口中的「黃老闆」、「香港黃先生」確實拿出了實在的作為才贏得這些阿尼的信賴。

在 1992 年 CERS 重新發現她們之前，東竹林尼姑寺彷彿只是美國探險家洛克書上的一張照片，沒有聲音也只有黑白的活在一個被阻隔的山頭上。一開始是為了整修大殿的壁畫而來的，不過看了阿尼們擁擠髒亂的居住環境之後，CERS 就決定要幫她們蓋新的宿舍。2000 年新的宿舍落成，大殿的壁畫得以開始修復，有了乾淨衛生的基本生活條件後，阿尼們又許下三大願望。當然，那個負責成全她們的阿拉丁，自然就是 CERS 了。

2016 年的春天，CERS 又再回到東竹林尼姑寺，團隊中沒有一個人算得出來這是他們來的第幾趟了。身為這些阿尼的老朋友，我卻有種一切如同昨日，然昨日永不再來的感慨。藍天之下，山頭終年覆雪的巴拉更宗神山依然在保護著他的子民，2000 年宿舍落成時的那張團體照片色彩依然火紅，阿尼們許下的心願也全都圓滿成就。只是，當年的那些老尼姑們多已隨風飄零結束了這一世的修行；寺院中庭，水泥地取代了黃土地，兩棵蘋果樹早已不見身影；現代化的廚房屋頂鋪了白色磁磚，所以再看不見佛光由木縫中灑下的光景；幾乎人手一機的年輕阿尼們，生活像是從天邊走到公路邊，與俗世俗人沒有距離的同步著。

世界變化之快，讓現代的探險家都逃不過一個共同的宿命，HM 說，當他們發現了某些文化或自然的閃爍亮點時，常常這些亮點在他們有生之年就熄滅了。於是，「文化保護」與「生態保育」就自然而然地加入了 CERS 這條 30 年的探險之路。而探險事業的定義，也因此被擴大了。CERS 不僅牢記探險初衷，也隨時保有創新方式的彈性作風，做為一個總是要面對新道路的探險家，HM 的座右銘讓

Getting 87 Tibetan nuns to take a group photograph with oneself was something quite unusual and that someone must be a person liked and trusted by these nuns. That very person was HM, whom these nuns nicknamed "Boss Wong" or "Mr. Wong from Hong Kong".

Before the CERS rediscovered the Dongjulin Nunnery in 1992, all that was known about the nunnery by the outside world was a black and white photograph showing it standing in solitude on a remote and almost unaccessible hill slope. The photograph was taken by an American explorer and put in a book which he wrote. The CERS' original project at the nunnery was to mend and repair the wall paintings in its main hall. However, when the Society found that nuns' living quarters were very dilapidated and congested, it decided to also build new quarters for them to improve their living conditions. In year 2000, the wall paintings were mended and repaired and the new quarters built. The nuns were very happy and they regarded CERS as their wish fulfilling god. They made three further wishes which the Society also subsequently duly help them fulfill.

In spring 2016, CERS once again visited the nunnery. None in the CERS team making the visit could recall how many times they have come to the place. The 2006 group photograph with the nuns, taken to commemorate the completion of the quarters, was still so colorful. The sky above the snow capped Balaganzong Mountain, which local Tibetans regarded as their guardian angel was still so clear and blue. Some of the older nuns in the photograph had since passed away. The dirt courtyard in the nunnery was now paved with concrete and the two apple trees were gone. The kitchen now has a modern look, with clean white porcelain tiled walls. The old kitchen wood walls with

人感動：“I serve, by leading.” 我走在前面，我做給大家看，這就是我要說的。

跟隨 HM 的腳步到今日，我才逐漸感受「探險」的真義。「尋找知識的路程」並不會是一條康莊大道，常常是需要他人的啟發或帶領的，所得到的知識或答案也常常與先前所擁有的觀念是對立或衝突的。只是不知這一路走來，HM 是否也曾經為這樣的衝突而有所遲疑呢？

cracks through which sun light could come in were long gone. Almost every nun in the nunnery had a mobile phone and they felt like having moved back to civilization from a primitive world.

Changes in today's world are so fast that all explorers are facing a new challenge. Whenever they discover a subject, be it concerning culture or the nature, worth of study and investigation, that subject, in today's rapid changing world, is likely to vanish and die away within a short span of time. So conscientious explorers like CERS are committed to promoting people's consciousness in cultural heritage and environmental protection while performing exploration work. CERS has been doing exactly this since its inception. So HM is proud to say."I serve, by leading".

那一年，最後一個離開西藏的傳教士・
沙智勇神父

Father Savioz, the Last Catholic Priest
to Leave Tibet

神父指著牆上老照片裡的人說：「他們全都在西藏服務過，留了鬍子的是 Coquoz 神父，天祥的這個教堂就是他創立的；Lovey 神父後來成為大聖伯納堂的院長；冰箱上的這位是 Tornay，他被西藏人給殺害了……」這是 HM 與沙智勇神父的第一次見面，那時沙神父重感冒中。

沙神父是讀了 HM 於 1984 年發表在《國家地理雜誌》上的文章時，寫信告訴 HM 他的親身經歷的，於是，兩人就成了有著西藏緣分的忘年之交。沙神父是最後一個離開西藏的傳教士。

1919 年出生在瑞士的沙智勇神父，在瑞士大聖伯納堂服務了六年之後被派往中國傳福音，那時他二十七歲。他先在昆明學習中文，然後進入茨中學習藏文，1947 年進入雲南藏區，1949 年時被派往阿墩子（今天的德欽）藏區的一個偏遠教堂，之後更進駐西藏的鹽井。1952 年成為最後一個被新中國逐出藏區的天主教神父，爾後來到台灣，在花蓮天祥的山區，直至退休才回到瑞士。

想要在西藏宣揚天主教，就跟要求藏人放下酥油茶開始開喝咖啡一樣的艱辛。而這件艱難的任務一開始是由法國巴黎的外方教會開始的（1853－1931），然而高原上的教會讓許多法國傳教士失去了生命。於是就由較為熟悉高海拔的瑞士教會接下了這個任務，繼續在那個長期以來以「異教」聞名的地域傳播天主教福音。經過了兩年的談判與十八個月的時間，終於在瀾滄江與薩爾溫江間三千八百公尺高的啞口建成了一座類似瑞士教會的療養院。這個地方成為三萬名跨越拉札山口的腳伕在艱苦的長途跋涉中可以歇息的避風擋雪之處，身心靈都能得到補給的安身之處。

不只如此，這批傳教士還在這裡設立教會、學校、孤兒院，甚至一座葡萄園。葡萄發酵後成為彌撒所需的酒，當然，以酒佐餐的附帶用途也不可忽視，教士們的酒發展成為今日中國西南地區最有名的「雲南紅」。

Pointing at an old photograph on the wall, Father Savioz told How Man, "They have all served in Tibet. The one who has a beard was Father Coquoz. The church in Tianxiang was set up by him. This was Father Lovey, who later became the head priest of the Grand Saint Bernard Mission Church. The one on the fridge was Tornay, he was later killed by the Tibetan."

In 1984, after reading a National Geographic article about Tibet written by How Man, he wrote to How Man about his experience there. They then became friends. Father Savioz was the last Catholic Priest to leave Tibet.

Father Savioz was born in 1919 in Switzerland. His career as a Catholic priest started in the Grand Saint Bernard Mission Church in his birth place. After six years there, he was sent to China. He was then 27. He first learned Chinese language in Kunming Yunnan. Afterwards he went to Cizhong to learn Tibetan. In 1947 he went to the Tibetan area in Yunnan. In 1949 he was sent to Adunzi (today's Deqin) to take charge of a remote chapel. And then afterwards he was sent to Yanjin, Tibet. In 1952 he was expelled and he was the last Catholic priest to leave Tibet. After his expulsion in Tibet, he went to Tianxiang, Hualien, Taiwan, where he stayed until his retirement. After retirement he returned to Switzerland.

Preaching Catholicism in Tibet is a very difficult task. It is like requiring Tibetan to quit yak butter tea and switch to coffee. First attempts to preach Catholicism on the plateau were made by the French between 1853 to 1931. There was little success and many missionaries died because of altitude sickness. Later Swiss missionaries were sent because they were highland people and were therefore considered more suitable. The Church first spent two whole years to

沙智勇神父就是那個稀有族群中的最後一人，在西藏境內唯一的一座教堂（當年叫 Yarkalo，今日的鹽井）服侍、宣道，對象是高原上篤信佛教的藏族。在那個年代要在高原上宣揚天主教已經是個不可能的任務，又遇到了中國政局不穩定的狀態，被驅逐出境還算是個好的結局，慘遭藏人殺害的 Tornay 神父，則是另一個悲傷的故事。傳教士們過人的意志力不得不令人佩服。對於 HM 來說，這種身在險境的經歷應該也是沙神父如此吸引他的重要原因之一吧。

紀錄高原這些鮮為人知又重要的史實是 CERS 的工作重點之一，更何況，當年沙神父這些奉獻者所散播的種子確實結出了一些果實：在這個老教堂周圍的村民裡，竟然以天主教徒居多。此外，瑞士大聖伯納教堂和法國海外傳教團都請求 CERS 尋找當時一些與教會相關的遺物，也就是在 1952 年中國驅逐外國傳教士時沒收的書籍和個人用品。由於 CERS 將保護項目擴及到雲南湄公河上游及怒江一代的古老天主教堂，那麼，沙智勇神父所擁有關於天主教在西藏的記憶當然也就格外珍貴。

HM 對於有故事的老人向來有著無比的耐心。他不止曾經到台灣天祥山區訪問過沙神父，更在他退休回到瑞士馬爾提尼後多次拜訪。年事已高的神父對於幾小時前發生的事情沒印象，卻對半個世紀前的日子、人物與事件準確無誤。艱苦的歲月總是比較容易留在心頭，難以磨滅。每當他拿出一本書、一張剪報甚至一張照片時，眼睛都會閃現光芒，彷彿那個年輕的沙智勇又回到高原上了。

幾次的見面，沙智勇神父不僅講了記憶所及的故事，更提供了 CERS 許多老照片以及大聖伯納教堂檔案室的相關資料。最珍貴的是一支長達五十分鐘的紀錄片，這個影片由與沙智勇神父一同入藏的 Detry 神父所拍攝，是關於一群瑞士教士從大理經過傈僳族地區進入西藏的長途行旅。他們渡過瀾滄江、薩爾溫江，途中在好幾間

obtain the Chinese authorities' approval to send missionaries to the plateau. Afterwards, another 18 months' time was spent building the first Catholic institution there. And this was a sanatorium on a 3,800 m mountain pass in the upper stretch region of the Lancang and Salween Rivers.

Later other institutions like chapels, schools, orphanages and a vineyard were also set up by these Swiss missionaries. The vineyard was meant to produce red wine to be used in religious ceremonies likes masses. Today, this vineyard has become the wine maker of the famous "Yunnan Red" wine.

Father Savioz was a member of these missionaries. Life as a Catholic missionary on the plateau was not easy in those days. The main reason was that Tibetans were largely ardent buddhists. Another reason was because of the political turbulence and instability at the time. Getting expelled was already lucky. The unlucky ones might even get killed. Father Tornay was one among them. In his days in Yarkals (today's Yanjin), Tibet, Father Savioz was the priest of the local chapel, which was the only Catholic chapel in Tibet. Despite all the hardships, he succeeded in, turning a considerable number of Tibetans living near his chapel into Catholics.

As one of the CERS' s missions was to unveil and record matters and events related to the plateau. Father Savioz' s experience was most valuable to How Man. The Grand Saint Bernard Mission Church in Switzerland and the French overseas Missionary Group, on the other hand, had also sought help from CERS in their attempts to find and retrieve articles and belongings that their missionaries might have left behind in China.

Every time How Man met Father Savioz, he would listen patiently and

教堂打尖，影片中甚至還有當地居民從事各種民俗和宗教活動的影像，都是十分有價值的資料。這些都曾經被展示在 CERS 中甸古城的博物館，未來也將被珍藏並展示在 CERS 中甸中心的博物館內。

2003 年，CERS 成功協助了當時 84 高齡的沙神父回到西藏，重新探訪他的教區。沿途，沙神父儘管睡的不踏實，身體也有些微恙，但一心想回到年輕時的那個教堂的心卻是異常熱烈。在茨中教堂時，沙神父雖然沒有主持彌撒，卻與數百位天主教徒一起禮拜、禱告與唱詩。他帶著 HM 到教堂附近的墓地，站在兩位去世的神父的目前祈禱，並嘆息著原來角落的修女院已經蕩然無存了。他摘了教堂前院結的一顆葡萄給 HM，就在這裡，法國傳教士將第一顆葡萄種子帶進中國，儘管 HM 覺得滋味過酸，但對於沙神父來說，再沒有比這個更有滋味的葡萄了。HM 說，這葡萄滋潤的是沙神父的心田而不是味覺。在德欽縣城，他見到了一位名為「瑪麗亞」的藏族婦女，瑪麗亞一見到沙神父馬上跪下，淚眼婆娑，兩人以藏語交談，沙神父彷彿回到了當年。

2003 年十月十三號，夜幕降臨的時候，沙神父終於回到了他此行的最後目的地－茨卡洛教堂。老神父回來的消息很快就在鎮上傳開，教徒們從四面八方趕來，大家的情緒都非常激動，神父也為這些教徒舉行祝福禮。隔天清晨，沙神父與同行的法國羅林神父以及三位藏族修女在小房間內舉行了一個小型的彌撒，在這個遙遠的西藏小教堂裡，沙神父將這個彌撒做得莊嚴神聖。彌撒結束，沙神父滿臉笑意。五十年之後，沙神父終於在他的「教區」茨卡洛教堂舉行了一次彌撒。彌撒，對於多數的傳教士和教徒來說是多麼輕易的事；然而，這個清晨的小彌撒所流露的是多麼厚重的祈禱、盼望與想念！年輕沙神父的傳教之途艱難險谿，所幸，與八十四歲的他終於在此相會。天堂也許曾經遙遠，但那時那刻，變得近在眼前。

HM 曾經在 2008 年的探險筆記裡這樣寫著：「阿爾卑斯山的雪開始飄下的時候我正抵達瑪爾蒂尼的火車站。鐵軌上停著漆成紅色的

attentively to the old man telling his stories on the plateau, How Man
had met Father Savioz many times, both in Tianxiang, Taiwan and
in Switzerland after his retirement. While he tended to forget recent
events, his memories on distant events were clear and accurate. Every
time he pulled out a book, a photograph or a news cutting to show
How Man a certain event, his mind was so sharp and precise and his
eyes were filled with brightness.

In these meetings, Father Savioz also provided How Man many old
photographs and church records. The most valuable piece of record
was a 50 minute film taken by Father Detry, who was sent to Tibet
together with Father Savioz. The film showed the group of Swiss
missionaries traveling in Tibet, showed them crossing the Lancang and
Salween Rivers, showed them staying over in Catholic chapels during
the journey, and also showed local people performing ceremorial/
religious rites. This film and the records are now kept as archives in
CERS's Zhongdian Centre. They are shown and exhibited to visitors
from time to time.

In 2003, Father Savioz was 84. This year CERS succeeded in helping
him make a visit to his former diocese in Tibet. Because of excitement,
he could not sleep well on the way. In the chapel in Cizhong, he
attended a mass together with several hundred local Catholics. After
the mass, he took How Man to the cemetery where he prayed for his
two colleagues buried there. He was also saddened to see that the
former nunnery had disappeared. And then he took How Man to
the vineyard set up by the French, picked a grape for How Man and
for himself. To How Man, the grape tasted quite sour. But to Father
Savioz, it was the best tasting grape he had ever eaten in his life.
On the way to Deqin, he met a Tibetan woman called Maria. She

特別列車－聖伯納特快車。車身畫著一隻聖伯納救難犬，後面跟著長長一串小狗，長度跟列車相當。車窗上則畫了著名的插圖－聖伯納教會的教士們穿著黑袍、戴著圓邊帽、踩著雪橇滑下阿爾卑斯山的雪坡。我想起此刻收納在我背包中的那張 DVD 中的一個影像：幾位神父正在西藏的雪山上滑雪，裡面有一位年輕英俊、頭戴法式軟帽、口銜菸斗的，正是沙智勇神父。」

2013 年沙智勇神父在瑞士瑪爾蒂尼結束了他在地球的一生；HM 帶著對他的回憶前去茨中教堂參加莊嚴的彌撒。彌撒中教堂停了電，彷彿是沙神父向這裡的教徒眨了眨眼，輕輕告別。沙神父熱愛揌粑，也喜歡酥油茶，咖啡杯裡的威士忌比咖啡還多；他的一生彷彿被濃縮在了居住二十多年的小屋牆上的幾張圖裡—中國、雲南、台灣天祥和阿爾卑斯山脈雪嶺的衛星雲圖。

recognized him and immediate knelt in front of him, tears in her eyes.

Shortly before nightfall on October 13, 2003, he finally arrived his destination the likalo chapel. The local Catholics had already learned of his coming and they gathered together to give him a warm welcome. He reciprocated by giving them the Catholic blessing. The next morning, he and his French colleague Father Luo Lin jointly performed a small mass for three local nuns. He was obviously very delighted for being able to return after half a century at the age of 84. His look was full of happiness, as if he was experiencing heaven.

In 2008 while on the way to visiting him, How Man had written the following lines in his diary "It was snowing when I arrived at the Martigny railway station. The station had a train there. As decoration, the windows of the train were painted with images of missionaries in black robes and round hats skating down a snow slope in Alps. This immediately reminded me of the DVD in my backpack which contains the images of several Catholic priests skating on a snow mountain in Tibet. The youngest of them, who wore a soft French cap, pipe in his mouth and looked very handsome, was Father Savioz."

Father Savioz passed away in 2013 in Martigny, Switzerland. The chapel in Cizhong held a farewell mass for him. In fond memory of him, How Man went to the chapel to attend the mass. During the ceremony, there was a sudden, short stoppage of electricity, as if the spirit of the deceased had blinked his eyes to bid farewell to attendants of the mass. People all missed him. Father Savioz liked yak butter tea and roasted qingke barley flour, he also liked coffee and whisky. His stories and experience in Tibet will remain in How Man's memory for a long long time.

東竹林尼姑寺的阿尼們正等著每天下午的酥油茶時光。2000
Dongjulin Nunnery nuns enjoying butter tea in the afternoon. 2000

東竹林尼姑寺，是個出家眾的寺廟也是年輕阿尼的學校，更多時候像是個大家庭。

Dongjulin Nunnery, an extraordinary temple, also is a school for the nuns, and it's like a big family.

阿尼們沿著東竹林尼姑寺外牆準備迎接活佛來臨。

Nuns lining up along the wall welcoming a Rinpoche.

東竹林尼姑寺大殿的壁畫，阿尼們曾經試著修復，拙劣隨興的筆觸依然清晰可見。

Ancient murals in Dongjulin Nunnery. Nuns attempted to restore it. The botched restoration efforts are still vivid.

當 CERS 為阿尼們建了新的宿舍以及修復大殿的壁畫後，懂得漢語的阿尼常常會說感謝「黃老闆」，並且很喜歡跟大家合照。

CERS built dormitory for the nuns and restored the murals. Nuns who speak Mandarin would often thank Boss Wong and like taking pictures with everyone.

七歲噶瑪巴的坐床大典 1992
Seven years old Karmapa at enthronement ceremony in 1992.

左：在西藏，即使政府規定了出家的年紀，但很多人還是選擇年幼出家。

(left)In Tibet despite government has regulated when one can become a monk or nun, however many still choose to become a monk or a nun at young age.

扎西活佛為 CERS 達摩祖師洞旁的閉關小屋焚香、煨桑、祈福。2016
Ronpoche Tashi burning incense, giving blessing to the Damo Master Cave meditation house built by CERS. /2016

CERS 的達摩祖師洞閉關小屋位在山崖邊，靜靜地與大自然合而為一

Damo Master Cave meditation house is situated right above the cliff. Silently it becomes one with the nature.

經幡之內、經文旋轉，人類雖顯得渺小但彷彿卻更靠近真理。

Pray flags flutter and sutra wheel turn. One should be humbled.

沙智勇神父與黃效文多年來已經成為忘年之交，個性急躁的黃效文卻在老人家身上顯露無比耐心。

Long-time friend of HM, Father Savioz. Father was very patient, unlike HM.

茨中教堂，年輕時的沙神父曾在此學習藏文，隨後進入鹽井。法國的傳教士也在這裡種下了從家鄉帶來的葡萄。

Church in Cizong. Yong Father Savioz once studied Portuguese there then entered Yanjin. French missionary brought grape and planted here.

地處四川德格的白雅寺跟黃效文有著非常特殊與深厚的緣分，他是在這裡被告知自己
是蓮花生大師的第二十五位弟子。

Deep connection between HM and Baiya monastry in Dege, Sichuan. He was told that he
was the 25th disciple of Padmasambhava.

〈黃・土〉 #Yellow・Land

在藏族的色彩觀裡，黃色是最高貴的象徵，是高僧活佛的專用色。在佛教的方位意義中，代表南方的寶生佛，即為金黃色。在藏族的戲曲中，戴著黃色面具的角色代表的是高僧大德。

黃色，也代表了土地與興旺。

Tibetans consider yellow as the most noble color. So living buddhas wear yellow robes. Statues and pictures of the Ratna Sambhava of the South are painted gold yellow, and Rinpoches and master monks in Tibetan dramas wear yellow masks. In Tibetan culture and tradition, yellow also represents prosperity of the land.

HM 最早也最長的一次探險是在 1975 到 1976 的八個月間，他靠著開一輛 VW Van 及徒步背著所有的家當，走遍拉丁美洲。Donte esta el proximo pueblo?（最近的一個市鎮在哪裡？）雖然他的西班牙語早就成為過去，然而當時那種無所畏懼的精神卻延續到今天。到底是甚麼樣的靈感讓他從拉丁美洲走向青藏高原呢？而這三十年的每次出走，又有多少次會讓他回想起年輕氣盛的那個自己呢？當我們年輕的時候，總是會想，不知道十年、二十年、甚至三十年後的自己會是甚麼樣子？在哪裡？又過著甚麼樣的生活？「轉換跑道」可能對一般人來說是再平常不過的事情了，但是這個從年輕就很清楚自己興趣與才能的 HM，卻好像從沒想過自己會做除了探險外的任何事。清楚 HM 的人，很容易發現他的好動與沒耐心，但是在「搶救一切美好的事物」這樣的初心之下，HM 又完全把耐心發揮到極致，三十幾年來堅持同一個夢想。

HM 曾經在高原上看過像舊約聖經裡的那種畫面：「身穿長袍的男人趕著一群羊，從大約一公里處向我走來，他的步履又慢又輕，還不時停下歇息，羊群也就在他面前吃草。差不多有一個小時那麼久吧，人和羊終於來到距離我面前兩百公尺的範圍內。這些羊可不是普通的羊，那人也不是普通的人。這是一群二十五隻的野生岩羊，而那放牧人，是個僧人。」

寬闊的谷地、深邃的溝壑、起伏的沙丘、蔚藍的湖泊、綠色的沼澤地、高山積雪融化的溪流，又有著大片的天然草場與高山屏障，幾乎與人類隔絕，這樣的美地，當然應該是高原動物生活的理想樂園。高原的生存條件雖然不易，但動物們在世代的繁衍下，早已經找到跟大自然和平共存的方式；可悲的是，

How Man's first and longest expedition was the one he made between
1975 to 1976. It was for eight months in Latin America. He drove a
Volkswagen van and the contents in his rug sack were all his gears and
belongings. He often found himself in the middle of nowhere and if
he was lucky to meet someone, he would say" Donte esta el proximo
pueblo (Where is the nearest town) " Long gone were the days where
How Man needs to speak Spanish, as he has shifted his exploration
region from Latin America to the Tibetan plateau. What made him
turn his interest and attention to the Tibetan plateau instead? In
expeditions he made in the Tibetan plateau in the subsequent 30 years,
did he still remember this first expedition, and what his mind and
feeling were then ? Making change in life (e.g. changing job, interest
or style of living) is an ordinary matter for any body and many people
have done that in their journey of life. How Man is different, he sticks
to exploration whole heartedly throughout. Since he was young he
was strongly interested in exploration and he knew he had a talent
for it. Another important reason for How Man to be so "addicted" to
exploration is his determination to use it as a means to help save and
preserve nice things from vanishing. So far 30 years he stands by his
dream unyieldingly. Those who know How Man well know that he is a
bit impatient and sometimes restless in usual daily life. However, when
it comes to exploration work, he is painstakingly well thought and
patient.

On the Tibetan plateau, How Man often saw sheeps grazing the pasture
with a herdsman, sometimes a monastic, behind, or wildlife stand
looking at him with alertness in the distant hill slope. On this remote

曾幾何時，這些美好的事物在青藏高原上顯得特別脆弱。在人類與文明入侵的這幾十年來，許多高原動物們痛苦不堪，瀕臨滅絕。於是，保育動物就成了 CERS 這幾十年來非常重要的任務，也是 CERS 長年支持與贊助阿爾金山保護區的主因。當然，探險途中遇到被一噸重的野氂牛追趕而落荒逃逸的精采片段，也成為了聯繫著那片土地、探險成員與 CERS 最津津樂道、百說不膩的回憶。

piece of land, these are beautiful glaciers, lakes, rivers, grasslands, valleys, etc. Because of the high altitude, the weather condition and other conditions for survival are harsh. Indigenous wildlife, however, have developed ways to survive under these hash conditions and mingle harmoniously with nature. In recent decades, however, human activities have gradually encroached on this previously very tranquil and peaceful land and bring the existence of the wildlife into jeopardy. For this reason, CERS has since its inception taken wildlife preservative as one of its major goals. The Society is a strong supporter and sponsor of the Arjinshan Nature Reserve. On one occasion when the Society's exploration team was doing a project deep in the mountain, it was attacked and chased by a huge and ferocious wild yak. The team narrowly escaped. This episode has become a subject that Society's members often talk about in subsequent years.

藏羚羊．不再唱悲歌

No More Tragedies for the
Tibetan Antelope

牠們的悲慘命運，竟來自於自己那身溫柔輕暖的皮毛，一種名為
「shahtoosh」的羊毛。在世界頂尖的時裝店內，一條 shahtoosh 的
披肩可以賣到八千到一萬美金，比相等重量的黃金還要昂貴，難怪
會有「軟黃金」之稱。

1998 年的夏天，HM 氣極敗壞地打了一通電話給台灣好友：「我剛
從阿爾金山保護區出來，天殺的，我們看到了被盜獵者屠殺的成群
藏羚羊的屍體……」在高原上旅行的人都知道，藏羚羊這三個字代
表的不僅是一個動物學名，他們的繁殖地可以算是自然世界保留得
最好的秘密之一。雄藏羚羊那對長達六十公分的長角，遠望就像一
隻獨角獸。牠們如風一般、可與人類保持安全距離的奔跑速度，讓
他們變得少見與高傲。而 1998 那一年，CERS 連續發現七百零六隻
被屠殺的藏羚羊屍體；隔年六月，保護區的武裝科學考察團在這裡
遭遇了兩個盜獵集團，他們所獵殺的九百零七隻藏羚羊，七橫八豎
的被散落在山溝谷內，有一個足球場的面積那麼大。

翻閱早期的探險記載，半個世紀前的青藏高原還可見到藏羚羊成群
遊蕩，估計有上百萬隻；而在 2000 年的時候，想在高原看到藏羚
羊已非易事，悲觀的估計，應該是在四萬隻以下，牠們面臨絕種的
命運。因此，在短短的十幾年內，藏羚羊不得不改變習性以應付那
些會影響牠們生存的人為活動，像是盜獵和採金。

回想 1998 年的那次高原考察，雖然因為目睹了藏羚羊被集體屠殺
而使得隊員們氣憤與悲傷，但 CERS 也成功地觀察、拍攝和錄影了
藏羚羊遷徙到產羔地的最後階段，包括生產過程與初生數日的哺育
情形。這是科學家超過百年追尋而首次鑑定的羚羊產羔地。CERS
甚至哺育了一頭被母親遺棄的小羊羔，然後次日再讓牠們團聚。當
下，HM 也向保護區的成員們承諾將不惜一切籌措資源與經費，絕
不再讓藏羚羊的繁殖季節成為流血季節。

The Tibetan Antelopes' tragic fate comes from their soft and tender fur, called "shahtoosh" by people in the fashion circle. In world class fur fashion shops, a lady's shahtoosh shoulder cape can fetch a price between eight to ten thousand US dollars. Tibetan Antelopes' furs are therefore called "soft gold".

In summer 1998, furious How Man spoke over the phone to a friend in Taiwan "I just returned from the Arjinshan Nature Reserve. I was so angry, I saw hundreds of dead Tibetan antelopes. The God dammed poachers have killed them for their furs." Travelers on the Tibetan plateau all know that the Tibetan antelope is a precious creature. However, very little was known about their life patterns on the plateau. In particular, how and where they give birth to their offsprings is perhaps the most well kept secret in the world. Male Tibetan antelopes have horns which can measure up to 60 cm in length. Tibetan antelopes are fast runners. Timid and extremely cautious, they always keep a safe distance from men and look at them elegantly. In the 1998 incident, How Man saw 706 freshly killed Tibetan antelopes. In June the next year, deep in the Arjinshan region, an armed conservatory research team saw two gangs of poachers. The team later found 907 dead Tibetan antelopes scattered around a place about the size of a football pitch in a valley.

Reports by early explorers to the region indicated that, at their time, large herds of Tibetan antelopes could often be seen. Later, in 2000, sighting of them has become very rare and their population was estimated to be less than 40,000. Over the years, to avoid getting killed by the poachers or the illegal gold miners, the Tibetan antelopes are believed to have forced themselves to change their living and

「曾經身為《美國國家地理雜誌》記者的我，深知照片的力量。我發誓，要把美麗的藏羚羊照片帶回文明世界，也要將盜獵者屠殺後所棄置的母羚羊及成形胎羊的殘體影像公諸於世。」此後，HM 更在 CNN、Discovery 等國際媒體上廣為宣傳。那些照片不只是藏羚羊美麗身影的見證，也讓世界上許多有名有利的人不寒而慄。

畢蔚林博士，CERS 最重要的生物學家，從 1998 年目睹藏羚羊被屠殺的景象後，連續四個夏季，帶著自己訓練出的隊伍在阿爾金山保護區，為藏羚羊的產羔區巡邏以及做田野調查。這個隊伍總共只有二十四個人，看管著比台灣還大的遼闊土地，海拔都在四千公尺以上，即使是夏季，溫度也經常在零度以下。在這個保護區內開車行走幾百公里，沒有任何支援，除了身體必須夠刻苦耐勞外，靠的就是一定要保護藏羚羊的那股熱情與堅持了。

所有的付出都是值得的，2001 年六月二十九日，HM 在他的探險日誌中寫道：「抵達的第一個清晨，帳篷內的氣溫紀錄是攝氏零下五點四度，高原上的夏天依然嚴酷。這次回來特別有意義，因為那些偷獵藏羚羊的壞蛋們竟然消失的無影無蹤。經常性的巡邏，果然起了遏阻的作用……總結了四個季節的產羔研究，大家一致認為必需在產羔區繼續監視以確保母羚羊與小羊羔受到完全的保護。更令人興奮的是，我們決定將研究範圍擴展到保護區內的其他有蹄類動物，像是野氂牛和藏野驢。」

2008 年北京奧運，藏羚羊成為吉祥物之一，電影《可可西里》與環保人士的宣傳也讓人們注意到了藏羚羊的珍貴與存亡問題，高原偏遠公路邊也開始出現了保育動物的標誌，我們很難去說這是誰的功勞，但可以肯定的是，如果沒有 HM 那些又美麗又殘酷的照片和影像，「shahtoosh」披肩的狂熱就不會退卻，CERS 確實善用了影像與媒體，也因而改變了藏羚羊差點被滅亡的命運。

migration patterns,making life even harsher for them.

The encouraging thing about CERS's 1998 expedition to the Arjinshan was that it succeeded, first time in the history of wildlife exploration, in filming and recording the Tibetan antelopes' migration to the destination where they would give birth to their offsprings, the actual birth giving process, and how mothers cared and nursed their newborns in next few days. In the observation and the filming process, CERS saw and rescued a new born that was abandoned by his mother because he was too weak to get up on his feet. The CERS team cared and nursed him and later returned him to the herd. CERS was very touched by what it has seen and vowed that it would do all it can to help ensure that the Tibetan antelopes are adequately protected from poaching activities.

"I have worked as a reporter for the National Geographic Magazine and I know that the power of media photographs. I therefore vowed to bring the photographs of massacred Tibetan antelopes (many of which were still unborn, pulled out from their mothers' womb and skinned) home and publish them to let the world know the atrocity the poachers have committed." These photographs were published by many popular media including CNN and The Discovery Channel. As well as shocking the world, they also made the rich celebrities who take pride in wearing shahtooshs feel ashamed.

In summer time in the next four years, Dr. William Bleisch, CERS Science Director, organized for a team of professionally trained volunteers to help the Arjinshan Nature Reserve patrol areas where pregnant Tibetan antelopes would migrate to and give birth. The team

HM 的腦子裡總是裝著奇怪的想法，這一次他所想的是，或許也應該好好的來研究一下，這些年年月月在極端氣候下追逐野生動物的野生動物科學家們，他們的行為肯定跟他們研究的動物是差不多的。如果有可能，跟隨 HM 的影子也很想研究 HM 的腦袋是怎麼樣的構造，到底是比較像有哲學意識的牧羊人，還是永不停歇、酷愛奔跑的珍貴藏羚羊呢？

「自豪的牧羊人 在廣闊的大草原上
生活變成了一種旋律
響徹世界的盡頭
我將不厭倦地守護著我的羊群
安詳地在肥沃的牧草地上吃草
孕育自家鄉搖籃的
我的傳統 歌謠 及故事
我將帶著他們到遠方」
　　　　－烏仁娜《在草原上》

has only 24 members and the area of the Arjinshan Nature Reserve is very big, bigger than Taiwan. The altitude is above 4000 meters and temperature can often drop below 0℃ even in summer. Team members needed to drive several hundred kilometers to travel from one point to another without support. They were tough guys but what really made them persist in their work was their love of nature and their devotion to protection of wildlife.

The efforts by CERS were proved to be effective. On 29 June 2001, HM revisited the Arjinshan Nature Reserve. He wrote in his expedition log, "Spent last night in tent. Temperature -5.4℃ , still freezing cold despite summer. Very pleased to learn that there have not been any poaching activities over the past four years. All agreed that the patrol programme should continue and the animals to be covered in this protection programme should be expanded to include the wild yak and the wild donkey."

The 2008 Beijing Olympics Games has chosen the Tibetan antelope as its official mascot. The movie Kekexili and appeals by environmentalists have aroused the world's concern over the danger of extinction of the Tibetan antelope. The authorities have also began to put up signs on roads in the Tibetan plateau region to educate people on wildlife protection. It is hard to say who should be credited for triggering off all these good works. But definitely How Man's crisp sharp and nice pictures depicting the cruelty of the poachers and the miserable fate of the Tibetan antelopes played a very important role in discouraging the high society from wearing shahtoosh. And no doubt this helps reduce/ eliminate people's urge for the fur, thus saving the animal from the danger of extinction.

How Man is a man full of strange ideas. Each time he has a new idea, he would seriously examine and pursue it, like scientists tracing and studying wildlife under harsh weather conditions in the wilderness. If How Man's shadow has such ability, he would definitely love to read into How Man's mind to ascertain what are the elements that make him both like a philosophical minded shepherd and an ever-running Tibetan antelope.

"The confident shepherd led his sheep to a wide, rich and undisturbed pasture at the edge of the world. The sheep grazed peacefully and the shepherd was silently doing his prayers and meditation. It was such peacefulness and tranquility that provide all the nourishments and inspirations for our people to form and develop our traditions, culture and thinking, and to spread them to places afar."

Lines from Wurenna's "Over the Grassland"

黑頸鶴・信守承諾一輩子

Black-necked Cranes, A Life-long Pledge

黑頸鶴，無疑地，是跟著 CERS 一起成長的。而這個項目的歷時之長與取得的成果，也都超出了 HM 原來的想像。CERS 與黑頸鶴的關係，如同黑頸鶴彼此的伴侶關係：一個永遠的承諾。

1995 年二月，HM 在他的探險筆記上寫著：「那位六十二歲的老人說，在他年輕時的『光輝』歲月裡，他起碼打落了兩百隻黑頸鶴，有一次還用自製的火繩槍一槍打下了好幾隻。以殺一隻坐牢七年來算，這個老頭子恐怕得在牢裡坐到 35 世紀呢。」老頭坦言，若不是現在健康不如以往，他還會再去打獵。說到底，對於雲南這一帶的人來說，黑頸鶴不過就是鵝的一種，他們叫牠做「老雁鵝」。

科學上來說，全世界有十五種鶴類，中國佔了九種，黑頸鶴是當中最罕見，也是唯一終生生活在高原的。黑頸鶴是候鳥，每年三月集群離開越冬地雲貴高原，然後北上青藏高原，在湖泊與河流等濕地與沼澤之中築巢，四月下旬開始繁殖並養育幼鳥；十月下旬再飛到海拔略低的雲貴高原、青藏高原東南部和中印、中巴邊境過冬。

CERS 從 1988 年就開始觀察黑頸鶴的繁殖與棲息地，那時候除了知道這是中國最罕見的鶴類之外，對牠們的數目與生活習慣都了解極少，據報只有不足一千隻。後來在中國科學家和國際鶴類基金會的多次觀察與點算中，才得出 1995 年的數字約為五千五百隻。但這對於繁殖率低的黑頸鶴來說還是過少，仍然需要保護才能使之繼續延續。

其實，就情感面來說，黑頸鶴也有充分的理由應該被保護的。在中國的歷史上，鶴一直被視為一種神仙之鳥，除了高雅脫俗罕見以外，從官服上的圖騰到鄉間農民的年畫，鶴的象徵意義早已深入民心，牠是很多成語與傳說中的主角，仙鶴更代表著福、壽；牠們的求愛與終生配偶方式更象徵著夫妻或生意夥伴上長期穩定的關係。

The Black-necked Crane was CERS's research subject since the Society's early days. Relationship between the two has never been broken since, just like the life-long companionship of a male and female black-necked crane.

In February 1995, How Man wrote the following lines in his expedition diary, "The 62 year old man said he reckoned that in the good old day when he was young, he had shot down more than 200 black-necked cranes. He said he used a home-made flint lock shotgun to do that. His best record was one shot that downed several cranes. If he still does this now, on the basis that one kill can land him in jail for seven years, he would need to stay in jail until the 35th Century. " The old man said if he was still healthy and agile, he would still go out to hunt these birds. For people in rural areas in Yunnan, like this old man, the Black-necked Crane is just a delicious game meat on their dining table. No wonder they nicknamed the bird "big goose".

There are 15 species of cranes in the world, nine of which can be found in China and the Black-necked Crane is rarest species. The Black-necked Crane is a migratory bird which spends its whole life on lands with high altitude. In March, Black-necked Cranes would leave their winter habitat at the Yunnan-Guizhou Plateau and go north to the Tibetan Plateau. They would stay in lakes, rivers and wet lands there to mate and to raise their off-springs until the end of October. When they would fly back to places with lower altitude, such as the Yunnan-Guizhou Plateau, the south east part of the Tibetan Plateau or places along the India-Pakistan border, to pass the winter.

In 1988 when CERS first commenced to study the Black-necked

然而，黑頸鶴與有賞鳥天堂之稱的貴州威寧縣草海濕地，幾十年來的關係就複雜多了。1970 年代，此地的公社為了爭取更多的農地，因此排乾湖水，加上氣候變化，使得來越冬的侯鳥因而減少，其中受創最重的就是黑頸鶴；1975 年時，牠們的數量從過往的幾百隻減為可悲的三十五隻。1982 年政策翻轉，草海濕地重新蓄水，1984 年黑頸鶴的數量就增為三百五十隻。到了 1985 年，自然保護區成立了，草海成為黑頸鶴最早的三個保護區之一，另外兩處則是香格里拉的納帕海和青海東南地區的隆寶灘。

根據 CERS 的調研，人類對黑頸鶴的威脅主要是在冬天，那時黑頸鶴會飛到較低的雲南地區過冬，跟人類因此有了接觸。鶴容易被偷獵當成食物，而鶴群會以農民收成後田裡剩餘的馬鈴薯為口糧，當春天來時，農民播下的種子有時也會被鶴吃掉。這衝突每年都會上演，因此 CERS 開始了一個解決農民與鶴間衝突的計畫，以確保黑頸鶴每年都能在最南端的棲息地平安度過。

這個計畫必需從對村民的教育做起，包括向當地居民宣傳黑頸鶴受國家保護的重要性，並在區域學校中加入鶴鳥課程及野外觀察學習，也獎勵人們舉報偷獵行為、成立省級保護區以及控制濕地生長區；除此之外，也同時引入賞鳥團以幫助當地經濟，讓村民知道，若好好的做好保育工作，黑頸鶴，可以變成大家的重要資產。現在，保護區附近的村民都知道黑頸鶴是受到保護的鳥，黑頸鶴也成為草海濕地的圖騰和標誌，吸引著許多外來遊客，甚至外國賞鳥團，也因此提升了村子的經濟實力。

2009 年，CERS 成功拿到批准，活捉五隻黑頸鶴，為牠們配上衛星跟蹤器，以此進一步了解這些特有種的行為、遷移路線及目的地。

黑頸鶴的保育計畫不僅讓鶴的數量穩定並逐年成長，也同時讓 CERS 也學習到，在保護這些珍貴動物的同時，也必需將牠們同居

Crane, the world knew very little about these birds. All that was known was that it is a rare species of cranes, and that its population was estimated at under 1,000. Later, in 1995, reports published by China's Science Academy and the International Cranes Research Foundation estimated the Black-necked Cranes population at 5,500. These reports however stressed that the number is still dangerously low, and that the efforts and measures to save them from extinction must continue.

Cranes are held as heavenly birds in Chinese tradition and culture because of their stately and elegant look and appearance. Therefore their image often appears on paintings and on rich people's and high government official's dressings. The Black-necked Crane, in particular, is seen not only as a symbol of elegance and longevity, but also an icon of fidelity and truthfulness towards one's spouse.

At the Caohai wetland in Weining County, Guizhou Province, Black-necked Crane experienced many ups and downs over the past several decades. In the 1970s, the local commune, in order to acquire more farm land to grow crops, drained the Caohai wetland and used the place for farming. This, together with climate change over the years, resulted in a steep decline in the number of migratory birds going there to stay for the winter. The Black-necked Crane was the species that suffered most. A 1975 survey showed that their number had dwindled from the usual several hundred to only 35. Fortunately in 1982, a change in policy resulted in Caohai being reinstated back to wetland. In 1984, the number of Black-necked Crane staying for winter there went up to 350. In 1985, the Caohai wetland was gazetted as a sanctuary for the Black-necked Cranes, together with Napahai in Shangrila and the Longprotan wetland in Qinghai Province.

人的生活一併考慮進去，人類和動物若能找出和諧共存的方式，那
才是雙贏的局面。

「天空中潔白的仙鶴
　請將你們的雙翅借我
　我不往遠處去飛
　只到理瑭就回　」
　　　－ 倉央嘉措 六世達賴喇嘛

CERS's research shows that Black-necked Cranes' threats come mostly from human. In winter time they stay in lower places such as Yunnan where there are far more human activities than in their summer habitat on the remote Tibetan Plateau. Plant bulbs are one of the foods they feed on and when they stop on farm lands to search for food they often get killed by the farmers.

To help them escape such ill fate so that they can spend the winter safely in Yunnan, CERS have launched various programmes in the local community. These included educating people at the grassroot level to love and protect the nature, to strictly observe the law on protection of wildlife and to report poaching activities. The Society also made suggestions to the local authorities on ways to improve the management of the wetland, and to operate bird sighting excursions for tourists. These would help boost the local economy and the economic benefits would provide great incentive for all the local people to take active measures to protect the wetland and the birds.

In 2009, upon approval by the local authorities, CERS successfully captured five live Black-necked Cranes and planted electronic chips on them. They were then released to allow the Society through satellite to keep track of their movements flight routes, and places where they stop, etc.

These programmes have resulted in a steady grow in the numbers of Black-necked Cranes over the years. A lesson the Society learns from the success of these programmes is the best way to protect nature and wildlife is to make the local people truly understand and realize that if they support the protective measures, it would be a win-win situation

for both sides, otherwise both sides would suffer heavily.

"Oh you white crane,

  please lend me your wings,

  I will not go far nor linger long,

  just a short stay at Litang and be back."

--Tsangyang Gyatso, The Sixth Dalai Lama

純種藏獒的愁眉深鎖

The Sad Faced Pure Bred Tibetan Mastiff

「這裡就是 Chili 的墓園了，牠還曾經上過中國郵票呢。」HM 語氣平靜，但我很清楚這隻藏獒在他心中的位置，要不然 HM 也不會特別在中甸中心他自己的宿舍外，留下這一塊空地給 Chili 了。

一百年前，清朝的隨軍醫官全紹清，在他拍攝拉薩的眾多照片中有一張藏獒與其主人的照片，照片的下方寫著：「這種紅眼、獅型的動物野性十足，很難馴服。由於沒有人敢去馴養和餵食，一般買狗的同時也要將主人一起買下。」1982 年，當 HM 第一次帶領《國家地理雜誌》探險隊前往西藏時，他也曾經在文章中提及兇猛的藏獒；然而，不論是全紹清或者 HM，他們所想不到的是，這個對藏族牧民們來說威猛又忠心的夥伴，二十年後竟然也會面臨消失的危險。

CERS 在 2004 年夏天開始了第一次關於藏獒的大型考察，五輛車，十六名隊員進入高原評估藏獒的困境。這個考察涵蓋了六千公里，走了五個藏區中的四個，共 30 個藏區縣城。這次的考察是 CERS 決心要尋獲真正藏獒，好讓牠們免遭滅絕厄運的第一步。

公路的修建帶來了臨時民工與新移民，他們開商店餐廳，在各式生意走上高原的同時也帶來了低地家犬，和藏獒交配後，將高原上古犬的血統改變了，因此，要尋獲一隻血統純正的藏獒成了相當困難的任務。藏獒有各種顏色，但兩眼上面一定要有兩小團黃點，好像牠們的另外兩隻眼睛，那是最大的特徵，大大的頭跟身體不成比例，鼻嘴大，上眼簾斜垂，正是傳說中「愁眉深鎖」的那個調調。

必需要尋找來自不同地區的小藏獒，才能建立起具有差異性及帶疏離性的血統資料庫，而這些確實費了 CERS 好一番心力。那段時間，HM 成了帶隊尋覓金羊毛的 Jason。尋找小藏獒談價錢的爾虞我詐、第一隻小犬遵守中國一胎化政策的誕生（卻不在 CERS 的計畫之內），其實，從第一隻「15K」坐上 Land Rover 開始流口水的那一刻起，藏獒們就時刻不斷地給 HM 驚喜，當然，也包括 Chili 上了

"This is Chili's grave. His picture was once on a Chinese postage stamp." How Man told me with a calm voice. I know how important Chili was in his heart, otherwise, he would not have set aside a piece of land for his burial in CERS' Zhongdian Center.

In one of the photographs taken in Lhasa one century ago by a Qing Dynasty Chinese army doctor, a local man was shown posing for the camera with his Tibetan mastiff. The caption for the photograph reads "This red eyed lion like dog is of a species that is ferocious and difficult to tame. Even you buy one back, you don't even dare to go near to feed him, not to mention to tame him. So any person who really wants to buy and own one will need to buy also his master."

In How Man's writings about his first expedition to Tibet in 1982 with a team of explorers from the National Geographic Magazine, he had also mentioned the Tibetan mastiff, what he and the Qing Dynasty army doctor did not realize was that the pure bred Tibetan mastiff, which for centuries was the local people's faithful companion, was going to face the danger of extinction twenty years later.

In summer 2004, the CERS started a programme on the plateau to look for and procure cubs of pure bred Tibetan mastiff and to set up a breeding base to help ensure purity of breed would not lose. The 16 member CERS team went deep into the plateau in five cars. A total of 30 counties were visited, and over 6000 km in distance were travelled.

Pure bred Tibetan mastiffs were getting difficult to find because over the decades, many low lands dogs had come to the plateau with their inland masters. The influx resulted in a sharp increase in the population of the cross breeds and gradually pure bred Tibetan mastiffs

中國郵票，華爾街日報封面文章及 CNN。

CERS 把藏獒基地建在面向雲南西藏交界處卡瓦卡博神山的一處原始村落「古久龍村」，那裡海拔三千六百公尺，只有五戶人家。CERS 協助他們成為藏獒飼養員，當夏季藏民前往山上放牧時就把藏獒帶到四千公尺高的營地，回到牠們最習慣的生活條件裡。

然而，這個神山下的計畫還是趕不上市場的變化。藏獒犬的復育已經停擺了好幾年了，因為投機者的介入把藏獒的價錢炒到一個天價。CERS 覺得如果把藏獒的幼犬交給藏人們，最終的命運也只是會被賣出去而已。而最近，藏獒的這股熱潮似乎開始退去，甚至還有報導說，有些不肖的繁殖者把不值錢的藏獒犬賣給了屠夫。

現在這個風景壯麗的地方有了新的經營管理者，王梅不僅是個佛教徒也是個成功的企業家，她正打算將這兒的房子變成生態旅館，服務前來朝聖的佛教徒與禪修的出家人。「這是一個對自然與文化保育有熱情的創意。我們希望王梅能為這個很棒的地方開創出全新的生命。」HM 說。

不知道接下來藏民會說些甚麼樣的故事給 Chili 的後代子孫聽；總之，CERS 永遠記得當年 15K 與 12K 坐上探險車的那一刻，他們流著口水，愁眉深鎖的樣子。

were difficult to find, unless in very remote places. Pure bred Tibetan mastiffs can have different colors but they all have a dark color patch just above their eyes making them look like having four eyes. They are big and strong and their heads and mouths are disproportionally big. Another distinguishing feature is their dropped eyelids, making their face looked sad.

CERS went to the very remote herdsman counties on the plateau to look for and procure pure bred cubs for propagation. These counties were also far apart to ensure genetic excellence of the future offsprings. The process was like Jason looking for the golden fleece in the ancient Greek fairy tale. Once a cub was identified, price negotiation with the owner began which often turned out to be difficult as many would ask for exorbitant prices. The first cub CERS purchased was Chili, who was very cute and lovely. The price was a high 15k. When he was taken on the Land Rover, he was so curious and interested that saliva came gushing out from his mouth. A scene which HM still vividly remembers. Chili's photograph later appeared on a Chinese stamp, a front page article on The Wall Street Journal, and on CNN.

The breeding base which CERS set up was in a remote, and primitive village beneath Mountain Khawakarpo on the Yunnan-Tibet border. The village had only five herdsman families and its elevation was 3,600 m. CERS entrusted the cubs to the villagers and gave them the necessary supports and training on how they should be fed, etc. In the summer season when the villagers went uphill to graze their livestock, they took the cubs along. The grazing ground's elevation was 4,000 m, the cubs would stay there with the villagers until the end of summer.

In subsequent years, many speculative commercial breeders had emerged. They made a lot of money selling pure bred cubs at first. Indeed at one time, pure bred cubs were sold at unthinkably high prices. But later, such speculative trading in pure breeds had died out because their population was gradually increasing. There were also rumors that some breeders are selling cubs that don't meet market demand to butchers. With these changes taking place, CERS had since discontinued its breeding base programme.

Stories about Chili and his descendants will continue to be told and heard among villagers and their children in the breeding base. And for How Man and CERS, they will never forget Chili's cute expression, with saliva gushing out from his mouth, when he was taken onto the Land Rover.

金絲美猴 vs. 傈僳獵手

Golden Monkeys vs. Lisu Hunters

自從 2001 年在芒康被金絲猴札西的迴旋腿踢中膝蓋之後，HM 就跟金絲猴結下了不解之緣。

金絲猴是地球上最稀有的靈長類動物之一，學名是雲南仰鼻猴，是唯一一種具有人類般紅嘴唇的猴子，鼻孔朝天也是牠們的外貌特色之一。金絲猴幾乎全數生活在雲南西藏邊界海拔極高的地區，大約是三千八百米到四千兩百米之間。2001 年時僅存不到一千五百隻。

兩年之後，HM 聽說雲南維西響古箐有個金絲猴棲息區時，他馬上就踏上了這片土地，當這裡的傈僳族人以為他的注意力只是在金絲猴時，他卻決定了要先關注幫助傈僳族人，因為傈僳族文化的消失可能比金絲猴還更急迫。於是從整修破陋屋頂、重建荒廢學校、在三個村子的三十九戶人家中幫助了最艱困的兩戶，甚至保護了兩間碩果僅存的古老傈僳族房屋，並將它們改為後來的展覽館，其後陸續發展成保護了共二十一間的傈僳族建築群。在那十幾次的傈僳族考察中，HM 竟然耐得住性子沒有上山去看猴子，可見得在他心中有自己的一個秤，每件事的輕重緩急他排列的清楚。

那麼，影子又要問了：「到底是保育金絲猴重要，還是保護傈僳族的傳統文化重要呢？」

世界變化之快，讓很多的「探險家」也必需加入「保育」的行列，齊聲保育我們身邊危及的自然和文化遺產，HM 當然也是這樣的一個探險家，他讓 CERS 認識保育的緊急與重要，並且規劃合適的方案，且具體執行。但是，當世人開始把「永續發展」掛在嘴邊時，他卻對更具體的、具有「經濟效益的保護」有著一套見解。

很多人並不知道，其實 CERS 一直努力的在平衡自然保育與文化保護。就像，保護金絲猴這種旗艦物種當然很重要，但是傈僳族的文化也不能視而不見；某一方的保育不應當以另一方為犧牲品。CERS

The first time How Man saw a golden monkey was in Mangkang in 2001. It is a highly endangered species. Golden hair, red lips and snub nose are its characteristics. Golden monkeys are found in the Yunnan and Tibet border region, in places with 3,800 m to 4,200 m elevation. In 2001, their population was estimated at under 1500.

Two years later, HM learnt that people had spotted a golden monkey habitat in Xiangguqing in Weixi, Yunnan. He promptly went there to investigate. When he arrived, the local Lisu people (most were hunters in the past) thought that his interest was on the golden monkeys only and nothing else. When HM saw the villages, where these Lisu people live was in very bad shape and their traditional way of living and culture were fast dying out, he realized that helping them preserve these things should have priority. So instead of rushing into the forest to investigate the monkeys, he and his team started helping the Lisu people mend their houses, rebuild a school, and fully restore two collapsed traditional Lisu style sheds and turn them into exhibition rooms to display artefacts of the Lisu tribe. These works involved a total of 21 houses in three villages. The villages have since regained their traditional Lisu look.

In addition to clearly knowing his priority, How Man is also mindful about integrating heritage/culture preservation work with measures and means to give economic benefits to the local people. He knows that this is the most effective way to gain support for the preservation work he launched.

A family in Shangrila, Yunnan made its living by producing home-made raw yak butter. The family has for generations been working

要求自己的保育項目能夠在經濟上可行，並能長期改善當地村落的生活問題。只是靠尋求資金來解決問題已經是過去的方式了，能為項目提供多元化的經濟效益和附加價值才是長久的解決之道。

氂牛奶酪就是一個具有「經濟效益保護」的成功項目。2004 年由 CERS、威斯康辛大學與藏族人一起建立一個氂牛乳酪手工業。HM 知道，上等的奶酪就跟上等的紅酒一樣，絕對會受到世界饕客的喜愛，何況是來自香格里拉，這個世外桃源。用正當的手段為藏民找到一條他們從未想到的經濟活水，保護動物、保護環境的同時更保護了當地人的生計，這就是 HM 所謂具有「經濟效益」的保護。到今天，「美香氂牛奶酪」年產 3 公噸，由兩個藏族家庭繼續經營著，2015 年更在法國得到難能可貴的金獎。

相同的概念，在 CERS 與傈僳族村民的共同努力之下，不僅保存了本土傈僳族山區部落文化，也促進了金絲猴居住地的生態旅遊，為村民改善了經濟。現在，響古箐甚至成為 CERS 很重要的教育中心之一。每到暑假，畢蔚林博士和中甸中心主任次仁卓瑪帶領著來自國內外的學生到這裡觀察金絲猴，也同時了解傈僳族的傳統文化，據說這裡也成為年輕學生們最感興趣的項目之一。從探險、保育到教育的這條路，CERS 走了三十年，也愈走愈明確。HM 曾說過，遠征的目的並不是去當第一個發現的人，好像很英雄；而是，我們怎麼去保護我們的發現。重點是內容，重要的是我們怎麼去演繹，然後給予保護、研究，以及教育。

關於那些生生不息並有著人類紅唇的金絲猴們，不論是大猴王繼續掌控一切，甚或小公猴可以趁虛而入，HM 都如以往一般，希望能在牠們某一個轉身或跳躍時，捕捉一張好特寫。

in this traditional industry. In the region, yak butter is used as fuel for oil lamps in monasteries and temples. Its price is low so the family could hardly make ends meet. The family therefore wished to quit this traditional industry and turn to other "modern" means to make a living. How Man knew of that and he promptly talked to the family into not letting the industry die out. What How Man did was to get professionals from the University of Wisconsin to help the family produce high quality edible yak cheese and help it sell the product abroad to boost its income. The cheese so produced was well received by the outside world and the family's business has grown and prospered since. The family and its fellow villagers were very thankful to CERS for its help which has enabled them to improve their income. CERS, on the other hand, was glad that the villagers' traditional yak butter industry did not die out. Nowadays, the village had two families producing the cheese and their total annual production was three tons. Branded "Mei Xiang Yak Cheese", the product won a gold prize in a gourmet festival in France in 2015.

In regard to the golden monkeys and the Lisu people, the CERS adopted a similar approach. By helping the Lisu villagers mend, rebuild and restore their houses back to their original Lisu style and shape, and by setting up the exhibition rooms to display artefacts, the Lisu people's traditions and culture were preserved. The place has since become a famous tourist spot because of the restoration and the nearby golden monkeys. The tourists would stop over there before proceeding to the forest behind to watch the golden monkeys and this created job opportunities for the villagers. During summer vacation every year, CERS' Science Director, Dr. William Bleisch and Education Officer, Tsering Drolma would station themselves in the village to act as guides

for students and tourists visiting the place. During the guided tour, they would convey CERS' message on the need for all to contribute toward cultural, heritage and wildlife protection and conservation. The Lisu village has thus become an important education base camp for CERS. How Man believes that an explorer's success is not judged by the fact that he is the first one to have discovered something rare and precious. The yardstick, he said, should be on whether he can subsequently devise measures to protect and preserve it so that the rest of the world can also appreciate it.

CERS' work has helped the Lisu people preserve their heritage and culture. The Society's education program there has also increased their as well as the tourists' awareness on the need to protect and conserve nature and its wildlife. The golden monkeys can therefore play, hop and swing freely for the tourists' cameras without fear.

成年的藏羚羊有著一對大羚角，牠們奔跑的速度快如閃電，令其他的動物難以追捕，但卻難逃人類槍枝的射擊。CERS 不僅找到藏羚羊產羔地，更成功地阻擋了盜獵者的恐怖行為，讓這美麗的生物繼續在高原安心的繁殖生活。

Grown Tibetan Antelope with a pair of big horns. They run fast, not easily preyed, but also not fast enough to dodge poacher's bullets. CERS not only found the Tibetan Antelopes calving ground, but also stopped the killings by the poachers. Now the beautiful creatures can roam freely on the Tibetan Plateau.

CERS 跑遍了三十個藏區縣城為了尋獲血統純正的藏獒，以避免牠們遭滅絕厄運。

CERS searched thirty counties in Tibetan region for pure breed Tibetan Mastiff. Bringing back the breed that was on the verge of extinction.

從高原上不同人家被帶回的小藏獒，牠們在 CERS 中甸中心成長茁壯。

Tibetan Mastiff puppies brought from highland. They grew up in CERS Zongdian Centre.

大片的天然草場與高山屏障，這樣的美地，是高原動物生活的理想樂園。動物們在世代的繁衍下，早已經找到跟大自然和平共存的方式。右圖為藏野驢。

Vast grassland and high mountain is an ideal living environment for the highland animals. (Tibetan Donkey)

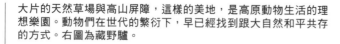

探險途中遇到被一噸重的野犛牛追趕，除了甘拜下風落荒而逃外，沒有第二個選擇。

Chased by a yak weighing about a ton. In that situation, one could only run for his life.

高原上的沙狐，由於靈巧速度快，因此非常難以捕捉牠的身影。

Corsac fox on the plateau. Nimble creature runs fast, difficult to catch with camera.

三十年的高原探險常常是為了再次目睹這樣的大氣象而出發，
感謝諸神在這段探險之路上對 CERS 的眷顧。

Nature is grand. Thank the divinity for bestowing blessings on CERS.

連續好幾年的冬天，黃效文都會獨自前往北海道，只為了跟這些高雅的丹頂鶴相聚。

For many years HM would travel to Hokkaido alone just to spend time with those elegant cranes.

每年都會到納帕海越冬的黑頸鶴，不僅是 CERS 長期關注的項目，
日久生情似地彷彿也成為 CERS 中甸中心的一分子。

Black-necked cranes fly to Napahai wetland every winter. It's one of
CERS' conservation project and has become part of CERS' family.

有著厚嘴唇的滇金絲猴，看起來還真像人類。靈敏、搗蛋愛爭王的
個性也跟人類相去不遠。

Snob-nosed monkey with thick lips, looks just like human. Agile, playful.

＜白・雲＞ ＃White・Clouds

壇城中的東方以白色來表現，在佛教中具有方位意義的白色金剛薩垂代表。高壽老人會在本命年穿上有日、月圖案的白色衣服以求吉祥。在藏族戲劇中，白色面具特指男性角色。

白色，代表雲。

In Mandela pictures of Tibetan buddhism, white stands for the east. Hence the directional icon for the east is the Vajrasattva. In Tibetan tradition, old persons in their year of fate, would wear clothes in white, with figures of the sun and the moon. It is believed such dressing will bring them happiness and peace of mind. In Tibetan dramas, white represents male persons or cloud.

與天相接 高原上的白雲 描淡了銀邊
與陽光遊戲
白雲跟神山吹噓著究竟誰的故事久遠
誰可以在夜裡躲過黑暗

那些將身體懸在半天空的逝者
與身上有著血盆大口的飛機
靜靜的 懷抱青春夢想
把遺憾藏在冰雪之下

茶屋小診所的味道 脆弱的飄向八方
自然無界 誰都不要上戰場
上個世紀的槍枝 在卡瓦卡博舉行了天葬
背了無數的雲朵在背上

阿里山的男孩不再打獵
繁華落印雲端
雲霧飄飄
祖靈的微笑在淡綠的茶色中
漾成一首溫柔的山地情歌

"The white clouds in the sky over the plateau

Have a dim silver lining.

They like to debate with the Holy Mountains on

Who have lived longer and who are immune from The darkness of

the night.

In the sky above the snow-covered horizon floats the spirit of those

who have passed away, and the ferocious looking airplanes.

In silence the spirits revive their youthful dreams and grief over

their unfulfilled wishes.

A new piece of sky then emerges and expands endlessly in all

directions above the horizon —

No more young men will be sent to the battle field under the new sky,

All guns and weapons will be disabled and permanently taken away

from the human world.

And then in the direction where you started your journey, you can

see the Gods coming forward to join you,

With a fatherly smile on their faces."

以死聞名的僰人懸棺

Hanging Coffins of the Bo people

不論是凌霄城、豆沙關或龍馬谷的任何懸棺，都無法讓後人看透僰人對於生命或死亡的態度。

從「他們是怎麼做到的」到「他們為什麼要這麼做」，這條路CERS走了超過二十個年頭，探索頻道與日本NHK也都被這些懸在半空的棺木所吸引並共同拍攝製作節目。重達五百磅（約二百二十七公斤）的棺木，要被放到七百多英尺（約二百一十三公尺）高的懸崖上，千年以前，沒有甚麼輔助工具的年代，究竟他們是如何做到的？更重要的是，他們為什麼要這麼做。是宗教信仰？還是為了躲避敵人或猛獸對屍體的破壞，所以要將他們「束之高閣」，並且還要接受日曬雨淋風吹。自從1985年HM第一次看到僰人懸棺時，就對這種特殊的葬儀深深著迷，歎為觀止取代了毛骨悚然。自此以後，HM說，僰人的鬼魂常伴他左右。

這些僰人的懸棺多位在雲南東北部和四川西南，熟悉以漢民族文化為思考基準的人一定難以相信，千年前竟然有人不願「入土為安」，反而把屍體高掛於懸崖，暴露在肉眼可見之處。死亡、葬禮和祭祖對漢民族來說是十分重要的，但是僰族對待屍體與亡靈的這種方式，完全打破了一般思維，即使從現在這個高度文明的年代回望，還是難以理解這種反地心引力的安葬方法。

有專家說，岩石或許是一個連結死者與上天的通道，因為懸棺是僰人死後登上天空的天梯。也有考古人類學家說，從古至今人們就相信死後升天，因此若把屍體放在離天近一點的地方或許也就離天堂更近了。不過被懷疑可能為僰族後代的何姓居民說，曾經有個故事流傳：千年以前這裡姓何的都是些做官的，他們相信若死後把屍體放在可以受到風吹雨淋日曬的地方，後代就會大為興盛，只是後來很多懸棺裡的屍體都被風吹走，結果姓何的這一族反而就一落千丈了。關於僰人的懸棺原因眾說紛紜，也都只是後代的傳說或猜測，並沒有任何科學上站得住腳的論述。

Hanging coffins of the ancient Bo people (a minority race in southwest China) can be seen in Ningshou City, Doushaguan and Longmagu. However, no one in these places could tell how the ancient Bo people managed to place their ancestors' coffins (often weighing up to 500 lbs) in holes and cracks on vertical cliff surfaces some six to seven hundred feet above ground. And was it for religious reasons that they did that ? Likewise no one can tell. Many years ago the Discovery Channel and Japan's NHK had produced a documentary on these coffins, which startled the world. CERS also started a study project on the subject.

HM first saw these hanging coffins in 1985. Since then, the questions how and why the ancient Bo people did that always hovers in his mind, to the extent that he could sometimes feel spirits of those lying in these coffins were around him.

The ancient Bo people's hanging coffin practice was totally against the Han people's belief that the spirit of the deceased may only rest in peace after the body has been buried underground.

Some say that ancient Bo people believed holes and cracks on vertical cliffs were paths to heaven so they placed coffins there to enable the deceased to go to heaven. Another saying, from a family surnamed Ho who was believed to be descendants of the ancient Bo people, was that their ancestors were officers in the Imperial Court generations after generations without fail. The success in their ancestors' career in the Imperial Court and the prosperity of descendants down the family line was solely due to the hanging coffin practice, they claimed. And then, later, they said, some coffins fell down the cliff because of damage of the supporting poles due to weathering etc. and the family began to encounter various difficulties and hardships, eventually leading to its total and irrevocable downfall.

不過，僰人違反自然的個性表現在了很多地方。HM 說僰人是擁抱矛盾的哲學家：他們單衣過冬、厚棉度夏；他們將亡者懸在空中，明知道有一天支撐的木頭會朽壞，棺木就會墜下……或許就是這種難以理解的挑戰吸引了 HM，所以才能把這個項目做得這麼長久與深入。

在這個懸棺的項目中，除了盡可能地找出這個習俗的可能原因外，還有另一個重點就是，僰人是否還有後代子孫的存在。具記載，明朝曾經在十六世紀討伐僰人，並將之趕盡殺絕，史稱九絲山大屠殺。不過，令人質疑的是，很難因為一場戰役就將一個民族全部消滅到一個不剩，更何況是擁有如此高超懸棺技術的僰族呢？CERS 希望能透過從懸棺中找出的先人骨骸以最先進的方式，找到 DNA 與僰人一致的後裔。這一條考古之路並非直通答案的大道，也許在過程中會衍生出更多的問題，也說不定會把大家帶進一個更大的謎團當中，說不定僰人早就把他們的秘密放在我們眼前，只是我們暫時還看不到而已，但這就是 CERS 所要追尋的不是嗎？

在某些項目的研究或保護過程中，我們可能無法快速的找到正確答案，但總會在過程中學習到或領悟到些甚麼，一點關於生命的線索或省思，就像 HM 那一年離開凌霄城時浮出的念頭：「即使沒有 DNA 測試，但我們不是全都帶有僰人的某種特徵嗎？我們不是都擅長把人捧到天上去，然後又任由他跌下來摔個遍體鱗傷嗎？有多少人會防患未然或亡羊補牢？答案說不定僰人早已留下，就藏在我們每個人的身上！」

HM 總是不改在關鍵時刻還是要幽默一下的個性，對著這些懸棺他又有了奇想：當我的隊員穩固棺木的功夫到家時，不如我也在懸崖上給自己留個位置。看來 HM 還是很享受那種被甚麼捧著，且高高在上的懸空感啊。

How Man would not say for sure whether these sayings have any truth in them. What he knows is that the ancient Bo people had a philosophy of doing things against the course of nature. These included wearing thin in bitterly cold winter and covering with thick cotton blankets in hot summer nights.

Another area which the CERS project aims to learn about is, are there any surviving descendants from the Bo people nowadays ? According to historical records, in 16th Century, the Ming Dynasty Imperial Court had waged a battle against the Bo people. In the battle, the Bo people, in entirety, were said to have been rounded up in the Jiusi Mountain area and massacred. CERS has doubts about this. It just doesn' t sound right that one single battle is sufficient to completely root out one whole race. Furthermore, the Bo people was not a backward people at the time, having regard to the advanced skill and knowledge they possessed. (Otherwise they would not be able to develop the method to place coffins on vertical surfaces of high cliffs.)

Extracting DNA from skeleton remains in the hanging coffins and comparing the data with modern people' s DNA might provide some clue. There is a long long way to go, and there is always a risk that this method will create more problems and unknowns that it can solve.

How Man believes that in a sense, we are all like that ancient Bo people. We flatter others, help them climb to dangerously high levels, and then would not give a damn when they fall back down heavily onto the ground. Perhaps the ancient Bo people' s DNA has long since got into our genes, and all of us are their descendants.

Himself being a person who enjoys being flattered and raised high up in the air, How Man is considering getting a place for himself when he next investigate a cliff with hanging coffins.

馬年轉第一神山‧岡仁波切

Circumambulation of Kailash
in the Year of the Horse

「這段旅程並不安逸，葡萄牙耶穌會教士佛雷爾回憶說，令人生畏的嚴寒和狂風把我的臉擦得疼痛難忍，使我大聲怒吼，『該詛咒的嚴寒！』在這個令人難以忍受的時刻，卡薩爾斯公主用熱茶來安慰我，透過翻譯她告訴我們要鼓起勇氣，因為如果她在我們身邊的話，高山和雪崩造成的危險都不會傷及我們。」這是美國作家約翰·麥格雷格在《西藏探險》中的一段文字，而這個耶穌會教士所詛咒的嚴寒所發生的地點正是岡底斯山。

藏人有很強的說故事能力，特別是運用了他們周圍的自然景觀。故事複雜的程度與彼此的牽扯，有點像希臘羅馬神話故事，只可惜，沒有太多人有能力將這些故事搬上大螢幕。神山，當然是西藏傳說故事中很重要的主角，祂們通常都有偉大的名字、性別以及所屬教派。西藏神山其中以岡仁波切為首，藏人將之視為宇宙中心，而神山岡仁波切正是岡底斯山的最高峰。祂不單是西藏佛教徒心中最聖潔的神山，也是印度教徒認定最神聖的地方之一，是 Lord Shiva 濕婆神的老家，是一個跨越宗教的神山。

2002 年，趁著馬年，CERS 跟著信徒們一起親身經歷了這個朝聖盛會，轉一圈就是五十三公里的路程。傳說馬年是釋迦摩尼佛的本命年，因此只要在這一年轉山一次便可多消十二世的業障。當然，多消一點業障並不是 CERS 選擇此時來轉山的目的。而是，馬年會聚集將近四十萬的信徒前來朝聖，在這個時間來做考察可以取得最多樣化且跨地域的資訊。

這一次，CERS 規畫的是兩天的行程，最初的十公里非常美好，只要順著其他朝聖者的腳步緩緩而行，沿途還一睹了岡仁波切的尊榮，這可不是想看就能看到的，若老天不賞臉，多數的朝聖者走完全程也無法親眼一見。第一天，大家前進了二十公里，黃昏時還攀登了一個五千六百米的山口，之後，不停下歇息也不行。

The extreme weather conditions around the Kailash region have been vividly described in many books written by pioneer explorers. Kailash is the highest mountain along the Gangdise Mountain Ridge on the Tibetan plateau. Kailash is considered as the most holy mountain by many peoples and religions. Tibetans and Tibetan buddhists consider the Mountain as the center of the universe and the holiest place. Hindus believe that the Mountain is the place of abode of Lord Shiva, the supreme god for destruction of the universe.

Every year religious adherents would do circumambulations of the Mountain to revere and show faith to their gods. For buddhists, performing the act in the year of the Horse is particularly important. This is because Buddha was born in the year of the Horse, and they believe that doing a circumambulation round Kailash in a year of the Horse would result in their evil karma in the previous twelve life cycles being pardoned. The year 2002 was a year of the Horse. That year CERS joined the tens of thousands of religious worshippers in doing the circumambulation of Kailash.

The purpose was more for better understanding the event and its significance in the worshippers' religious believes, than for CERS and its members to get rid of evil karma in their previous lives. HM and his CERS members completed the trek in two days. The first day was comparatively easy and not too tough. They just followed other pilgrims and moved on slowly. They were lucky the weather was good and they were able to see the grand, snow covered dome shape top of the Mountain at various points. Before night fall, they climbed up a 5,600 m mountain pass. After that, and totally exhausted, they rested for the night at a spot with lower altitude.

第二天得從四千八百米直上五千六百米的北面關口，再強悍的平地人也得在這段路途上謙虛而行。人們安靜地走著，有人揹著水壺，沿途燒茶；有人只拿著碗，餓的時候就跟其他的朝聖者要點糌粑充飢。大多數是藏人，也有信奉佛教的夏爾巴人和信奉印度教的尼泊爾人和印度人，當然中間也穿插幾個西方人。海拔高度讓隊員們只能緩步而行，HM 甚至每走大約十步就得停下喘息，儘管他已經在高原進出無數次，並且這次為了要轉山，還特意在高原先停留了三個星期，但畢竟身上流的血與藏族不同，還是需要比較多的氧氣啊。

很多朝聖者出現了高山症狀，但依然勉強繼續著，有年約六十的婦人因染病及過度疲勞而在路上往生；一名年僅二十八歲的年輕女子因為呼吸困難喝上別人好心遞給的糖水時嗆著昏倒，最後不治；奄奄一息的老人被年輕人攙扶著下山……。沿途所見卻讓 HM 有了不同的省思。

朝聖的目的到底是甚麼？不是應該為朝聖者帶來心靈的喜悅與心智的啟迪嗎？那麼，神山為何能看著這些信仰者在自己懷抱受苦甚至死去？這些人只有一個再單純不過的目的，那就是信仰。把一座山當成最高的崇拜對象，本就是人類對自然的原始崇拜行為，但，轉山與上教堂或進寺廟大不相同，這個過程牽涉到生與死，就不得不讓人多思考一些了。難道沒有人可以做點甚麼來減少這些心痛發生嗎？轉山朝聖不是一個突發事件，也有一條可循的路線，如果旅遊局或當地政府能設立幾個簡單的急救站或治療高山症的小診所，不就可以減少這些悲劇發生嗎？只顧著在山下設崗哨收費，把這個神聖的行為當作市場經濟來看待，怎不令人憤怒。

山口經幡飄揚數百米，朝聖著不間斷地向著唯一的目標前去，HM 佇足，五味雜陳的感動跟著經幡一起在藍天下飄動。拿起相機回頭再看一眼岡仁波切神山，山峰已全然隱沒在雲霧之中，這個離天最近的地方。

The next day they continued the trek on the 4,800 m high trail and proceeded towards another formidable 5,600 m high mountain pass. The trail was full of slow moving people. All were silent because they really did not have any spare energy or breath to speak. Some carried water and gas stove to make tea on the way. Some carried nothing except a bowl which they used to beg for water and food from others when thirsty or hungry. Most people on the trail were Tibetan buddhists but there were also Hindu Indians and Nepaleses. A few westerners could also be seen from time to time. For every ten steps or so, How Man had to stop to breathe, so this part of the trek was really tough for him. If he had not done the three weeks acclimatization on the plateau before hand, he would not have been able to complete the trek.

Many pilgrims developed symptoms of altitude sickness but they struggled on. An old woman succumbed to fatigue (and probably also some disease she might already had) and died on the way. A young girl who had breathing difficulties stopped to drink some refreshment fluid. She choked herself, fell unconscious and eventually also died. Many elderly persons who were too weak to continue the trek had to give up. They were carefully carried down the trail to lower places by their younger companions. Memories of these sad events have since always stayed in How Man's mind.

In doing the circumambulation, the pilgrims were seeking blessings from the Holy Mountain to enable them to have comfort of the mind and enlightenment of the soul. For some, they were risking their lives to do that. The local authorities should have foreseen such risks but unfortunately they had not done anything (e.g. setting up first-aid

那一天，HM 這樣寫著：「不管岡仁波切給的是祝福或詛咒，有一課是最有力的，有別於世界上被不同宗教你爭我奪的那些聖地，岡仁波切是被不同宗教和平共享的，千百年來，一直如是。」

stations along the trail) to address the problem. It seems that their concern, instead, was on collection of admission fee to participate the event. Hence all they did about the event was to set up an entrance booth at the starting point of the trail to collect admission fee.

As How Man's shadow I have been following his steps all the way. I now gradually understand the true meaning of exploration. The path an explorer has to go through to seek out the truth is always not easy to travel along. In addition to self-motivation, he also needs guidance or advice from others. His findings in the end might also not tally or even contradict with what people generally believe. For all these years, has How Man ever bothered by such thoughts ? Has his quest for truth ever been weakened ?

At the mountain pass several hundred meters ahead, prayer flags were flipping under the wind. Pilgrims were moving undauntedly towards it. Stopping for a short break, How Man took out his camera and wanted to take a picture. Just at this moment, unfortunately, a layer of cloud and mist emerged on the top of the Holy Mountain, making it invisible.

That day, How Man wrote in his expedition diary "A place revered and regarded as monumental by different religions is often a place where people of these religions would fight and kill each other to try to control. Kailash is not. It is peaceful all the way through. This is because it has an immense power to keep its worshippers, of whatever religion, in harmony and willing to share its blessings with different people."

卡瓦卡博的茶屋與診所

Teahouse and Clinic at
Mount Khawakarpo Circumambulation Route

關於探險，我總是預期挑戰或問題會發生，我就
是去解決它！

About exploration, I expect challenges and
obstables, and my job is to fix it and overcome it.

---How Man

美麗，經常是與殘酷雙生雙宿；梅里雪山，正是如此。但願你只是遙望、敬畏，而心中沒有「征服」或「人定勝天」這樣的妄想。

從雲南走滇藏公路，進入西藏的交界時，是無法錯過梅里雪山的。但，也很難真正看清祂的容貌，祂總是在雲霧的簇擁下。在藏文經典中，梅里雪山的十三座六千米以上的高峰，都被奉為「修行於太子神宮的神仙」，其中的主峰卡瓦卡博，更被尊為西藏的八大神山之首。

1987 年以前，人們對於卡瓦卡博的認識只有高度，六千七百四十米，祂的美與高與困難讓全世界的登山者垂涎。1987 年六月，來自日本上越山嶽會的登山者花了三個月的時間登上了五千一百米，歷經了冰崩、雪崩以及難以翻越的陡峭冰壁，最後宣告失敗，這次他們連卡瓦卡博的影子也沒看見。1988 年美國克倫奇登山隊闖進梅里雪山，但同樣失敗而歸，這一趟他們只上到了四千二百米。

最有名也最慘痛的征服梅里雪山事件是發生在 1990 年，那是由中日聯合組成的登山隊，隊員中有三分之一以上的人有過八千米以上的攀登經驗，且配備著先進的衛星雲圖接收器，且事前已經有過多次前導探勘。十二月二十一日，前鋒突擊隊成功地攀登到主峰西側 6470 的高度，離峰頂的垂直距離只有 240 米。但山神還是震怒了，突如其來的雲遮沒了山頂，接著就是狂風暴雪，登山隊長井上治郎，他是日本知名的氣象專家，從三號營地下令撤退，在山頂邊的前鋒人員直到第二天才平安回到三號營。

悲劇的真正發生是在 1991 年的第一天，暴雪將三號營地完全封死；一月三日，當三號營地跟大本營通了最後一次話後，就完全消失了，山神接走了這十七條生命，這是登山史上第二大的悲劇。1998 年 7 月 18 日藏民尚木達瓦近在四千米高的夏季牧場放牛回家時發現了冰川上五顏六色的東西。卡瓦卡博神山將這十七個人的遺骸遺物送回人間來了。

Beauty and cruelty are often very close together. The Meili Mountain is a good example of this. If you have the opportunity to admire the Mountain with respect from a distance, I hope the idea " I want to conquer it by getting to its top some day" will not arise in my mind, because the idea is a very dangerous one.

Meili Mountain is situated on the Yunnan side of the Yunnan-Tibetan border. If you travel along the Yunnan-Tibetan highway towards Tibet, the Mountain will come into your view as you move near the border area, provided that there is no fog or mist at the time. As this doesn't happen frequently, few travelers have the luck to see the top of the full mountain ridge. According to Tibetan folklore, the 13 main peaks (all over 6,000 m high) along the Meili Mountain ridge are palace residence of heavenly gods. The highest of them, Mount Khawakarpo, is one of the eight most revered holy mountains on the Tibetan plateau.

Prior to 1987, the world knew very little about Mount Khawakarpo, except its elevation – 6,740 m above sea level. Because of its beauty, and the fact that no one has ever got to its top before, conquering it has become the dream of many mountaineers and explorers. In June 1987, a team of mountaineers from the Japanese (Jouetsu Sangakukai) Mountaineering Club spent three months trying to summit it. They climbed to an almost vertical ice cliff at 5,100 m when they were forced to abort the attempt because of an avalanche. They felt very bitter as they did not even manage to see the summit. In 1988 the American (Nicolas Clinch) Mountaineering Club also try to summit it. They also failed and the highest point they reached was only 4,200 m.

The most famous and disastrous attempt was in 1990 by a joint

HM 曾經在探險筆記上寫過：「現代的所謂探險家，看見一座山便耐不住性子想要登上山頂去征服它。但真正傳統探險家看見一座山，很可能只去最低的山口。他追求的不是征服，而是尋找山背後所隱藏的，以擴大他對周遭的知識。」

為了紀念並以此為鑑，CERS 的中甸中心收藏著好幾樣那次中日探險隊在雪地裡被挖掘出的遺物，有照相機、底片、背包、眼鏡、登冰河鞋，甚至功藤俊二的筆記本。

這個美麗又殘酷的卡瓦卡博神山，至今還是高高地坐在雲端，令登山者扼腕，並接受信徒的朝聖與膜拜；尤其每到藏曆羊年，總是會吸引最多的朝聖者前來轉山，而這個梅里轉山，一轉就是十三天。

2002 年，CERS 開始了卡瓦卡博轉山項目，也就是在信徒們轉山必經之地的瀾滄江上吊橋兩頭各建一個茶屋以及小診所。橋的這一頭，是一間奉茶兼休息的地方，可以讓 CERS 在六十年一次的水羊年，也就是 2003 年，向十萬多名的轉山者進行普查。守著橋的另一頭的將是一間傳統藏式診所，將為這些長途跋涉的朝聖者提供基本的醫療服務。茶屋為轉山者奉茶，並順道調查高原上的大小情況，像是自然環境、野生動物、文化習慣、宗教信仰、教育、健康、兒童、婦女、老人等等，有了這些一手資料後，CERS 就可以進行各種社會、科學和行為上的研究。這不失為一種以逸待勞的探險方法，守在這裡就可以知道高原上的大小事，但，必須是在朝聖者蜂擁而至的這一年，錯過了就要再等六十年了。

這個茶屋與診所在 2003 年善盡職責，六個月內總共奉上了數千杯的酥油茶並照顧了超過 4,600 個轉山者的健康。保護與照顧神山的子民，是 HM 這個現代探險家向卡瓦卡博表達敬畏的最溫柔方式。不過十三年過去了，這地方已經毀了，接管的當地村民並沒有好好的維護這個地方；神山腳下的診所和茶屋，很不幸地成為管理者失職的個案。

Chinese-Japanese team comprising 17 very experienced climbers. One third of them had climbing experience at altitudes over 8,000 m. The team had all the advanced equipment to receive weather information from satellites and the like. And much survey and preparation works were done before hand. On 21 December, the climbers' forward party reached 6,470 m on the western slope of Mount Khawakarpo. Further ascending 240 m in vertical height would get them to the summit. It must be that their intrusion had annoyed the mountain god. Within minutes, a hail storm developed around the summit. Team captain (Inoue Jirou, a famous meteorologist) ordered retreat to camp 3. At camp 3, the team waited for one whole night for the forward party to return safely.

Real tragedy for the team came on the following days. The heavy snow storm went on non-stop. On the first day of 1991, the team reported that camp 3 where they stayed was totally blocked off by very thick snow. Two days later, on January 3, communication with camp 3 was totally lost. All attempts to contact the team failed. The mountain had taken away the lives of all the 17 team members.

Years later, on 18 July 1998, while taking his cattles to the summer grazing ground, a Tibetan herdsman Shangmu Dawa saw some colorful stuff on a glacier. These were later found to be bodies and belongings of the 17 team members. The god at Mount Khawakarpo has finally sent their bodies and things back.

How Man had once written in his expedition diary "A real explorer is not a man who wants to "conquer" a high mountain he sees." He respects it and doesn't want to conquer it. What he wants is offering buttered tea to pilgrims. Medical care and attention were given to 4,600 of them. Instead of trying to "conquer" Mount Khawakarpo, How Man had always wanted to revere and show respect to it. He believed the best way to do that was to give warmth and tender care to its pilgrims.

Thirteen years have since passed. The two huts are now deserted and left unattended because of remoteness of the place. The next Year of the Sheep will come some 60 years later, How Man hopes that, by that time, someone who share the same philosophy as him will emerge to restore and resurrect the teahouse and the clinic to provide the much welcomed services to pilgrims of this great mountain.

鄒族的過去、現在與未來

The Past, Present and Future of
the Tsou People

台灣阿里山的雲霧與神木一樣，具有魔力，特別是在清晨第一道陽光出現之前。你最好不要輕易的在起霧時許下諾言，因為除了山裡的精靈，連祖靈都會要你信守一輩子。

台灣島的阿里山脈與青藏高原完全是兩種不同個性的山林樣貌。青藏高原壯麗嚴酷，用盡力氣呼喊，也不會有回音。而阿里山脈卻擁有獨出一格的溫潤秀麗，像是仙人居住之地。特別是阿里山國家公園的這個區域，展現出的是人與山林共生共存的狀態。這兩處都一樣地擄獲了 HM 的探險之心。

阿里山鄒族的傳統房舍再建，是 CERS 在台灣唯一的項目。熟悉 HM 的人都知道他有很多台灣的好友，他也經常來台灣，甚至台灣的幾個外島都有他的足跡，像是金門、馬祖、澎湖、蘭嶼，和小琉球。他也喜歡台東的日出，海洋季風，但是阿里山鄒族的文化，更讓 HM 充滿了興趣。

CERS 的項目在達邦，是鄒族社區的中心，小鎮裡人口超過八百人，不到三條街區。其他住民散落在附近的山丘上，山谷裡，大多從事種植茶葉跟其他農業。

「以前他們喜歡獵人頭，現在自己的人頭數都變得這麼少了！」HM 還是不改喜歡開玩笑的個性，用這樣的方式提醒了我們鄒族的人口正在減少當中，現在已經不到七千人了。

更可惜的是鄒族的文化。不是說九族文化村那樣的形式不好，而是如果能夠將鄒族的傳統屋舍蓋在鄒族自己的土地上，並且給予下一代適度的教育，那麼每一代的鄒族人便可以更靠近自己的生命源頭，而不迷失在其他強勢文化及城市慾望之中。

五年前一個偶然的機會，透過安孝明（Amo）跟蒲慧玲夫妻讓 CERS 了解到鄒族的文化和它正在瓦解的狀況。這對年輕夫妻非常

In Ali Mountain, Taiwan, the morning mist, like the Shenmu (god tree), is considered to possess magic power. If one makes a ledge when the first ray of sunshine falls on the morning mist in Ali Mountain, he better keeps it. Otherwise the mountain spirit will join hand with the spirits of that person's ancestors to bring misfortune and ill fate to him. The saying goes.

The Ali Mountain Range and the Tibetan plateau are two different kinds of mountain areas. Each has its special beauty and character, and its own way of interacting with people who live on them. And both have attracted the attention of How Man as a heritage preservationist.

The CERS' only project in Taiwan is about the traditional houses of the Tsou people in Ali Mountain. Those who know How Man well know that he has many friends in Taiwan and that he has been to Taiwan and its outlying island many times. He likes Taiwan but what really attracts his interest is the culture of the Tsou people in Ali Mountain.

The CERS project site is situated in Dabang. This small town, with a population of about 800 people, is the community center of the Tsou people. These Tsou people live on hill slopes and villages. Most of them are tea farmers.

"Because they hunt people for their heads in the past, and the mutual hunting over the decades have reduced their population to the present size." How Man likes to joke. That of course was not the real reason. But it reminds people that there are less and less Tsou people as time passes. A recent estimate puts its population at less than 7,000.

Even sadder is the gradual disappearance of the Tsou people culture.

熱切地想要找回先人的過去。打獵是鄒族重要的傳統，但是大多都被禁止了。賴以維生的打獵活動所衍生出來的文化也隨之消失。現代卻簡單的房屋已經取代了鄒族傳統的茅草屋。安孝明與蒲慧玲都是鄒族的年輕人，對自己的文化不僅有認同感更有傳承的使命。他們夢想著重建傳統房屋，當作歷史的見證。CERS 對他們的熱情印象深刻，並承諾會幫助他們完成夢想。

有了海南島的經驗後，阿里山的項目終於有機會來實踐 HM「倒過來做」的哲學了。學會深知理想的管理人才是項目能否永續的最重要因素，因此這個鄒族房舍重建的項目先找到了適合的當地人選，才開始動手。安孝明和蒲慧玲當然是最佳人選。

於是三棟傳統鄒族的茅草房就在「過去、現在與未來」的概念下動工了。在鄒族「手工」與「手造」的建築即將失去的此刻，Amo 用著他那雙獵人的手和一顆熱情勇敢的心，開始打造了這傳統茅草房。蓋一棟房子光是備料就需要一年的時間，每個步驟都是靠著 Amo 的雙手親力親為，因此一棟房舍的完成，超過了兩年。

2016 年的九月初，HM 帶著台灣團隊驗收了兩間房，分別代表著鄒族的過去和現在。「過去」裡，沒水沒電，彷彿走進上個世紀，角落裡放的是弓箭和打獵的戰利品，飛鼠、山豬的頭顱和幾個大獠牙。「現在」裡有宿舍、廚房、浴室、餐廳以及一個展示區，展示著鄒族過往的獵人頭習俗，以及族人傳統樣貌。「現在」有著很強的教育功能，HM 滿意地說：「Amo 跟慧玲已經招待兩百多位鄒族的學生來這裡參觀了。孩子們來這裡不只是看看以前的茅草屋跟文物而已，他們也來學習怎麼使用傳統的刀來製作器具；怎麼用弓、箭來射箭；怎麼在傳統的石爐上生火煮飯；有時候還會被邀請在這兩棟屋子裡過夜。」

Although the local authorities have made some efforts to preserve minority peoples' culture, like constructing heritage houses, in the Nine Tribes' Culture Village, the Tsou people nonetheless thought that the purpose could be better served if their heritage house is built on their own land. This way, their people would have a stronger sense of identification.

Five years ago when How Man was in Taiwan doing a study on the Tsou people history and culture, he had the opportunity of meeting a Tsou couple Pu Hui-lin and her husband Amo. The young couple were literate and cultured people and they were keen to retrieve and retain memories of their ancestors' past to ensure their fellow clansmen would not forget them. The Tsou people's ancestors made their living by hunting and they lived in grass huts. Both have disappeared now. As a heritage preservationist himself, How Man totally shared the couple's feeling so he quickly pledged to help them fulfill their wish. How Man in fact glad to have met the couple who share the same values and ideas. He recalled that in the Hainan Island Li People project, the CERS had built traditional style houses but subsequently could not find suitable persons to manage them on a long-term basis. And the project therefore failed.

This time was different. The couple were people living there and they were dedicated. They would therefore be the best people to help manage the project.

The Tsou people project involved constructing two traditional grass houses. The work was done by hand by Amo in strict accordance with

「未來」呢？Amo 的未來肯定跟鄒族那個十歲少年的未來不會一樣，也許「未來」的茅草之上會是太陽能板，茅草之下完全由電腦控制，誰又知道呢？期待 CERS 與鄒族共同的「未來」。

the traditional method. Because of the painstaking procedures involved in selection of materials and construction steps, and because Amo was working single-handedly, it took him a total of four years to build the two houses.

In September 2016, How Man and his CERS team went to Taiwan to inspect the two project houses. The house that shows the Tsou people's past does not have electricity supply and fittings in it and crude and primitive giving vistors the feeling that they are back to the ancient days. Display items in the house include hunting bows and arrows, skulls and tusks of boars. The house showing the Tsou people's present and fitted out with a kitchen, a bathroom, a dormitory, a dining area and an exhibition area. Pictures and photographs about Tsou people's head hunting traditions, clothes and ornaments, etc. in the past, are displayed in this exhibition area. How Man and his team were glad to learn from Amo that since the opening of the two houses, more than 200 young students of Tsou origin had come to visit them. During the visit, they were briefed on things like their people's history and traditions. They were also taught how to use their people's traditional tools and utensils to meet their daily needs. Selected students were also invited to spend the night in the two houses.

As regards the future of the Tsou people, no one can say for sure what they would be like. One thing is sure and that is CERS will continue to support them in their efforts to preserve their culture and heritage.

坐看雲起 --- 駝峰飛行員

Watching the Clouds Rise
– The Hump Pilots

還有甚麼樣的故事能激勵探險家的「探險精神」呢？

如果，神山是離天最近的地方，那麼，飛越神山的那群人是否可以說是全世界、全人類歷史上離天最近的物種呢？二次大戰期間那些駝峰航線的飛行員又是用著甚麼樣的膽識飛越喜馬拉雅山呢？他們經歷的一切全都令 HM 這個探險家神往，因為再不會有比這更瘋狂的飛行事蹟出現了！

如果你恰巧是個飛行員，不論是客機或戰機，請想像一下你正坐在駕駛艙裡沒有加壓設備的 C-53 型飛機裡，你的飛行高度上限是兩萬六千英尺，你將從新疆往印度飛去，你即將從喜馬拉雅山西側穿過 K2 山區（K2 是世界第二高峰），你沒有導航，你得憑著過人的眼力才有機會平安降落在德里……。

當 2002 年 HM 與迪克‧洛斯（Dick Rossi）第一次見面的時候，HM 就清楚的告訴了這位曾是飛虎隊員也是駝峰飛行員說，自己對他感興趣的不是戰爭史也不是那種膚淺的中國民族主義，而是由衷欽佩這些飛行員的勇氣與冒險心，某種程度來說，這與 HM 的探險事業所需要的探險精神幾乎是一致的。

HM 喜歡把這些每次升空後就不計後果的駝峰飛行員比喻為「飛行創業家」，這種人愛冒險、有自信、就像現代社會的創業投資家。金錢報酬是必須的附屬品，更重要的是過度的刺激以及那種「不是一般人能做到的」挑戰與自信。這些飛行員們跟不可能動搖的大自然對抗，保佑他們的是命運，每一次成功完成任務，謝天謝大地。事實證明，這些藝高人膽大的飛行員們所擁有的勇氣與個性，讓他們在戰後即使選擇了不同的行業也都有傲人的成績。像是 Roy Farrell 創辦了國泰航空、迪克則成立了飛虎航空，是一家貨運航空公司，後來賣給了聯邦快遞，而探險出這條駝峰航線的飛行員陳文寬，不僅成功營運了當時的中央航空運輸公司，更在台灣成立了復興航空。

What are the things that inspire and impel explorers to venture into the unknown, sometimes risking their lives ?

How Man was fascinated when he first learnt of the stories of "hump pilots" in WWII. These were pilots who flew over the Himalayas, a dangerous act in those days. Unlike modern aircraft, their C-53 cargo planes did not have pressurized cockpit or any modern navigation system. Also these old planes could not fly above 26,000 feet. This means, when flying from China's Xinjiang to India, they needed to fly through gaps between the Himalaya and K2 (second highest mountain in the world) mountain ridges, and land in Delhi, India, with just their naked eyes.

In 2002 when How Man met Dick Rossi, a hump pilot, for the first time, he expressed his admiration for these pilots' courage. How Man believes that, without an adventurer's spirit and an entrepreneur's drive and determination, these pilots would not have been able to accomplish their flying missions time and again. Because of these qualities in their character, many of them were able to lead a successful career in various fields after the war: Dick set up the Flying Tiger Air Cargo Company (which later became the United Express), Roy Farrell founded the Cathay Pacific, and Moon Chin, the pilot who first mapped out and flew the hump route, set up the TransAsia Airways in Taiwan.

How Man has been in close touch with the hump pilot since 2002. This is not only because he was greatly attracted by their stories, but because he wanted to record these stories in history.

"We all know WWII and we now have peace. But many of us may

從 2002 年至今，HM 跟這些心中的英雄都保持著非常密切的關
係，不僅僅是他們的年代與生命故事深深吸引著 HM，更重要的是
CERS 希望能夠將這段驚心動魄的歷史盡可能地保留下來。

「儘管我們這一代的人都知道有過第二次世界大戰，但是多數的人
並不清楚現在的太平盛世是多少人的犧牲所換來的。我認為，這群
駝峰飛行員正代表了這些為和平而奮鬥的人。」相信 HM 的這段話
足以說明為什麼 CERS 會如此重視這些碩果僅存的駝峰飛行員了。

not know that the peace we now enjoy was won by the sacrifices and courageous acts of many people, and the hump pilots can best represent these heroes", How Man said. Not many hump pilots are still alive today, that's why How Man treasures his contact and connections with them very much.

翻越 K2 第一人・陳文寬

Moon Chin, the first to fly
over Mount K2

「當時我的秘密任務是要尋找中印之間的新航道,喀喇崑崙山像個巨大的牆把新疆跟印度平原隔開,我必須找到較低的高山啞口穿越。起飛後我將飛機駛向南方,因為 K2 西邊的啞口似乎較低,但仍舊是高過我 C-53 的飛行高度,所以格外危險。第一次嘗試時我遇上了雲層,濕度導致機翼結了厚冰,凝結的冰霜會使飛機重量增加高度下降,於是我向上拉升到一萬八千呎,結冰的情況反而好轉了,然後我看到眼前出現一個啞口,我把飛機朝那裏飛去,當印度平原似乎就出現在眼前的那一刻,我碰上了巨大的冰雹風暴,冰雹朝著擋風玻璃而來,風暴也帶走了視線,於是我跟副駕駛潘國定說,回頭吧,我們迅速做了個 60 度急彎,一脫離險境後,我們又馬上爬升到兩萬一千英尺高再度嘗試飛越啞口,這次沒有風暴等在另一頭,我們順利的滑過了 K2,我看見了印度平原上那條清晰的印度河,那是最好的導航了,將我們帶向新德里。兩個小時後我的 C-53 降落在了新德里機場……」。

半個世紀前的這趟冒險,現在聽起來似乎很輕鬆,其實卻是一個拿命去搏的不可能任務。陳文寬用著高超的飛行技術贏了,成為第一個飛越世界最危險山脈的機長,他的這條駝峰第二航線成為戰時中國西南最重要的備用運輸補給線。

一直以來,全世界的人都非常尊敬佩服那些以一己之力,在沒有先進儀器下飛越大洋或開發新航線的西方飛行員。在中國以及世界多數地方也都以為駝峰航線完全是美國人的功勞。大部分人並不知道其實也有很多技術極佳的華人飛行員同樣為中國航空的駝峰航線做了貢獻。然而這位在中國出生,美國籍的陳文寬卻是駝峰航線之所以存在的最重要飛行員。

陳文寬的冒險事蹟多如繁星無法細數,他令人欽羨的飛行生涯中也同時包括了許多機密與具爭議的飛行任務,從二次世界大戰、中國內戰、韓戰、越戰等戰役。

"At that time my secret mission was to find a new flight route between China and India. The Karakoram Mountain ridge was like a huge wall separating China's Xinjiang and the Indian plain. After take off, I flew towards the south as the mountain passes on the west side of K2 appeared to be lower. But they were still higher than the height at which my C-53 was flying so the situation was quite dangerous. In my first attempt to fly over the ridge I met a layer of clouds. Because of the moisture in the cloud, a layer of ice began to form on my wings and quickly grew thicker and thicker. The ice increased the weight of my plane and caused it to lose some height. I therefore pulled up to 18,000 feet. At this height weather was better and frosting of the wings began to ease off. And then a mountain pass appeared in front. I flew towards it. When I almost could see the Indian plain below, a hail storm developed in front and ice pellets were hitting hard on my wind shield blinding my sight. I and my co-pilot Pan Guoding quickly took a 60° turn back to exit the storm zone. And then we climbed up to a higher altitude of 21,000 feet to make a second attempt to pass through the mountain pass. This time we were lucky. There was no storm and we flew through safely, passing Mount K2 on our side. Soon afterwards, I could see the Indian plain below. By reference to the Indus River, which we could see clearly now, we flew toward New Delhi. And then in about two hours' time, my C-53 reached and landed in New Delhi Airport." With a calm voice, Moon Chin recounted to How Man his first flight on the hump route. Moon was held as one of the most courageous and skillful pilot because that flight. Until the end of the war, the hump route was China's most important supply route in the southwest.

There were good reasons for Moon to earn people's respect. Flying

還有一件輝煌的事蹟是值得不斷地被提及的。當年杜立德將軍進行東京大轟炸後迫降在中國境內，經中國人救起之後，他搭乘陳文寬的 C-53 準備飛越駝峰到加爾各答，同行的有三名機員以及七位付費乘客。當天美國大使館告知杜立德將軍緬北的密支那將在下午落入日軍手裡，當陳文寬在那天下午要降落密支那機場時，杜立德遞了張紙條告訴陳文寬說，這裡已經被日軍佔領了。但是陳文寬因為看到了一架 C-47 從跑道上起飛前往印度，於是不顧警告還是著陸了。

當時在機場上的眾多難民原本以為最後一班飛機已經飛離了，正打算離開；突然發現這架飛機從天而降，於是紛紛衝向這架 C-53。機門一開，人群搶著登機，原本機上只有二十八個改裝的帆布座椅，但是大批的人一下子全都擠了上來。艙門一關，陳文寬加足油門立刻滑行。「你知道你在幹嘛嗎？」杜立德緊張地問陳文寬。陳文寬卻信心滿滿地回答：「不用擔心，難民不會太重的！」

在那個熱血沸騰的年代裡，人們是把死亡當成家常便飯的，更何況是像陳文寬這樣的飛行員。結果，當他們成功降落加爾各答機場時，總共有七十個乘客下機；但是當行李艙打開時，又有八個逃難者跌了出來。陳文寬又為 C-53 創下了另一個特殊的飛行紀錄。

大戰結束時，陳文寬擔任中國航空公司的總機師，他載過的名人不計其數，其中也包括蔣介石及夫人。戰後他展現了生意人的天分，創辦了中央航空運輸公司，購買超過百架劃歸剩餘物資的飛機；1951 年他在台灣成立了復興航空，在 1983 年賣掉持股退休，搬回美國。

在這些年與陳文寬的相處中，HM 聽到的不是走入歷史的故事，而是仍然令人血脈賁張生命刻痕。這些無法複製的人生經驗，其實就是 HM 在這三十年的探險生涯中想要創造的：勇敢的、獨特的、具有時代意義且無法被後人複製！2008 年，陳文寬將自己收藏幾十年的珍貴照片及攝影底片交給 CERS。那些照片不僅述說了他個人的珍貴記憶，更是那個烽火年代的最好見證。這所有的一切也將豐

old airplanes like the C-53 without modern navigation aids along the hump route was indeed not something for those with less courage and skill. For a long time, people gave credit only to the Americans for opening the hump route supply line. They did not realize that many Chinese pilots like Moon had contributed to the success of the route.

After the hump route flights, Moon had also participated in many other similarly dangerous or secret/controversial flight missions including those during China's civil war, the Korean and the Vietnam wars.

One other thing about Moon worth mentioning is about his landing in Burma's Myitkyina airport very shortly before it fell into the hands of the invading Japan troops. He was flying his C-53 along the hump route to Calcutta India, with a plan to stop over at Myitkyina Burma. There were a total of eleven persons on the plane including the American General Doolittle. In a bombing mission on Tokyo, the General's airplane was damaged by flak fire but it succeeded in flying back to China to force land. Before boarding China's plane to Calcutta in the morning, the General received notification from the American Consulate that Myitkyina would fall into Japanese hands in the afternoon. When the plane was over Myitkyina and Moon was getting ready to land, the General went into the cockpit and passed a note to him which said that the place had already fallen. At this juncture, however, Moon saw a C-47 plane taking off from the airport runway. He therefore judged that the place had not fallen yet. So he landed despite the General's advice.

As soon as the C-53 stopped and the cabin door opened, a large crowd of refugees rushed forward and squeezed into the plane. The plane crew quickly closed the door and Moon promptly flew his plane into the sky again.

"Do you know what you are doing ? "the General shouted nervously.

富 CERS 在中甸中心的博物館。

2012 年，100 歲的陳文寬跟著 CERS 重新踏上緬甸，重訪了他七十年的未曾再踏上的土地。這次他可是跟著 CERS 的探險腳步前進的，他踏上了 HM Explorer 航行了伊洛瓦底江，也到了以往他只從空中俯瞰的茵萊湖，老飛行員說，從前從前……這個湖在夏季是個大湖，但到了冬季枯水期時就成了兩個小湖……時光流轉，緬甸整體來說雖然並沒有改變多少，但卻已經不是飛行員年輕時眼裡的那片土地了。慶幸的是，陳文寬的幽默與好奇心彷彿也跟著他的年紀一同成長，到了無人可及的境界了。

"No problem, these refugees shouldn't be too heavy for my plane to carry ", Moon said with confidence.

When Moon's plane finally landed in Calcutta, he found that his 27 seat plane had carried 70 persons with another 8 in the luggage compartment. Moon therefore has set another world record.

After the war, Moon worked as a Chief Flight Captain for the China Airlines. While in this post, he had many prestigious passengers on his plane, including Generalissimo and Madame Chiang Kai-shek. He later showed his business talent by procuring over 100 airplanes that were decommissioned from the U.S. military and set up the Central Air Transport Corp (CATC). In 1951 he founded Taiwan's Transasia Airways. In 1983, he sold his shares to retire in the United States.

How Man and Moon have known each other for many years now. Both have a unique and adventurous experience in life that they are proud of and other people would envy. In 2008, Moon gave How Man many precious photographs taken in early days. These photographs, now kept at CERS' Zhongdian Centre, give people a good idea what the community and people's livelihood were like in China in the war years.

In 2012, Moon, now aged 100, followed How Man and traveled on the Irrawaddy River in CERS' river boat HM Explorer. He was last on Burmese soil some 70 years ago. The old pilot told How Man that he could still remember looking down at the Inle Lake from his airplane in the old days. He said the Lake was a big piece of water in summer time but in dry water season, the big piece of water would shrink to become two small lakes lying close together. He said despite the long lapse of time, he did not see any big change in things in Burma and he was glad to be back again in peace time.

飛虎王牌・飛越駝峰735趟—迪克・羅西

Dick Rossi – The Ace of AVG
who had flown the hump route 735 times

我們遠征的目的並不是去當第一個發現的人，好像很英雄；而是，我們怎麼去保護我們的發現。重點是內容，重要的是我們怎麼去解釋，然後給予保護、研究、教育。

It's not about being the first one to discover something new. It's about preserving our findings. Research it, and give interpretation to it.

---How Man

當迪克‧羅西第一次踏上中國的時候，他從一個 26 歲的海軍飛行教官搖身一變成為飛虎隊員。然而一年之後，當陳納德將軍解散飛虎隊時（正式名稱為美國自願團－AVG），他已經是坐擁六項戰績的王牌飛行員了。在那個砲彈比雨水還多的日子裡，飛虎隊總共擊落敵機將近三百架，擊斃敵機駕駛員二百人；在有紀錄可考的歷史中，沒有任何一個飛行中隊可與他們相比，也因此「飛虎隊」張牙怒吼的圖案，不僅在天空飛翔，更刻劃在人們的心中成為「英雄」的符號。離開飛虎隊的迪克，對於充滿挑戰的冒險飛行情有獨鍾，於是加入了中國航空公司，成為駝峰航線的飛行員。

自從日本打進緬甸，不爭氣的英軍又節節敗退之後，中美的路上補給線就被切斷了，於是這條長達八百公里，穿越世界屋脊喜馬拉雅的駝峰航線，就成為一條空中命脈。這是一條史上最悲壯航線，因為全程幾乎都在海拔四千五百米到五千五百米之間，最高處還必須翻過七千米。想想看這些並不先進的 C46、C47 運輸機，沒有壓力調節艙，若不是靠著飛行員的勇氣和過人的飛行技術，簡直就是另一種敢死隊。在戰況最危急的那三年內，駝峰運送了六十五萬噸物資，卻墜毀了五百架運輸機，失去了一千五百位飛行員。

戰爭結束，迪克總共飛越駝峰七百三十五趟，姑且不論危機四伏的戰鬥機時間，迪克說：「我這一輩子總共在飛行艙裡待了兩萬五千個小時左右！」

很顯然，迪克‧羅西在中國的青春歲月影響了他的一生。他後來成立了一家航空運輸公司，叫飛虎航空，儼然同時紀念了自己生命中的兩大冒險事蹟；這家航空公司後來賣給了知名的聯邦快遞。

多年以來，迪克一直是「飛虎會」的主席，對每隻飛虎的下落都追蹤了解，只是每年的聚會人數一次比一次少，令人不勝唏噓。他的車庫裡塞滿了過去光榮的一切，曾與飛虎相關的書籍、剪報、郵票

When Dick Rossi came to China as a member of the AVG (American Volunteer Group), he was 26. Before that, he was a flight instructor in the navy. A year later when General Claire Chennault decommissioned the AVG, Dick was already held as the "ace" pilot of the Group, with six outstanding and unmatched battle records behind him. In its fighting days in skies over China, the Group shot down nearly 300 Japanese airplanes killing 200 pilots of these planes. As no other fighter squadron could match this record, members of the Group were deemed as heroes by people in China. They called them "heroes of the 'tiger-planes' " and this was because the nose of the planes was painted like a tiger. After the AVG, Dick continued his flying career and adventurous life by joining the China National Aviation Corp as a hump pilot.

By that time, Japan has defeated the British in Burma, cutting off the land route between India and China, totally stopping China from getting the much needed supplies from this land route. The hump air route was therefore opened, which soon became China's lifeline for supplies from the outside. The 800 km hump route ran through air spaces with the hostile weather conditions. The route was over a high plateau so most of the time the airplanes flying this route were flying at altitudes between 4,500 to 5,500 m and at several sections, they needed to climb to over 7,000 m and fly between mountain gaps. The airplanes used were the C-46s and C-47s which were not advancely equipped. The cockpit was not pressurized so pilots were exposed to the risk of altitude sickness. Flying the hump route therefore required a lot of coverage and very good judgement and skills. A total of 650,000 tons of supplies were flown into China from this route during the war, enabling the country to continue its fight against the invading

到每年聚會的小冊子等等。2005 年，中國官方邀請了飛虎和中航兩隊隊友以及二次大戰的其他美國人到北京慶賀大戰結束六十周年。迪克說，中國國家主席向他敬酒，他享受了一次英雄式的歡迎。其實，不管有沒有這樣的款待，飛虎和駝峰飛行員早就是中國人民心中與天、與白雲齊高的英雄了。

2006 年底，迪克捐出了許多珍藏的紀念品給 CERS，有高價並簽了名的印製品以及好幾件當年飛越駝峰航線的無價之寶，這些所代表的不僅是飛虎或駝峰的勇敢故事，應該更是這位飛虎英雄對於探險英雄的一大肯定吧。

Japanese. A total of 500 planes crashed while flying the route, costing the lives of 1,500 hump pilots and crew members.

By the end of the war, Dick had flown the hump route 735 times, each time putting his life to danger. "Looking back, I can't image I have flown 25,000 hours over this dangerous route," Dick said.

Dick's experience in China must be very unforgettable for him. After the war he set up an air cargo company and he named it "Flying Tiger" Air Cargo Company. In his days in China, he and his buddies in the AVG were referred to as pilots of the tiger planes by the Chinese people. Dick later sold his company to the United Express to retire.

For many years, Dick was Chairman of the Flying Tiger Association. He kept contact with all members of the association and organized annual meetings for members to get together. With the passage of time, fewer and fewer members came to the annual meeting. Dick has collected a large quantity of books, newspaper and magazine articles, and stamps about the AVG and the hump flights. He has also kept publications of the Flying Tiger Association on its annual meetings of members. In 2005, China held a ceremony to commemorate the 60th anniversary of the end of WWII. Dick and other surviving hump pilots were invited as guests of honor and they were greeted by China's president at the ceremony.

In 2006, Dick donated many articles of souvenir value concerning the AVG and the hump flights to CERS. These articles were very precious because they bear witness to the hump pilot's heroic acts in the war.

比爾・邁爾的告別飛行

Bill Maher's Farewell Flight

要有甚麼樣的交情，比爾・邁爾才會把他的最後一次飛行留給那個人呢？尤其是對這些把飛行看做第二生命的駝峰飛行員！也許是英雄惜英雄，當比爾・邁爾對 HM 說：「效文，你來之前，我已經想了兩個禮拜，我決定把這一刻留給你！」一向反應伶俐的 HM，這次可是一個字都回不了；比爾又說：「總有一天要結束的，現在正是時候。」這一年是 2007 年，比爾・邁爾八十八歲，距離他第一次單獨飛上天空，已經有六十八個年頭了。這一趟飛行，比爾載著 HM 飛向威斯康辛的「奧許寇許航空展」，這個航空展從 1969 年開始，每年都吸引了多達一萬架小飛機來參加，可以說是航空界的「胡士托」，HM 想參加這個航空展已經好久了，沒想到竟然能搭乘比爾的這架西斯納 T-210 單引擎機前來，真是奇妙的夢想成真。

在與比爾的多次相處中，HM 聽了許多關於這些駝峰飛行員的故事，比爾說：「你知道，當年我們都是些不合群的怪胎，很難管束，這也是為什麼後來我們有這麼多人創業成功……我的老朋友 Christy 兩年前過世，我在他的葬禮中說，Christy 是個混蛋，但他是我們的混蛋，我們都喜歡他……」（Fletcher Christy Hanks 飛越駝峰航線 347 次，並且曾經在 1997 年，高齡 79 歲時率領一隊人馬進入緬甸找到一架當年在駝峰航線失蹤的 C-53 運輸機）在那個青春的歲月，在那個瘋狂的年代，每個人都有著比藍天更高的志向，也同樣培養出了無可替代的革命情感。

對這些「資深」駝峰飛行員來說，重複地述說著戰時故事，如何飛越喜馬拉雅山、如何在黑暗中躲避敵機，都已經成為媽媽說給小孩的床邊故事一樣的熟練與自在。只是，過去永遠不會過去，他們把大好青春拿去冒險的這個舉動已經無關乎個人，而是一個時代的使命。Louis Stannard 在他的《上海日記》中非常簡潔地用三個詞描述了那時中航飛行員的生命：貪婪、冒險與性。也許這第一個和第三個已經在比爾年過九十的生活裡黯淡了下來，但是那冒險的心，卻

Like most hump pilots, Bill Maher took flying as the most important thing in his life. In 2007 after Bill passed his 88th birthday, he said to How Man, "I've been thinking for two weeks about my farewell flight. I am too old now and it's about time I should end my flying life. To mark this occasion I would like to invite you to join me in the cockpit for my last, farewell flight." How Man readily agreed. This farewell flight was made 68 years after Bill's first flight, in his single engine Cessna T-210 plane with How Man, and they were flying to participate in the Oshkosh Wisconsin Air Show. The fair was an annual event attracting thousands small planes each year.

How Man had known Bill for many years and had heard many stories about the hump pilots from him. He told How Man, "In our days flying the hump route in China, many of us were sort of eccentric and untamed but each got some peculiar qualities in his character that made him a successful person. Christy was one of them. He was very successful in his career after the war. He passed away two years ago. You know what I said in his funeral – I said in our days as hump pilots in China, we all liked him and we nick-named him Wretch. But he was our wretch our buddy and we will miss him." Bill was referring to Fletcher Christy Hanks, who flew the hump route 347 times. In 1997, at the age of 79, Christy led a team deep into a remote jungle area in Burma trying to find a C-53 plane flown by one of his close buddies that went missing over that area during the war.

The old hump pilots still vividly remembered how they flew over the Himalayas in bad weather and how they dodged enemy fighters in darkness. Perhaps the reason they took on these dangerous missions was to satisfy their adventurous urge as young persons. But they had

一直延續到了他的最後一次飛行，甚至，他的每一次開車。而 HM，也同樣拿出他的冒險之心，跟著比爾一起飛行。

HM 曾經在他的探險筆記中寫到比爾，HM 說，在比爾開車帶我去餐館吃晚飯的路上，我開始擔心他現在這個歲數的協調能力，他轉彎速度之快，有幾次車子差點衝出路面。三年前我就注意到他開飛機比開車安全，因為天空很大沒東西可撞。

我於是開始想像那個穿著棕色皮夾克的年輕比爾，那個馳名中外的「血幅」就貼在他的背後，上面有著中國國民黨的黨徽，還有幾句中文，請求民眾在飛機失事或遭到擊落時協助飛行員。我彷彿又看到他走上他的 C-47，揮手比了一個帥氣的動作，然而坐在副駕駛座位的另一個飛行員，竟然是 HM，一個跟比爾有著一樣勇氣與冒險心的當代探險家！

made valuable contributions to the Allies winning the war. In his book "Shanghai Diaries", writer Louis Stannard succinctly summed up the three forces that motivate the hump pilots, and these were greed, adventure spirit and sex. For 90 year old Bill, perhaps greed and sex had long died down, but adventure spirit was still very active in him. This could be seen from the way he drove on the highway each time, and flying his plane in his farewell flight with How Man.

How Man had noted in this diary that when Bill drove him to the restaurant for dinner on one occasion, he was worried because he was driving so fast that the car almost veered off the road on several occasions. He said his observation about Bill three years ago was right, that his flying was safer than his driving, because the sky was empty and had nothing for him to hit upon.

When Bill was standing next to his plane, about to do his farewell flight, his appearance first gradually blurred in my vision and then, moments later, his image showed up again as a young hump pilot. On the back of his jacket, was the standard war time printed note requesting Chinese people to rescue him and take him to safety if his plane was shot down or crashed. How Man as his co-pilot was standing next to him. The image of the plane also gradually blurred and re-emerged as a war time C-47. With a wave of hands, he and How Man climbed into it and flew off.

僰人的懸棺是 CERS 從 1990 年代就開始的項目。無獨有偶，菲律賓也有懸棺的習俗。

Bo people's hanging coffins has been one of CERS' preservation project since 1990. Hanging coffins can also be found in the Philippines.

帕米爾高原的柯爾克孜族羊毛氈房，有如蒙古包。

At the foot of snowy mountains on The Pamir, tents made of wool yurts, similar to mongolian yurt.

傳說中卡瓦卡博神山的妻子緬之姆，白色山峰絕不輕易顯現。

Mt. Khawakarp's wife Montesano rarely reveals its snow white peak to the world.

駝峰飛機與飛行機師。（資料照片）
The hump pilots and their planes. (archive picture)

百歲駝峰機長 左起：陳文寬，楊積，Peter Goutiere
Centenarian pilots. Moon Chin Chen, Jack Young,
Peter Goutiere (left to right)

早期的鄒族人與庫巴（資料照）
Tsou people and the gathering house in the past. (archive picture)

CERS 在台灣阿里山達邦的項目，手工打造完成了兩棟傳統房舍。/2016
CERS project in Alishan Dabang Taiwan. Two traditional Tsuo houses built by hand. 2016

＜藍・中間＞ #Blue・Middle

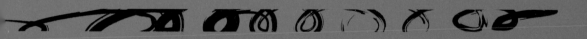

藍，是中間位的顏色。

以中間方位意義的「不動如來佛」為象徵。探險學會的
三十年裡，與許多人發生了錯綜複雜的緣分，不論這些緣
分是純粹的巧合或互相幫助或惺惺相惜，都是在中間位置
支撐 CERS 一路向前的無形力量。

Blue is the color for things and matters in the middle. It is also
the color of the Buddha of Akshobhya in Tibetan Buddhism.
In the 30 years since the CERS's formation, the Society has
interacted and developed relationships with many people. These
interactions and relationships are very intricate, have, as if by
fate, gradually formed an invisible midway force that support the
Society in achieving its missions and goals.

如果沒有最後一個鄂溫克人，黃效文就不會有自創探險學會的想法；有了 Don Conlan 的鼓勵，探險學會的成立就更義無反顧；如果沒有台灣好友如蔣彥士先生與李國鼎先生在最艱難時的大力支持，也不會讓探險學會順利地走到今天；如果沒有全世界許多企業家的慷慨支持，探險學會也達不到現在的規模。古巴女子何秋蘭對粵劇的熱情與奉獻感動了 HM；探索陳文寬先生與沙智勇神父的故事時，HM 也從中得到了莫大的勇氣並相信了盼望的重要。與高原上的藏人，特別是好幾位活佛們的機緣，也全是佛祖庇佑。探險並非一人所能成就的事業，若沒有龐大的後勤隊伍，就不可能有任何的出發或抵達。「這些人」都是黃效文這三十年事業版圖中缺一不可的，而「這些人」在中間位所放射出的光芒與價值，也將如太陽一般，日日為 CERS 注入無窮的能量。

How Man would not have wanted to set up his own exploration society if it wasn't for finding the last surviving Ewenki. His determination to do so would not be so strong if it wasn't for the encouragement by Don Conlan. The Society would not have been able to pass its most difficult time if good friends in Taiwan like Jiang Yan-shi and Li Guo-ding had not emerged to give their support. Without the generous support of them and of others the Society would not be able to grow to its present size and scale. How Man was deeply touched by the contributions by Cantonese Opera Singer, Ho Chau Lan in Cuba. The stories of Moon Chin Chen and the Catholic Father Savioz have given How Man great encouragements and these all helped consolidate How Man's belief that he could make the Society a success. His cordial relationship with the local Tibetan people and the sincere friendships with the living buddhas became across on the plateau must also have resulted in silent blessings from them which made his expeditions successful time after time.

How Man was grateful to all these people. They were the hidden force/influence in the middle which helped How Man to steer his Society in the correct direction all these years.

The Last Reindeer Herder
in How Man's Memory

最後一個馴鹿牧人・黃效文的謬思

所有的故事都必需有個開始，就像每條河川都會有個源頭一樣，HM 為什麼會從美國《國家地理雜誌》的第一線記者退下而成立香港中國探險學會呢？決不可能毫無緣由或線索可循。也許時間還沒久遠到需要用「從前從前……」來做開場，但絕對可以從 1983 年他對鄂溫克族的那個採訪開始，那最後的馴鹿牧人卻是 HM 人生事業的轉折點。

今年八十六歲的瑪麗亞索是最後一個馴鹿牧人，若按照鄂溫克人的本意－「來自森林的人」來說，瑪麗亞索也是最後一個鄂溫克人，因為她只有住在帳篷裡才有家的感覺。HM 認識瑪麗亞索的那年，瑪麗亞索只有五十出頭，而 HM 現在的年紀都要比那時的瑪麗亞索大上十幾歲了。他們其實已經是三十多年的老朋友了，也難怪瑪麗亞索會在 HM 幾年前去探望她時，為他唱情歌了。

1983 年當 HM 為國家地理雜誌做最後的馴鹿牧人時就意識到了中國少數民族的珍貴傳統正在快速瓦解中，尤其是像當時總數只有 166 人的鄂溫克族瓦庫特部落。於是 HM 開始在那趟採訪中蒐集少數民族文物，也因此成為 CERS 現在相當重要的資產之一。那次的採訪也讓 HM 發現單是文字和照片並不足以記錄眼前活生生的文化，於是他也開始用著那時自己並不擅長的影片來記錄所見。

外地人前來這裡多是為了紀念鄂溫克人曾經在此放牧過的馴鹿，HM 完全不是。他從一開始就清楚他的目標是探尋鄂溫克人及他們的歷史。由於幾十年前森林被大量砍伐後，直接影響了鄂溫克人的狩獵生活，以及與狩獵生活息息相關的文化和住宅。

HM 重返瑪麗亞索家中的那年是 1988 年，這次為的是拍攝瑪麗亞索的先生拉吉米製作鄂溫克人特殊的器具和日常用品，也同時跟著拉吉米和安道一同進入雪中打獵。那趟行程也同時記錄了最後一位薩滿（巫師），牛娜。如今這些人都已經不在了，他們所代表的生

Every story has a beginning, like every river has a source. If people look at why How Man decided to step down as a reporter of the National Geographic Magazine and set up CERS, they will find that his reporting of the Ewenki people in 1983 was the "turning point."

Mariasol is now 86, she is the last Ewenki and reindeer herder in the world. The Ewenki is a minority people in Northern China and the word Ewenki means "people from the forest". Mariasol is considered the last Ewenki because, for all these years, she is the only Ewenki that still lives in tent. In her mind, no place is more like home than inside a tent. When How Man first met her in 1983, she was around 50. For more than 30 years they have known each other. No wonder when How Man visited her a few years ago, she was so delighted that she sang love songs for him.

In the 1983 National Geographic reporting of the Ewenki reindeer herder people in their last settlement in Wakute, the population of this minority people had already dwindled to 166. The artefacts that How Man collected, together with the articles he wrote and photographs he took in connection with the reporting, were therefore very valuable and had now become important CERS assets. During that reporting, How Man also realized that the quality of reporting would be greatly improved by incorporating camera footages. From that time onwards, How Man started to use also video/ movie camera to conduct reporting.

The Ewenki was people that lived on hunting and reindeer herding in forests. In the 1983 reporting, How Man sadly realized that what caused the Ewenki population and culture and tradition to dwindle

活型態與傳統也一起走入了歷史，所幸，CERS 盡可能地把這些都記錄了下來，直到今日，這些少數民族的影像紀錄成為了 CERS，甚至整體人類文化珍貴重要的財產。

2012 年冬天，HM 又再度帶著 CERS 的成員重訪瑪麗亞索。瑪麗亞索給 HM 唱了一首又一首的歌，還演奏了先生拉吉米生前最愛的口簧；而 HM 回報的是在 iPad 上播放 1988 年拉吉米所錄下的影片。一切如同昨日，然昨日永不再來，臨走時，瑪麗亞索又送給了 CERS 珍貴的禮物：那是一套馴鹿的鞍子、鞍毯與鞍袋（內部以樺樹皮撐起，外以駝鹿皮覆裹）。

三十年的探險之路所帶給 HM 最難以估量的，就是這些人的情誼，從瑪麗亞索到她的先生拉吉米、兒子何協，與女兒德卡莎，每個人都用最原始的真心以對。這種特殊的情誼，不需要雙方在一起很長的時間，只要起到關鍵性的作用，就值得了。無疑地，這最後的馴鹿人確實起了關鍵性的影響，他是讓 HM 成立探險學會，以致力於中國邊陲自然與文化保護的導火線；而就這個初心來看，HM 也確實在這個領域做得很不錯。或許，那最後的薩滿牛娜早已預見這一切，所以才會將裝著一隻木頭鳥的靈盒＊送給探險學會吧，因為探險學會就像 HM 的孩子一樣。想起瑪麗亞索那天即興唱給 HM 的歌，她唱到：「……下雪的季節裡，你們這樣的一群人來找我，就像黃色的小鳥落到我的帳篷上一樣……」優美的旋律中，帳篷內的火爐前，笑容上了每一位探險成員的臉，沒有比這個更溫暖的冬天了。

＊ 靈盒：從前每當有嬰兒出生，牛娜都會做這麼一個木盒子。年輕的鄂溫克族人根本沒有聽過，更別說看過了。

and vanish was the rapid disappearance of forests several decades ago. The idea of setting up an exploration society to help people understand this alarming situation and win their support in nature and heritage preservation also arose in his mind.

In 1988 How Man visited Mariasol for the second time. This time it was for the purposes of filming her husband Lajimi make Ewenki people's traditional tools and utensils, as well as doing hunting with him in snow in the forest. The visit was concluded with an interview with last Shaman (witch) of the Ewenki people, a lady by the name of Niuna. Now both Lajimi and Niuna have passed away. Records and camera footages of this visit are kept by CERS as some of its most valuable assets today.

In winter 2012, How Man led a CERS team to visit Mariasol again. She was so pleased and delighted. She sang song after song for How Man. She also played musical pieces with her late husband's jaw harp. How Man reciprocated by showing her the footage he made in 1988 visit on his iPad. All were very happy and their 1988 meeting was like yesterday. Before departure, she also gave How Man some presents: a reindeer saddle, a saddle blanket and a saddle ride pouch. How Man was greatly impressed by her hospitality.

One of the things How Man treasures most in his 30 years expedition career is his friendship with sincere and unsophisticated people like Mariasol. Her son Hexie and daughter Dekeska also joined her in meeting How Man with a sincere heart.

How Man's encounter with Mariasol the last Ewenki reindeer herder has played an important role in making him decide to set up the

CERS. Under How Man's leadership, CERS performed very well and quickly became famous among people in the exploration and natural preservation circles. It seems like that the Society's success was already foreseen by the Ewenki Shaman Niuna. Before How Man departed her, she gave him a spirit box as present. In Ewenki tradition, when a new baby is born to a family, the Shaman will give the family a spirit box that she had consecrated. The box will ensure, according to Ewenki people's belief, the healthy growth and bright future of the newborn. Niuna knew that, to How Man, CERS is his dear newborn baby, and that the baby would grow up well and have a bright future.

The night before departure in winter 2012 was a memorable moment. Despite the bitter cold outside, the air inside Mariasol's tent was warm, cordial and filled with her soft singing voice. Until now How Man can still remember words in one of her songs, "My dear friends, you come from afar to see me in such cold weather. I am so happy and glad because your coming is like beautiful yellow birds coming down to rest on my tent."

她是古巴人・她是粵劇名伶

She's a Cuban,
She Sings Cantonese Operas

每件事情做到最好就是門藝術

When a thing is done to it's very best, it's an art.

---How Man

何秋蘭，今年 84 歲，有個中文名字，粵語也十分流利，然而卻是個不折不扣的古巴人。坎坷的身世讓她曾經和媽媽一起在街頭乞討；四歲時和媽媽一起被好心人方標收養。方標熱愛粵劇，也因此開始了秋蘭跟粵劇這長達八十年的熱戀。

HM 在哈瓦那見到秋蘭，聽著她述說自己是如何愛上粵劇並成為花旦的過程。臉上的重彩、身上的戲服、勤苦得來的基本功夫、傳神的唱腔和演技，幾乎完全遮掩了她是個古巴人的事實。

哈瓦那有四家粵劇團，秋蘭曾是其中一家的當家花旦，但自從 1959 年革命之後，所有的劇碼都禁止以中文演出，秋蘭也只好在中文報社當撿字員以維生。

「我正在練習帝女花，這是五十年代很受歡迎的一齣戲，我從來沒有表演過，但我真的很喜歡裡面的調調，我希望能在今年春節慶祝會上演出一段……」秋蘭告訴 HM，把 HM 當成自己粉絲一樣的與他分享著關於粵劇的一切。

2014 年秋天，CERS 邀請了秋蘭以及美玉前來香港參加石澳的沙灘粵劇節。美玉今年 86 歲，是二分之一的華人，她跟秋蘭不同，學習中文的時間不夠長，所以必需用拼音死記，常和秋蘭一起搭檔演出。

CERS 之所以邀請這兩位古巴女士訪問香港有兩個主要的原因。第一個是，秋蘭對於中華文化和藝術的熱情感動了 HM，也啟發了 HM。HM 想和香港人分享她的熱情，特別是那些將一切視為理所當然的年輕人；我們的下一代是多麼不重視中華文化，也不懂當前所擁有的穩定與繁榮得來多麼不容易。人們很容易不滿於現實，卻忘了今日的局面是前人長期的犧牲與堅忍所換來的。希望秋蘭的故事能讓這些只追求生活享樂而忽視生命價值的年輕人有些許省思。

Ho Chau Lan is a Cuban. She's now 84, speaks fluent Cantonese and is a keen lover of Cantonese operas. She has a miserable childhood. When she was four years old, poverty had driven her and her mother to beg on streets in Cuba to make a living. Later, she was adopted as daughter by Cuban Chinese Fang Biu and it was then that her miserable childhood came to an end. Fang Biu liked Cantonese operas and because of his influence, Ho Chau Lan also became a keen lover of Cantonese operas.

How Man met Ho Chau Lan in Havana. She told How Man how she started learning to sing Cantonese operas from scratch. She told How Man how to dress up and put on make-ups for different stage plays, and the basic singing and dancing skills required for these plays. During the meeting, How Man almost totally forgot that she was a Cuban.

Ho Chau Lan used to play the key female role in one of the four Cantonese opera companies in Havana. However, after the Cuban revolution in 1959, Cantonese operas were banned in Havana, forcing her to work as a typesetter in a Chinese newspaper to make a living.

"I like to sing 'The Last Princess of Ming Dynasty' " she told How Man.

"The solo part sung by the princess was so beautifully written. I always hope to have the opportunity to sing it on stage on Chinese New Year day," she said.

In autumn 2014, CERS invited Ho Chau Lan and her singing partner Mei Yuk to come to Hong Kong to participate in the Cantonese Opera Festival held on Shek O Beach. Mei Yuk is two years older than Ho Chau Lan. Her mastery of Cantonese is not as good as Ho Chau Lan

第二是，HM 深深覺得秋蘭對粵劇的熱情與奉獻應該得到獎勵。那麼何不讓她完全沉浸在粵劇中一個星期呢？每年秋天在石澳的海灘都有個粵劇節，2014 年的這個粵劇節，秋蘭和美玉來了，這個星期有別於她們在古巴半世紀的貧乏生活，她們享受了夢想中的粵劇情節，忠孝節義、兒女情長、英雄高歌。甚至有一個下午，CERS 安排了十一名樂師組成的完整樂團為秋蘭和美玉試演伴奏。

這趟中國行的壓軸，是秋蘭回到養父方標位在廣東開平的老宅子。秋蘭手持三炷香，祭拜方家祖先；方標本人離開故土後就再也沒有回來過，而如今他的異國養女卻站在方家牌位前祭拜，方標在天之靈必定甚感寬慰，他所收養的女兒承接了他對粵劇的愛好與投入，這樣的家族傳統將繼續下去，儘管是在一個離故鄉很遙遠的地方。

這個「項目」完全不同於以往 CERS 所做的一切，你無法估算出其中的付出與所得，但又如何？秋蘭代表的是對於傳統文化的熱情與執著，她的故事感動鼓舞著在這個領域上奉獻心力的每一個靈魂。若秋蘭的人生故事代表的是良馬，就且讓 CERS 成為這個故事的伯樂吧。

so each time they sang together Ho has to help her make phonetic transcriptions of the lyrics.

There were two reasons for How Man to decide to invite the two old ladies to come to Hong Kong to participate the event. First, their unyielding love of Chinese art and culture despite all the hardships has deeply impressed How Man. How Man hoped that their stories could help young persons in Hong Kong foster love and interest for traditional Chinese art and culture. He also hope that the stories would make young persons in Hong Kong realize how fortunate they were to be born in Hong Kong, where the society is stable and making a living is easy. The second reason was that, being a kind-hearted man, How Man wanted to help the ladies make their wish come true, as the wish was so humble and so dearful to them.

The ladies were very happy singing on the stage in the Festival.

During their stay in Hong Kong, CERS arranged for them to sing on stage for a second time. That was done in an afternoon. CERS hired 11 instruments musicians to provide the music accompaniment for them to sing.

Before returning to Cuba, CERS accompanied the ladies to the ancestral house of Fang Biu, Ho Chau Lan's foster father. Fang had already passed away. The house was in Kaiping, Guangdong. There Ho Chau Lan performed religious rituals to worship her foster father's ancestors. Fang left the ancestral house for Cuba at a very young age. Until his death he never had an opportunity to return to worship his ancestors. When his foster daughter was performing the worship ceremony, his soul in heaven must be filled with comfort and happiness.

Exploration Museums

Stops on the Path of Explorations

若你開始對探險學會的項目有一點了解了，不知道心中會不會有這個疑問：為什麼這個探險學會有這麼多的展覽中心，甚至博物館？

讓我們回望 1961 年，看看那個有點叛逆的少年黃效文。小學六年級時，他讀的是 A 班，此後他的成績像溜滑梯一樣，一路下滑，中學一年級時到了 B 班，二年級進了 C 班，最後在畢業時勉強維持在五年 E 班。他暱稱自己讀的這班是 5Aa 班，意思是五年級藝術班的 A 班。後來他進了威斯康辛大學，主修新聞及藝術。他於是有了很多機會參觀世界各地的博物館，其中有很多令他印象深刻的博物館規模並不大，感覺卻很親切。當他在美國《國家地理雜誌》工作的時候，那裏甚至有自己的博物館，叫做「探險家之廊」。

HM 的探險學會並不是要跟《國家地理雜誌》走一樣的路，但是所有的這些主題博物館都是後來探險學會的靈感來源。當然，最主要的是 HM 希望學會所有的工作成績能夠被好好典藏，並成為有教育意義的展示，有一天甚至能成為後代研究中國偏遠地區的重要資料來源，因為有太多的物件和文化影像現今都已成為如煙的往事。學會所收藏的有形的物件包括千百件的文物、錄音、錄影、筆記、手稿、幾千本書籍、超過二十五萬張的幻燈片以及持續增加的大量攝影資料。

「規模小但聚焦」是學會設計博物館的原則。從小 HM 就知道適時地不循傳統，偶爾走走極端反而會有意想不到的效果，也就是在這樣的原則下，探險學會所設計的博物館或展覽廳當然會帶給觀者驚喜與樂趣。

就以響古箐的展館為例，這裡主要傳遞的訊息是：自然與文化都是需要被保護的重要遺產。滇金絲猴分布在雲南和四川，是特有種；由於盜獵和棲息地的流失，金絲猴瀕臨絕種。而傈僳族的分布與金絲猴的棲息地有重疊，他們的傳統也在消失當中；例如，打獵相關

As you know more about the CERS, you might wonder why it has so many exhibition venues and museums.

Let us look back to 1961. How Man was then a Grade A primary school pupil. However when he rose to secondary school, his school results went down year after year. In year one, he was Grade B. In year two, he was Grade C. And then in year three to year five (end of secondary education), he was Grade E throughout. Talking about his secondary secondary school days. How Man likes to say that in his case the Grade E was in fact an enigma for Grade A, because his teachers did not want him to turn proud and lose his talents. After he finished secondary school in Hong Kong, he entered the University of Wisconsin to study journalism and art. While studying there, he had the opportunity to visit many museums. Some of these museums gave him very good impressions. They were not big or grand, instead they were small but they all had well thought-out themes which make them very interesting and informative. When working in the National Geographic Magazine, staff there set up a "Explorers' Corridor" for themselves which they referred to as the magazine museum.

After setting up the CERS, How Man knew that the Society's educational goals and missions would best be achieved by displaying its exploration findings and results (photographs, videos, films, publications, etc) in what he called "small but focused" museums. To date, the CERS has set up many such theme museums. More than 250,000 slides, films, videos and photographs, and thousands of artefacts, publications, original manuscripts and records are now kept and exhibited in these museums.

的習俗在法規下逐漸遭到侵害，人類五千年的歷史濃縮在了傈僳族的百年生活內 -- 從採集漁業迅速演變到農耕。

在傈僳族獨特的建築風格消失的同時，探險學會成功的保存了二十一間傳統的傈僳族木楞房，並且將一條條木楞編號拆解後在村邊重建，這些重建的傳統房舍除了提供遊客住宿之外，也特別設置了小型展覽室以展示並介紹傈僳族的文化與文物，這能夠讓對金絲猴有興趣的民眾也同時了解那個區域人文的一面。這個概念有點像遺址博物館，只是，來參觀的民眾不只可由「遺物」窺視過去的傈僳族，更可以在村中感受到現在傈僳族的真實生活。響古箐這裡也成為探險學會每年夏天實地教育的最好場所。

探險學會也曾經在中甸納帕海濕地保護區旁設置以黑頸鶴以及其他高原候鳥為主角的博物館。這個博物館的特色是不僅有文字圖像的展示，只要時間對了，這些主角會帶給你驚喜，親自出現在你眼前。

中甸古城邊的「探險歷史博物館」是一個有著六個小展覽室的老房子，曾經藏有探險學會最豐富的資料：前芬蘭總統曼納漢在 1906 至 1908 年的絲路探險功績、中國飛行史（包括 1914 年第一個華裔美國飛行員）、二戰時駝峰航線相關資料圖片、中國少數民族文物、以及不可細數的藏區與佛教文物。遺憾的是，當自然文化遇上了經濟開發，似乎不得不讓道而行。但樂觀地來看，這個「探險歷史博物館」將被收進即將完工的中甸中心博物館內，屆時將會有更豐富的內容可對外展示。異地重生會有不同的挑戰，也一定會帶來等量的驚喜，就像 2012 年五月的那趟行程，原本想探索入藏新路，雖然沒達成原本的目的，最後卻在一場突如其來的大雪中，幫助了查拉山口外一間寺廟的屋頂修建。一切就像西藏人說的，都是因緣際會。

放在時間長流裡來看，或許，探險學會的某些博物館或展覽室是短暫的，但都是這三十年來的過程結晶，也都對探險、研究、教育和

The main theme of the Xiangguqing Museum, for example, is to educate people on the importance of wildlife and heritage preservation, using the golden monkey and the traditional style Lisu people sheds as examples. Golden monkeys almost went into extinction a decade ago because of illegal poaching and lost of habitats. Also living in these habitats for generations were the Lisu people. They were people who made their living by hunting and fishing, using traditional tools. The sheds in which they lived were built of wood, primitive in look but blend in well with the jungle environment. Like the golden monkeys, these heritage sheds were facing the danger of extinction, something everyone will regret.

The museum is situated in 21 traditional Lisu style sheds which CERS has restored in a Lisu village. The village is located on the edge of a piece of forest now demarcated as a protection zone for the golden monkeys through efforts by the CERS. The forest is one of the few places in China where golden monkeys can still be spotted. Tools and utensils which the Lisu people used in the old days, pictures and articles concerning their culture, rites and history are displayed. Also exhibited in the museums are pictures and information and education materials on the golden monkeys, and on the need for protection of wildlife and the natural environment. The museum has now become a popular education centre for university and secondary school students on school holidays, during which CERS staff members would station there to act as their tour conductors.

Another example of theme museum is the one about the black-necked cranes in the Napahai marshland in Zhongdian. Black-necked cranes are migratory birds on the Tibetan plateau. They spend the summer in

保育起了相當的作用。在日以繼夜地奔波當中，在一個項目接著一個項目之間，博物館就像是個長串文字的逗點，他可以讓人稍微停下腳步，看看自己做了甚麼，又帶給了人們甚麼。期待中旬中心博物館的開幕，看看這次不守規矩的 HM 又將帶給我們甚麼驚喜！

Napahai attracting hundreds of visitors to come forward to see them. On the perimeter of the marshland, CERS set up many notice boards containing pictures and information about the bird to increase visitors' pleasure and interest in their bird watching tour. The notice also convey messages on the need for all to contribute towards wildlife and environment protection.

One further example is a six room museum which the CERS set up on the edge of the old town area in Zhongdian. Subjects for exhibition there include the silk road exploration in 1906-1908 by former Finnish president Mannerheim, Chinese aviation history (which includes the life of the first Chinese pilot), the Hump Flight Route in WWII, the minority people cultures and Tibetan buddhism. Due to the imminent redevelopment of the old town area, this museum is set to be relocated to the CERS Centre Museum soon. After relocation, the museum will have a completely new look with more exhibits and display materials.

In its 30 years exploration work, CERS has amassed large quantities of information and data on many subjects. The theme museums which the Society has set up are stops on the long exploration path. They enable the Society to take short breaks from time to time and to use these breaks to review its past work and prepare itself for new challenges ahead.

鄂溫克獵手阿力山大。
Ewenki hunter Alexander

1983 年的鄂溫克家族
An Ewenki family in 1983

藏東南察隅縣僜人
Teng people of southeaster Tibet Zayu.

位於中國東北的鄂溫克人被稱作是最後的馴鹿牧人，他們
住帳蓬，放牧馴鹿的傳統，今日已消失。

Ewenki, the last reindeer herder in the northeast of China.
They no longer living in tents or herd.

女時代的何秋蘭，不僅身段好，她的粵劇扮
相亦十分迷人。（何秋蘭提供）

Young Ho Chau Lan. Beautifully dressed in
Cantonese opera dress. (photo provided by
Ho Chau Lan)

何秋蘭與母親以及養父方標合影。
（何秋蘭提供）

Ho Chau Lan with her mother and the Chinese
father, who adopted her. (photo provided by
Ho Chau Lan)

何秋蘭到香港參加石澳粵劇節時，於 CERS
石澳 1939 著戲粧留影。（攝影：李伯達）

Ho Chau Lan visited Cantonese opera festival
in Shek O, Hong Kong.

Photographed in CERS' 1939 Shek O building,
by Xavier Lee

甘肅南部瑪取縣的神山祭慶典，稱：龍打，
即風馬旗飄空中之意。

Longda flying in the sky during a ceremony
to pay respect to a local sacred mountain at
Marqu County Southern Gansu.

四川甘孜州德格縣新路海的冰川湖泊，位於
瑪尼干戈外十公里處。

Alpine lake Xinluhai is fed by glacier in
Dege County of Ganzi Prefecture of western
Sichung, 10 km from Manigangguo.

湄公河支流瀾滄江流經寮國北部的景致
Nam Tha, a tributary of the Mekong River in upper Laos.

成立探險學會的小木屋，位於美國加州帕薩迪納山中。1986
CERS was found in Angeles National Forest cabin in Pasadena in 1986

探險學會位於中國雲南的中甸中心
CERS Zongdian Centre in Yunnan China

學習古錢 – 外圓內方。

心裡有清楚的原則，對外待人處事要懂得圓融、妥協。

Old Chinese coin, square inside and round on the outside. With principles inwardly and demanding on oneself, but flexible outwardly when dealing with others.

---How Man

畢蔚林博士 William Bleisch, PhD

1986 年在美國聖地牙哥，畢蔚林去聽了一場黃效文的演講，那是他第一次知道這個人。1987 年，當時畢蔚林在加州理工大學做博士後研究，他拿了一筆研究中國黑冠長臂猿的經費，黃效文對畢博士說，「你有錢，我有車」，然後他們就一起進入了雲南南部無量山的森林之中。畢博士關心的一直是瀕臨絕種的生物，黃效文關心的則是傳統文化的流失；於是 CERS 決定同時以自然與文化的保育為宗旨。從那之後，畢博士就跟探險學會一起合作多個項目，也開始了他在中國各地進行野生動物與自然保育的開端。

1992 年，畢博士成為野生動物保護協會的研究員；1998 年起的三年時間，畢博士全心在阿爾金山藏羚羊的保護上；直到 2012 年，他才成為探險學會的全職工作人員。他的專業知識給了探險學會非常大的幫助，若沒有他的投入那些關於野生動物和生態保育的項目是絕對沒有可能達成的。

那麼，在探險學會的這些年來的項目裡，畢博士覺得最成功的是哪個呢？「我覺得是白馬雪山旁的響古箐，學會成功的做到了一邊保護還一邊可以讓村民有自己的生活……」畢博士的中文其實說的很不錯，只是看著他的老外臉，一般人都不覺得他能說出流利的中國話。這個位於雲南維西的「金絲猴保護」加「傈僳族文化保護」項目，恰巧證明了 HM 在 1987 年就確定的學會宗旨：同時做到自然與文化的保育。事實證明，自然（野生動物）與文化（人類文明）是可以共生共存的，不需要為了刻意保護某一方而犧牲另一方。

三十年來，畢博士跟著學會一起累積了人生的厚度和廣度，他甚至開始學佛，把自己的生命看得很淡。我曾經跟著畢博士一起在達摩祖師洞轉山，看著他虔誠地為佛像敬拜與獻哈達時，我突然也有一種感覺，或許在 HM 的心中，畢博士也是一個「項目」也說不定。

William Bleisch, Ph.D.

Join CERS 2002

In 1986, William Bleisch attended a speech given by HM in San Diego. It was the first time he learnt of HM. In 1987, Dr. Bleisch was doing post-doctoral research at Caltech, he obtained research fund for a project on the Chinese black crested gibbon. HM told Dr. Bleisch, "You've got money, and I've got a car," so they ended up working in the forest of Wuliang Mountain at the southern Yunnan Province together. Dr. Bleisch's concern was protection of endangered wild life, while HM's focus was preservation of vanishing traditional culture. After How Man founded the CERS, he decided that its mission should be nature and culture conservation. Dr. Bleisch subsequently worked together with CERS on many wildlife and the natural conservation projects in China.

In 1992, Dr. Bleisch became a researcher at the Wildlife Conservation Society; for three years since 1998, Dr. Bleisch dedicated himself to the protection of the Tibetan antelopes at Arjin Mountain. He didn't become a full-time staff at CERS until 2012. His professional knowledge provided CERS enormous help on wildlife and nature conservation.

When asked which project he thinks is the most successful? Dr. Bleisch said it was the one in Xiangguqing near Baima Xueshan. "We managed to conserve things while enabling nearby villagers to live their normal life". Dr. Bleisch actually speaks fluent Mandarin. With his westerner looks, one can hardly believe he speaks Mandarin so well. The "Golden Monkey" conservation and the "Lisu Tribe" culture

HM 曾經打趣地說過：「我把雲南介紹給他，他的回報就是介紹叢林裡的螞蝗給我。」

此刻，在伊洛瓦底江的 HM Explorer 上，畢博士站在船頭，穿著他的筒裙（longyi），滿意地在河面上放出自製的風箏，順著江邊的風，這風箏一下子就輕巧的飛上了天。

How Man：
一個好好的準教授，哈佛、洛克菲勒博士、加州理工，出鬼（軌）了，跑到中國去探險研究三十年，還討了個會收拾他的中國老婆。

preservation projects in Yunnan, he said, proved that nature and culture conservation can be done at the same time, and that wildlife and human being can co-exist in harmony. These are also the CERS' firm convictions.

Thirty years with CERS, Dr. Bleisch has now got much in depth life experience than before. He now practices Buddhism and views life much differently than before. I have accompanied Dr. Bleisch to do circumambulation round the Damozong cave, and when I saw him pray and made khata offering, I thought to myself "maybe How Man sees turning Dr. Bleisch into a buddhist is also a CERS project too". HM once jokingly said "I introduced Yunnan to him, and in return he introduced to me jungle leeches".

As the HM Explorer traveled on the Irrawaddy River, Dr. Bleisch stood at the bow in his longyi, flew his hand-made kite over the river like a young boy. With the river breeze, the kite soon flew in the sky. Youth has returned to his heart.

How Man:
Harvard, Rockefeller, Caltech PhD, a professor-to-be, decided to sidestep the normal path and venture into China to do exploration and research for 30 years, and to even marry a Chinese wife who treats him like a slave.

DON CONLAN

前 The Capital Group 總裁暨首席經濟學家

我應該不用告訴你驅使 CERS 前進的人是誰。黃效文是一個非常好奇的人，他的興趣非常廣泛，也有用之不盡的決心跟行動力。他同時對處在危急處境的動物、鳥類、人 — 整體的文化，都非常的關心。那些我們可能聽過，但不會太注意的事，直到有一天他們消失了，一切都太晚的時候。HM 特別的地方就是他總是可以事先察覺到，看得夠遠，看到在發展中的亞洲生態跟文化上即將發生的災難。但是他不會讀過了或是提過這些事就算了，他是真的會為這些人、事、物付出的。在災難發生前就開始動作，很多時候就在即時的那一刻趕上，這就是 CERS 非常獨特的地方，過去這三十年他們在世界上做的就是這些。

1986 年 CERS 一開始的時候我就認識 HM 了，我可以告訴你好多他著手的項目，剛好都在關鍵時刻將許多即將消失的一切即時救回來。他的創意跟具說服力的文字跟攝影的天賦讓他可以去西藏拯救搖搖欲墜的古老寺廟、黑頸鶴、野生藏羚羊、海南島原住民的房屋，還有其他很多很多搶救回來的項目。他的經費常常不足，但是熱誠跟活力卻是滿滿的。

我很榮幸的稱他為我很特別的朋友。

How Man：
一九八零年代第一次見到 Don 是在我洛杉磯國家森林裡的小木屋家中。Don 在附近也有一個周末會用的小木屋。那裡有十四個這樣的小木屋藏在深山裡，裡面住著來自大城市裡很特別，也有些古怪的人。我們一開始就成為互相忠實的好朋友，而這份友誼隨著 CERS 的成立已經來到了三十年。Don 是支持我們最久的其中一位。與他的對話，無論是在洛杉磯，西藏高原或是緬甸，總是知性的。他總是熱愛研究，對一切感到好奇，也就是「好奇」這個特質，讓 Don 還有我，永保年輕。

DON CONLAN

Retired President and Chief Economist, The Capital Group

I probably don't have to tell you that the driving force behind The China Exploration and Research Society. How Man Wong is an incredibly curious-minded person with an amazing range of interests and inexhaustible determination to follow them through. He also carries a deep concern for animals, birds, people – entire cultures that are at risks, that most of us let pass with little notice – until they are gone; when it's too late.

How Man's special knack is to be able to see far enough ahead, the impending ecological and cultural disasters that are constantly looming in developing Asia and, for that matter, all over the world. But he doesn't just read about them or talk about them – he DOES something about them ahead of time, often just in time. That is the special niche in the world that CERS has filled for the past three decades.

I have known How Man from the beginning of CERS in 1986 and I could tell you of many projects that he has undertaken that managed to pull something from the edge of extinction, often in the nick of time. His creative and persuasive writing powers and his photographic talent have managed to help save the crumbling ancient monasteries of Tibet, the black cranes of China, the wild Tibetan antelope, the indigenous buildings of Hainan island, among many other redemption projects, often with insufficient funds, but always with abundant enthusiasm and energy. It has been my pleasure to call him my special friend.

Judith-Ann Corrente

大都會歌劇院，主席跟執行長，紐約州
羅倫斯威爾中學，受託人，勞倫斯維爾，紐澤西州

黃效文形容自己是個探險家。但是實際上他的工作比探險家還要廣。透過他致力於教育的付出還有他與生俱來的教學能力，HM 可以毫不費力地點起別人對探險的熱情，然後跟隨他們的腳步踏出去，遠離舒適圈，走進那環境裡去學習。

我第一次見到 HM 是透過一位我們在羅倫斯威爾中學共同友人的介紹。他跟我建立一個合作關係，將羅倫斯威爾的學生跟教師帶到 CERS 在中國跟緬甸的項目去實地學習。我發現我自己也越來越被吸引去跨越界線，拓展我的體驗。用兩個星期的時間徹底的視察緬甸的鄉村；用十六天的時間，旋風式的縱橫交錯於寒冷的雲南省，甚至單純的發現香港的另一面。特別是聆聽探險家大師本人說話，他把我也變成了一位忠實的探險家，開始探索一個完全不同的世界。CERS 是這世界上很特殊的寶藏。

How Man：
身為第一批畢業於普林斯頓大學的女學生，這本身是一項創舉，但是 Judith 無畏的冒險精神超越了她在學術跟教育上的成就。沒有多少人會飛私人飛機到中國或是緬甸，然後開始一段進入野外，生活簡樸的短程旅行。Judith 就是這樣做，她把通常要兩天的行程集中在一天，只為了要第一手看到 CERS 的項目。毫無疑問地，我信任她當我的顧問，當我迷失的時候，當然不是在野外的時候。

Judith-Ann Corrente

President and CEO, The Metropolitan Opera, New York, NY

Trustee, The Lawrenceville School, Lawrenceville, NJ

Wong How Man describes himself as an explorer. But his vocation is actually much broader than that. Through his commitment to education and his natural teaching ability, How Man effortlessly ignites in others the passion to explore and learn in environments far beyond their comfort zones.

I first met How Man through a mutual friend from The Lawrenceville School. As he and I formed a partnership to bring Lawrenceville students and faculty to work on CERS projects in China and Myanmar, I found myself drawn increasingly to stretch beyond the boundaries of my experience too. Thoroughly scouring the countryside of Myanmar for two weeks, crisscrossing frigid Yunnan Province in a brief whirlwind of 16 days, even simply discovering the other side of Hong Kong, but especially listening to the master explorer himself, have made me a committed explorer of a vastly different world as well. CERS has been an exceptional gift.

How Man:
To be among the first graduating class of women at Princeton was a pioneering feat, but Judith's intrepid adventure for exceeds academics and education. Not many would fly private jet to China or Myanmar and then went on a rough-it excursion into the wild. Judith did just that, cramming usual overnight trips into long endurance day-trips, just to visit remote CERS sites first hand. No doubt I trust her as my advisor when I feel lost while not in the field.

陳盛泉 Eric Chen

聲寶集團副總裁．贊助 CERS 長達 24 年

若以人生的興趣來分，HM 很明顯的被分在了探險的那一組，Eric 則被分在了歷史學家的那一組。只要是對他有些認識的人，一定會折服於他記憶「歷史年代」的功夫。那可不是他在跟你見面的前幾分鐘才準備好的，而是多年來對於歷史的興趣，讓他變成了一個類似史記上身那樣的達人。Eric 辦公室裡舉目所見都是歷史相關的書籍，很容易讓人忘記他其實是台大電機系畢業的，並且在四十歲之前就當上了台灣新力的總經理。

「我會認識黃效文就是在 1992 年 YPO（青年總裁協會）的大會上，那時他是受邀前來演講的貴賓，我才知道原來這世界有人在做這麼特別的事。再加上每個男孩都有那種冒險探險的心，都希望自己是印第安納‧瓊斯，去追尋所羅門寶藏……我小時候確實很喜歡看《索羅門寶藏》……」從那之後，Eric 就跟 HM 成了好朋友，兩人年紀相差 364 天，算是同個年代的人，也因此 HM 這樣一個探險家對 Eric 來說，就好像是從電影和書本裡走出來的英雄一樣。

Eric 的記憶力好到可以清楚的回憶當時 HM 演講的細節，「我還記得是在亞都飯店，HM 那時的國語很不好，所以中英文夾雜的說著他的長江源頭探險的事情，不過完全不影響他說故事的魅力。他現在的國語說得愈來愈好了，我們還一起去馬祖，他還可以用他的國語跟當地人對話，不過，跟當地人喝酒就要靠我了，哈哈哈。」Eric 爽朗的笑聲，好像也把我帶去了他們的旅行當中。問到跟 HM 一起坐吉普車進藏區的經驗，Eric 說，「我去過中甸兩次，記得 2004 年 3 月 17 號我在高原上接到朋友打來催票的電話，然後我在 21 號回台灣，我的兒子繼續跟著 HM 在高原上走。」接下來就出現了 CERS 喜歡傳誦的「對牛彈琴」的有趣探險插曲了。都說是因

Eric Chen

Sampo Corporation. Vice President. CERS Sponsor for 24 years.

Eric and How Man have very different interests and hobbies. HM is
interested in exploration in the wilderness while Eric is an historian.
Anyone who knows Eric is amazed by his incredible memory on
historical topics. Rome wasn't built in a day, his wealth of knowledge
is accumulated over time making him an expert in history. Eric's office
is full of books on history that one might forget he was an Engineering
graduate from National Taiwan University. His engineering
background has enabled him to become General Manager of Sony
Taiwan before the age of forty.

"I met How Man during the 1992 conference of the Young Presidents'
Organization where he was a guest speaker. It amazed me that someone
out there is doing something so unique. You know inside everyman's
heart lives an explorer, we all wanted to be like Indiana Jones at some
stage of our lives, to go after King Solomon's treasures. I have indeed
enjoyed reading 'King Solomon's Mines when I was a young boy."

Eric and How Man became close friends since that meeting, their age
difference of only 364 days means that they are people of the same
generation. To Eric, How Man is like a real life hero straight from the
movies and books. Eric still clearly recalls the details of How Man's
speech during that conference. "I remember that it was held at The
Landis Hotel in Taipei. How Man's Mandarin was not as fluent back
then. His speech on the expedition to the new source of the Yangtze
River was delivered in a mixture of English and Mandarin but it did
not affect his story telling ability at all.

為在高原上的漫漫旅行實在是太無聊了，所以某天下午在高原上，Eric 的兒子突發奇想拿著一支笛走到氂牛前開始演奏了起來。我們當然也不難想像那個畫面，廣闊的高原上，藍天白雲，熱血少年與黑色老氂牛……。

當然，能夠讓一個成功的企業家持續二十四年的贊助，HM 沒點真本事是不能的。「HM 從探險到保育，真的做了很多有意義也有意思的事情，光是保護藏羚羊這件事就很令人佩服。我很喜歡 HM 個性上的直接不掩飾，我自己也是這樣的人，不喜歡拐彎抹角的，所以當他每次和我見面，都會很清楚的告訴我又做了些甚麼，或者需要甚麼幫助，我會一直支持他的。知道最近幾年 CERS 開始把觸角往東南亞延伸，希望也會有好的成績；不過他在西藏雲南做的那些也希望可以繼續經營下去。」

CERS 能夠這麼順利的走到今天，不得不感謝像 Eric 這樣的企業家的贊助，不僅是企業支持，很多時候甚至是來自他們自己的私人贊助。「三十年很不容易的，但最重要的是 HM 你要好好的保持身體健康，多培養一些好的人才來繼續這樣的事業，還有啊，我們兩個人都一樣不要碎碎念，不要太嘮叨……」Eric 邊說邊笑，好像也發覺自己要開始對老友 HM 碎碎念了起來。

在離開 Eric 辦公室前我們談到了下西洋的鄭和、孫立人將軍，以及黃仁宇；天南地北的聊著歷史人物以及書寫歷史的人物，又再次感受到了 Eric 對歷史的熱愛。

最後 Eric 問了一句：「HM，緬甸真的很好玩嗎？」我彷彿看見一個十歲的 Eric，閃爍他天真好奇的雙眼，問著同樣十歲的死黨 HM 說。

"His Mandarin has improved a lot since then, when we travelled to the Matsu Islands he was able to communicate comfortably with the locals in Mandarin. However, he still counts on me when it came to drinking with the locals." I then asked about their experience in Tibet. "I've been to Zhongdian twice. I remember getting a call from a friend urging me to go back and vote while I was still on the plateau, I then returned to Taiwan on the 21th, leaving my son to continue the trip with How Man", recounts Eric.

Eric proceeded to share with me a popular story circulating in CERS about a boy that 'playing music to a cow' (this is an old Chinese proverb which is equivalent to the Western saying of talking to a wall). So happened was that Eric's son found travelling around the plateau and the mountains a little uneventful, and as a way to entertain himself he picked up a flute and started playing to a nearby yak. Whether the music was beautifully played was not known, but the scene in which it was played was very beautiful: backdrop of green grass, crystal clear blue sky, a hot-blooded young man and an old yak.

Without doubt, having the support of a successful entrepreneur for consecutive 24 years, HM must be doing something meaningful and right. Eric has expressed the following about HM. "How Man has devoted so much of himself to the cause of conservation. The conservation of the Tibetan Antelope alone deserves immense respect. I like How Man's frankness and sincerity and I much prefer people who are direct and genuine like him. So every time we meet, he would tell me exactly what he has been working and whether he needs assistance. I will continue to support his cause. I am pleased to hear CERS' plan to expand to South East Asia, I wish it will achieve good results there

How Man：

唉，不容易呵，當了十多年學會董事，開會從台灣過來，每年晚會又飛過來多次，不是簽張支票慷慨一下這麼簡單。我是不喜歡求人幫助的人，若非知道對方心甘情願，根本不願提出。Eric 嘛，我都知道他是出於本心幫忙的，否則不會放下高球棒來參加我們的活動。

Cao Zhong Yue

Yunnan Institute of Geography researcher.
Join CERS 1993

"I spent more time with How Man than with my parents!" Cao has clear
and beaming eyes, he is Han by ethnicity, but skin tone like Tibetan.

"I've been very fortunate to work under Mr. Wong. Our expeditions
journeys have covered more than half of China. On the surface it looks
like we are just helping HM to realize his dreams. It is much more than
that because our work is really meaningful and, after so many years,
CERS has become my life." Cao always refers How Man as 'Mr. Wong,'
his way of showing respect. He said Mr. Wong is his teacher, from whom
he has learnt many things he didn't previously know. He has been with
How Man for over twenty years, starting as a driver. He has since gathered
much experience and skills in expedition work and is now an important
member of CERS. Cao is very clear how demanding How Man is. He was
in charge of Damozong cave restoration project last year, and this year he
produced a satisfactory result.

Cao has travelled with How Man for a long time and been to many places.
But still there often were places he never heard of that HM would want
him to go. He often wondered, when this happened, "how on earth he
knows that such a place exits in China?"

How Man:

**There was a year when Cao's wife was in a medical emergency,
prevented him from joining our expedition. Later, he told me he made**

a pledge as long as wife's health improves, he would quit smoking. He quitted smoking and his wife got better. Recently his wife fell ill again, I asked Cao what's his pledge this time. Would it be start smoking again? Fortunately his wife recovers well.

張帆

雲南大學雲南省地理研究所所長。1991 年起參加探險學會項目至今，他的專業是生物學，專研鳥類，也是石灰岩洞穴專家。

「1991 年初的一天，黃效文來到我任職的雲南省地理研究所演講，演講的內容是關於長江和長江源頭探尋。坐在聽眾席中的我一開始就感到很驚奇，那英文 How Man Wong 是這次演講的主題？還是字拼錯了，應該是 How Man Wrong－人類如何做錯事？他的身體看上去那麼瘦削，還戴著副眼鏡，怎麼可能會是個探險家呢？一個自然地理學概念上的江河與源頭的問題，怎麼包還了那麼多精彩的人文與歷史內容？」那一年，張帆才二十八歲；而黃效文，四十二歲。

在那之後，張帆成了 HM 的御用助手，跟著上高原溯三江源、保護黑頸鶴、保護僰人懸棺等等，在此之前，張帆的人生全都活在三千公尺之下，但是自從跟探險合作後，他的人生被帶到了全新的高點。

在湄公河的探險船上，張帆驚覺，他的大半人生都是跟著探險學會一起走過的。這條辛苦的路上，張帆也曾對探險學會的方向給予重要意見，但更多的是彼此互相扶持的革命情感。

「如果說人生路途上一次的相遇是緣分的話，那麼長達二十五年的風雨相隨、生死與共就只能用『命中注定』來解釋了。感謝上帝將我的興趣與職業搭配得如此完美的同時，還給我安排了這麼一位亦師亦友的帶路人！」

How Man：
我介紹他給別人都說「將來的將」、「麻煩的煩」，他都要趕忙修正。乒乓球也可算是高手，我都告訴別人打贏了他再來找我吧。他確實是學會用來擋駕麻煩事的高手，能處理最複雜的人事及政治上的難題。

Zhang Fan

Director of Yunnan Institute of Geography, Yunnan University.
Expert in biology, birds, and caving.
Join CERES 1991

"On a day in the beginning of 1991, How Man gave a speech at
Yunnan Institute of Geography where I worked, he talked about
Yangtze River and exploring the source. I was sitting there wondering
if the spelling is incorrect. Shouldn't it read "How Man Wrong"
instead? He looked so thin and wearing a pair of glasses, he didn't look
like an explorer. However, the contents of his speech, as I remembered,
was superb, addressing not just on geography but also on cultural and
humanity matters." Zhang was 28 years old, How Man was 42.

Since then, Zhang became How Man's right hand man, taking part in
the expeditions to the source of the three rivers on the plateau, and in
the black neck cranes, and the Bo people's hanging coffins projects.
Before joining CERS, he has never been to places above 3,000 meters.
By joining CERS, his life as reached a new height, literally.

On board HM Explorer on the Mekong River, Zhang suddenly realized
that half of his life was spent with CERS. Recalling his eventful years
with the CERS, he was glad and happy that the Society had all along
been heading towards the correct direction. Apart from leadership, he
believed the success was also due to comradeship among the Society's
staff.

"I am glad that God has given me a career that matches my interests so
well. I am glad too that HE has also arranged for a good mentor and

teacher to guide me."

How Man:

I always introduce him to others as "Jiang" – as future, "Fan" – as trouble in Mandarin, and he would always hurry to correct me. He is good at table tennis. For those who wanted to play table tennis with me, I always told them that I would play with them if they could beat Zhang. Zhang is also good at keeping troubles out of CERS and is most skillful at dealing with human resources and political issues.

Karl von Habsburg

奧地利皇太子，Blue Shield 總裁

我第一次聽聞 CERS 跟黃效文這名字是在二十年前一趟跨大西洋的飛機旅程上。機上雜誌有一篇很有趣的文章，描寫在地球上最後一位真正的探險家跟他的學會。這個未知的世界非常的吸引我，我跟太太決定，一定要跟故事裡的主角見面。

那時候我太太正在準備黑水城的珍寶展覽，寶物是由俄國探險家科茲洛夫在一九零八年從塔克拉瑪干沙漠裡一個秘密的城鎮取出，帶到聖彼得堡，歸檔後從此隱身，直到被她挖出來。很清楚的，只有 HM 是那個可以帶我們去黑水城的人。

那趟旅程並沒有成行，許多原因是遠超過 HM 可以控制的。不過我們卻開始了很棒的友誼，幾趟令人難忘的旅行帶我們到中國非常偏遠的地方，那種只有 CERS 才到得了的地方。

我一直都喜歡帶著小孩一起出國去冒險，HM 讓這些旅行變得非常有紀念價值。我永遠都不會忘記一九九八年我帶著兩個比較大的小孩，一個兩歲一個四歲，跟 HM 一起去麗江。這個美麗的古城位在令人驚嘆的山區裡，我女兒都還記得，這是她人生最早的記憶裡其中之一。如何？這如果是你第一個記憶！

另一趟旅行也是我永遠也不會忘記的，HM 邀請我陪他跟他的團隊去中國大西部的藏羚羊產羔地。那是二零一一年的夏天，當時我父親的身體況狀很不好。我告訴 HM 如果父親的狀況變得更差，我有可能接到通知後得馬上趕回家。HM 告訴我他可以隨時安排我回家。要知道海拔五千公尺以上，遠離柏油路，安排回家可不是件容易的事。然而，當我們一抵達這趟旅程最偏遠的地方時，電話來了，我必須馬上回家。在 HM 的安排下，超有效率跟心胸寬大的 Berry Sin

HRH Karl von Habsburg

Archduke of Austria and Chairman of Blue Shield

The first time I came across the names CERS and How Man Wong
was on a transatlantic flight 20 years ago. There was this fascinating
article in an inflight magazine, portraying the last true explorer on the
planet and the organisation behind him. Feeling strongly attracted to
the uncharted, my wife and I decided it was necessary to meet the man
behind the story.

My wife was working at the time on an exhibition of the treasures of
Khara Khoto, taken from the secret town in the Taklamakan desert by
the Russian explorer Kozlov in 1908, and brought to St. Petersburg,
where it lay hidden in an archive, until unearthed by her. It was
immediately clear to us, if anyone could take us to Khara Khoto, it
would be How Man.

The trip never materialized at the time, for reasons far beyond How
Man's influence. But what did materialize was a great friendship, and
some unforgettable trips to the more remote corners of China, only
accessible to CERS. I always like to bring my children when venturing
abroad, and it was How Man who made some of the most memorable
trips possible. I will never forget a journey in 1998 with How Man
and my older children, at the time 2 and 4, to Lijiang. The wonders of
this ancient city in the most stunning mountainous setting is still one
of the earliest recollections of my daughter: how about that as one of
your first memories!

In another trip I will never forget, How Man invited me to accompany

一路陪著我，我於是及時趕到家，跟父親做最後告別。

CERS 跟黃效文已經成為保育偏遠地區文化跟環境的指標，對規劃可持續的探險來說也是。我的工作是保護文化資產，因此我必需到非洲跟亞洲的偏遠地區與戰亂地區工作，每當我遇到棘手的狀況時，我第一個想法就是：HM 會怎麼做？他的原則像是「當你沒有備案 B 跟備案 C 的時候，永遠不要出發」，還有「跟別人請求原諒比拿到許可來的容易」，這些對我起了很大的幫助。

HM 從來不把中國看待成一個孤立的地方。像是薩爾溫江的項目，茵萊湖，或是飛越駝峰的飛機，他總是把鄰近的國家一同放在對的背景裡。CERS 一直以來扮演著保育中國文化與自然非常重要的角色，未來也會繼續。這一個國家擁有獨一無二的歷史文化，並且有這樣的一群人這樣費盡心思的付出，人們跟大自然可以倍感榮耀了。三十年只是個開始！

How Man：
當 Karl 遇到問題的時候會想到我，這似乎也是合理的，也許我是個麻煩製造者，或者麻煩總是會跟著我。他的車隊曾經在廷巴克圖的溫泉區故障，他馬上就想到跟我一起的旅程中，也曾經發生過好幾次類似的狀況。Karl 進入軍事衝突區去交涉仲裁文化資產是非常危險的事，但也是我最欽佩的。

him and his team to the birthing grounds of the Tibetan antelope in China's Wild-West. It was the summer of 2011, and my father with at years was of very frail health. I told How Man that I might suddenly receive notice to come home, if my father's situation deteriorated. How Man told me he could facilitate my transport back home anytime, not an easy feat when you are at over 5000 meters altitude, and days away from the next gravel road. Once at the remotest point of our expedition, the dreaded call came and I had to rush home. How Man organised it, and accompanied by the ever efficient and big-hearted Berry Sin, I made it back in time to say a last good-bye before my father died.

CERS and How Man Wong have become the benchmark when it comes to preserve the culture and ecology of remote places, but also definitely when it comes to organising sustainable expeditions. My professional work with Cultural Property Protection is leading me to remote and embattled places in Africa and Asia, but whenever I come into a difficult situation my first thought is: What would How Man do? His principles like 'never depart without a plan B and C', but also 'it is always better to ask for forgiveness than for permission' have saved me more than once.

How Man has never seen China as an isolated place. Projects like the ones on the Salween River, Inle Lake or the planes crossing the hump, have always put it in the right context with its neighbours. CERS has played, and will play in the future, an incredibly important part in preserving China's multifaceted culture and nature. A country with such an unmatched wealth in history, people and nature can be proud of professionals protecting it with unmatched dedication and

sophistication. 30 years is just the beginning!

How Man:

It seems appropriate that when in trouble, Karl should think of me, be it because I am a trouble maker, or trouble tends to follows me. I remember when his convoy broke down at the hot spot of Timbuktu, he too thought of the multiple similar incidents when travelling with me. His motivation to be present at military conflict zones to negotiate and arbitrate on behalf of cultural heritage sites is extremely dangerous, and most admirable.

黃毓芳 EuFang Hwang

旅館設計師 Hotel Designer

阿芳與 HM 的認識比較戲劇性，並不是那種聽了演講慕名而來或者經過朋友特別的介紹，而是在香格里拉飛往昆明的飛機上，那是2003 年。阿芳回憶說，那時剛好陳盛泉坐在旁邊，因為同樣來自台灣，所以兩人聊起天來，陳盛泉向後指著一位先生問阿芳：「妳在藏區那麼久，不認識坐在後面那一位嗎？他是 Wong How Man 妳一定要去認識啦！」

「我是到了中甸中心，深入的了解 CERS 所做的項目之後，才開始認識黃效文這個人的。發現他帶著探險學會在藏區做了保育黑頸鶴、藏羚羊和藏獒犬這些事情，有點被感動耶……HM 真是個不可多得的人才……之後我們才開始有往來，直到海南島的項目，才算是真的跟 CERS 在工作上有實質的接觸。」不論是 CERS 的員工或者 CERS 的好友，幾乎每個人都知道阿芳這號人物，不僅僅是因為她在旅館設計這個專業領域的突出表現，更是她爽朗熱情的個性。

「我是不知道 HM 跟藏區的緣分是從何而來的，我一到藏區就愛上了這裡，就覺得我一定要住在這裡，並且在藏區做點甚麼。結果有一個人叫做黃效文，他已經為這裡做了這麼多事了，他前輩子一定跟這裡有甚麼極為特殊的緣分！」離開了舒適的美國加州和自己創立的事務所，阿芳一進入藏區就是 12 個年頭，但她其實喜愛的不僅是藏族文化，就連麗江的老房子以及沙溪的老馬店，都有阿芳保護少數民族傳統建築的自有方式。

2009 年阿芳成為 CERS 海南島項目的一員，辛苦地跟著夥伴們一起把黎族「金字型」的傳統房舍保留下來。「能在那樣偏遠的地方做洗手間、汙水處理這些，是很難得的經驗，我們盡量就地取材，還

EuFang Hwang

Hotel Designer

The meeting between the two was a little dramatic. It wasn't meeting aThe meeting between the two was a little dramatic. It wasn't meeting at a speech or introduced through friends. It was on a flight from Shangri-la to Kunming in 2004, when sitting next to Eufang was Eric Chen, also from Taiwan and a board director of CERS. It led to a sequence of events.

"After visiting Zhongdian Center, have a better understanding of CERS' projects, I then started to know How Man. I was a little moved when I learnt that CERS he led has done so many projects in Tibet, like protecting black-necked cranes, Tibetan antelope and Tibetan mastiff. How Man is the one and the only. We remained in contact. However it was until the project in Hainan, I started actually working with CERS" said A-fang. CERS staffs or friends of CERS almost all know A-fang. She excels at designing hotels. She is full of life and very passionate.

"I didn't know what fate would bring me to Tibet and get to know How Man. I fell in love with Tibet the minute I came here, and I knew I had to live here and do something for Tibet. Then came this person How Man. He has already done so much for this place. He must had some unique connection with this place in his previous life!" said A-fang.

After leaving the comfortable life in California and the firm that she founded, A-fang has been in Tibet over 12 years; she not only loves

用了河邊的石頭……整體的條件很不好，但是最後覺得很開心，因為我們做到了！」雖然有時候員工都會說黃老闆的想法變化很快，並且非常主觀，但是阿芳卻也中肯的說：「如果不是 HM 的眼光和過人的行動力，根本就不可能有所謂的海南島『項目』的出現，這也就是我很佩服他的地方。這就是 HM。」有才華的人還能彼此惺惺相惜，真的難能可貴。

2016 年九月初，HM 前往台灣阿里山驗收第二間達邦的傳統房舍。這個阿里山的項目阿芳也參與其中。

「探險學會三十年了真的很不容易，我很希望未來 CERS 可以做更多台灣的項目，因為學會很多贊助人來自台灣。也希望 CERS 能給台灣學生暑期上課的機會，讓台灣的孩子能透過不同的角度來瞭解保護自然和文化傳承這些事的重要性。探險學會做了這麼多事，也該讓更多的台灣人，特別是台灣年輕人知道在這個世界上，甚至就在亞洲，有人在努力做這些事。」我很贊同阿芳的這個建議，因為在多數台灣人的心裡，通常會認為 CERS 所做的「探險」和「保育」這類型的工作是很「西方人」的，並不知道原來華人世界裡有個黃效文，能帶著自己的觀點，做出這麼多傲人的成績。探險家不在故事書裡，而是真真切切的活在現代，此刻，就在我們的眼前。

How Man：
阿芳也可算 CERS 的手足了，一次她在台東為我的手傷開刀，另一次在川藏高原為我的腳傷再度動刀。當然在野外活動時她的烹飪也是一流的，也算文武雙全吧。我很欣賞她的室內設計，很有心思，能把冷冷的房子弄得像個窩，從這點我很重視她對學會建築維修中所提的意見，也佩服她能在任何場合大方地為阿芳穿上她的藏裝。

Tibetan culture, she has great passion for preserving minority tribe's traditional architecture. She has restored houses in Lijiang and Shaxi.

A-fang became a member of CERS Hainan project in 2009, the team painstakingly restored the traditional houses. "It was a precious experience, working in the remote place, building toilet and waste water management. We used what's available to us. We used river rocks even. The working condition wasn't great, but we did it and were very happy about that". Sometimes staffs would say How Man changes his mind rapidly and is very willful. But A-fang responded "If it wasn't for How Man's vision and quick to action, there would be no Hainan project. This is what I admire about him". These two people with great talents and discerning eyes see talent in others.

In the beginning of September 2016, How Man went to Alishan in Taiwan to inspect the second traditional house in Dabang. A-fang also participated in this project.

"CERS has been around for thirty years and it is not an easy job. I hope CERS in the future will do more projects in Taiwan, because a lot of supporters are from Taiwan. It would be great if CERS would give summer internship to students here, making kids in Taiwan understand the importance of nature and culture conservation, letting them see it from different angle. Let young people here know that there are people dedicated their efforts to that". I agree with A-fang's suggestion, because many Taiwanese think that "exploration' and "conservation" is very western, they didn't know in the Chinese world, there is HM, the real life explorer.

How Man:

A-fang is considered one of CERS' key members. One time in
Taitung she performed a surgery on my hand, another time on my
foot while on the Sichuan-Tibet plateau. Her cooking in the field
is first class. She does everything. I appreciate her interior design
works, very thoughtful, always have ways to make a place cozy, so I
value her opinions when it comes to restoring architectures. I also
like her good taste in dressing herself up in Tibetan costumes for
important occasions.

高希均

遠見、天下文化教育基金會董事長

黃效文曾是美國《國家地理雜誌》第一位華裔文字及攝影記者。長久以來他的探險、寫作、攝影、實地採訪、田野工作以及所發表的十多本中英文著作都呈現了他對新聞、探險、保育、古蹟與環境的熱情。三十年前他就利用太空梭上的最新儀器，發現了長江的一條新源流，立刻引起轟動；他在中國邊疆設置的工作站，拍攝到了瀕臨絕種的稀有動物，引起全球關注；近年來建造了一條探險船，在緬甸北部與印度、中國交界的河流上，觀察與紀錄逐漸消失的古蹟與村落。在菲律賓南部也以同樣手段對海洋珊瑚魚類做出研究。

這些包括新聞、人文、科技與探險熱情的第一手報導，使他在 2002年獲得了美國<時代>雜誌第一屆亞洲英雄的讚譽，稱他是「中國探險的今人中，成就第一」。CNN 曾有十二次報導他的紀錄。效文曾經說過：「今天很多記者探測別人隱私，尤其社會知名人士的隱私，若能以同樣工作熱情，用到社會有益及上進的主題上，他們都會成為現代社會、都市的探險家。」社會探險家所關心的不會是名人隱私，而是下一代人的未來。

過去三十年來大家都看到了黃效文在中國邊境對大自然的愛護、對生態保育的警告、對人類古蹟的關懷。所有這些都豐富地展現了這位人道主義者對地球上真善美的實踐。我依舊這樣的期待效文與CERS 的下一個三十年。(by 高希均)

How Man：
我認識高教授快五十年了，在我 1969 年初到美國威斯康辛州念書時便認識了，能在亦師亦友的路途上走了半世紀，真不容易。他創辦的天下文化出版社更前後出版了我的十七本書，令我們近年來更有機會見面聊天談及中國及台灣的各方面，更難能可貴。

Charles Kao,

Director of Commonwealth Publishing Group Cultural & Education Fund

How Man was the first Chinese reporter to work for America's National Geographic Magazine. His main areas of work there were exploration, field investigation, writing, photography and conducting interviews. In the course of his work he had written and published many articles and books. Reading these articles and books one will find that How Man is an ardent lover of nature and cultural and historical relics. And because of such love, he is totally devoted to protecting and preserving them.

Thirty years ago, through using the most advanced equipment on the Space Shuttle, he discovered a new source of the Yangtze River. He then physically went to the spot to confirm his finding and his expedition won the applause of all people in the geography and science circles. He also proceeded deep into remote and desolate regions in China to film endangered wildlife and to investigate the dangers these animals were facing. His findings shocked the world.

In recent years, he has built a river boat to facilitate his exploration team to study and investigation vanishing cultures and heritages along rivers in the China/Myanmar/India border regions. His team also studies and investigates coral ecology in waters in southern Philippines.

How Man's outstanding achievements has won him the honor "Among the selection of 25 Asian Heroes" by Time Magazine in 2002. The magazine described him as "China's most accomplished living explorer". His achievements and stories were reported by the CNN

no less than twelve times. How Man has once said, "Today's reporters like to probe and unveil other people's privacies, particularly those of the celebrities. If they can turn to study and investigate subjects that can promote the well-being of the society with the same degree of thoroughness and diligence, their contributions will be as big as those of the explorers. A responsible and public spirited reporter should have concern for the well-being of the next generation, not celebrities' privacy."

All of us can see How Man's deep concern and love for Mother Nature and for historical relics. In performing his Society's work, he always performs it with a humanitarian spirit and he always seeks perfection. I look forward to seeing the CERS progress and rise to further heights in the next 30 years.

How Man:

I have known Professor Kao for almost half a century now. I first met him in 1969 when I was a student in Wisconsin State and thereafter we became friends. His Commonwealth Publishing Group has published 17 books that I have written. Professor Kao is a learned person and I treat him as my respected teacher. In recent years I often have the opportunity of meeting him and chatting about things concerning China and Taiwan. I feel honored and privileged on all such occasions.

柯詩倫 Sharon Ko

畢業於美國加州伍德伯里大學室內建築系（Woodbury University）

2006 － 2009 為探險學會實習生，2011 － 2013 為全職員工，現為中甸中心博物館建築設計負責人。

Sharon 跟探險學會的緣分結在 2006 的夏天，當時她跟著教授 Ildiko Choy 到香港、拉薩與香格里拉，並且幫忙設計了古城博物館、納帕海的黑頸鶴觀鳥中心以及為藏獒中心生產室做了空間規畫的提案。但真正認識 HM 是在 2009 年的那趟香格里拉之行。「教授因為水土不服所以只好先回美國去了，我就代替他留下來並且到海南島帶學生和整理文物⋯⋯」Sharon 來自台灣，是個小留學生，曾經在 HM 的新書發表會上幫 HM 讀過幾段書中的中文，雖然念得不流暢，但卻看得出她的認真與努力，她就是這樣的一個大女孩，總是可以看到她認真專業的對待她的工作。

HM 常常會變成喜歡捉弄人的小孩，所以總是認真生活工作的 Sharon 常被 HM 弄得哭笑不得，尤其是牙刷被偷用的這件事，誰也不知道這個淘氣的 HM 到底是不是真的做了，但是 HM 倒是昭告世人了，「他開的笑話真的是愈來愈不好笑了⋯⋯」Sharon 直白又無奈地說；「但也是他的誠意打動了我，那時 HM 到 L.A. 都會來找我並且表示出希望我加入探險學會一起做點甚麼，前後總共有四次。我想了很久，HM 所做的事情的高度以及背後的重大意義都是無人能及的，而我當時手邊的那些商業案子似乎是個任何時間任何年紀都可以繼續的，再加上一些私人因素也想離開美國，所以就開始了我的雲南緣分。」

加入探險學會後，Sharon 主要是做文物展覽設計、空間規劃、照片展覽、文物紀錄以及在暑假協助帶學生做調研。現在 Sharon 最主要的工作就是中甸中心的博物館建造。

Sharon Ko

Department of Interior Architecture, Woodbury University
CERS intern 2006-2009
CERS full-time staff 2011-2013
Currently in charge of Zhongdian center museum architecture design

Sharon's relationship with CERS began in the summer of 2006, when
she followed professor Ildiko Choy to Hong Kong, Lhasa and Shangri-
La, to assist in the design of Old Town Museum, the delivery room
in the Tibetan mastiff breeding centre, and in the Black-necked crane
observing center project at Napahai. However, it was the Shangri-La
trip in 2009 that she got to know HM. "The professor had to return
to the United States as he got altitude sickness, so I stayed behind
instead. Subsequently I went to Hainan Island to lead the students
organize the cultural relics...." Sharon comes from Taiwan, went to the
US to study when she was young. On an event to commemorate the
publishing of a book written by HM, she was asked to read paragraphs
from the book in Chinese, she couldn't deliver it smoothly, but she
tried it very hard, that is Sharon. She's dedicated to her job and
serious.

HM has once made fun with Sharon by telling her that he has used
her tooth brush many times. She was embarrassed and thought that
his jokes were getting less and less funny. "But despite being funny I
know he is a good and sincere person. While I was in L.A. he came to
visit me four times, asking me to join CERS. I thought about it for a
long time. There is great meaning behind things HM has done, there is
no one like him. I can go back to the architecture field anytime at any

最令 Sharon 印象深刻的一趟探險是在她剛剛加入學會時的那趟怒江溯源之旅，倒不是因為路途艱難與突然而至的暴風雪，而是溯源後一起到了藏羚羊的產羔地。那時探險隊搶救了一隻小藏羚孤兒帶回營地，而 Sharon 就在帳篷內成為保母，負責照顧失去母親的小藏羚。Sharon 很清楚，若不是加入了探險學會，一輩子都不可能有這樣的機會跟藏羚羊如此貼近。「我很佩服 HM 對每一趟探險的計畫，還有遇到狀況時能夠當下做出判斷和決定……但是，他開的玩笑可是愈來愈不好笑囉！」Sharon 一定又想起了那個牙刷事件了！

How Man：
最近借了 Sharon 的瑞士刀一用，還她的時候加了一句：「那牙籤真棒！」她的臉色太好看了。

age, and with other personal reasons, I hopped on the plane, left the US and headed for Yunnan".

After joining the CERS, Sharon is in charge of designing relic exhibitions, spatial planning, photography exhibition, cultural documentation and assist summer interns with their survey. Presently her focus is building the Zhongdian Center museum.

Sharon's most memorable exploration was to the source of the Salween when she first joined CERS. It wasn't the blizzard, and the rough journey that made the exploration memorable, it was discovering the Tibetan antelope calving ground that made it memorable. The CERS team rescued a lone baby antelope and Sharon became her babysitter. Sharon knew if it wasn't for CERS, she would never have the opportunity to get so close to a Tibetan Antelope. "I am very impressed with HM's exploration planning. His response to unexpected incidents are also good. But, the jokes he made on me were not good", Sharon remembers the toothbrush incident again.

How Man:

Recently I borrowed Sharon's Swiss knife, when I returned the knife to her I said "that is one great toothpick". Upon hearing what I just said, the look on her face was most exquisite.

林百里 Barry Lam

廣達電子公司董事長／CERS 董事會主席

「他可以這麼隨興，活在自己的世界中，做自己喜歡的事情，他真的很幸福！」沒想到像 Barry Lam 這麼成功的企業家也會流露出對於 How Man Wong 這個探險家的羨慕之情。

每個人在這個世界上扮演的角色都不同，但無疑地，從 2016 年這個時間點來檢視，這兩位都可以站上成功者的舞台。Barry 和 HM 的人生志趣不同，也讓他們背負著不同的社會責任。但自從 1999 年瑞士銀行的一個晚宴後，這兩個同樣出生在香港的男人，生命就出現了共有責任、共同前進的那道緣分。HM 在中國藏區所做的文化保存和保育工作，正是 Barry 認為刻不容緩的工作，「那些文化當時若不保存，很快的就會被人類進步的腳步給消滅掉了。」Barry 說，也因此，Barry 完全地支持著 HM 的每一個項目。兩人結識後，很快的，在 2000 年的那個農曆年，Barry 就跟著 HM 一起到了中甸，看好了一塊兩人都喜歡的地，準備作為探險學會的基地。那裏，就是現在 CERS 中甸中心，是探險學會前往藏區工作的大本營。

「HM 念新聞，再加上在美國《國家地理雜誌》那段時間的訓練，所以他對探險項目的目的和戰略都很清楚，再加上方法創新，所以能夠獲得有相同理念的人和企業的支持……這三十年來，他確實獲得了很大的成就。」1966 年 Barry 到台灣念書，今年剛好五十年，他的人生和事業也同樣有著一般人所望塵莫及的成就。1966 年是個重要的年代，那年林百里來台灣，那年中國的文化大革命開始。雖然自己的工作領域是在電機電子，但是 Barry 沒有設限自己的觸角，他熱愛藝術與文化，應該也就因為如此，他知道 HM 保護文化的工作有多麼重要，所以他才這麼樣的支持著 HM。

Barry Lam

Chairman, Quanta Computer / CERS Chairman

"He is very lucky to be able to live his dreams, do whatever he desires as he wishes. "Surprisingly even a successful businessman such as Barry Lam could be envious of the life of an explorer - Mr. How Man Wong.

We all assume different roles in this world, but undoubtedly both of these two men have achieved great success. Barry and How Man have different ambition, which created different social responsiblity for them respectively. However, since a joint dinner banquet of CERS/UBS in Taiwan back in 1999, they have found a common interest and responsibility between them that has brought them together by fate.

The work How Man has done on cultural preservation and conservation in ethno-cultural Tibet has gained approval from Barry. "If we do not preserve these cultures that have been passed down from generations, it will eventually disappear overtime with sociocultural evolution," said Barry who wholeheartedly supports How Man in his cause. Soon after their meeting, during Chinese New Year in Year 2000, they travelled to Zhongdian together to pick out a piece of land that is to be the operation base for CERS. Nowadays it is known as the CERS Zhongdian Center, the base for exploring ethno-cultural Tibet.

How Man's qualification in journalism alongside his background with the National Geographic Magazine (US) has provided him with the necessary knowledge and tactics in research and exploration. His new approach has received support from his peers and various businesses.

「他啊，是個很高傲的人，也有偏見，他不喜歡的事情你跟他說一百遍他也不會去做……就我們學理工的人來看，他就是一個浪漫。我跟他一起上到梅里雪山看藏獒基地，大山大水的，HM 的世界就是那個樣子的……」我完全懂得 Barry 說的這句：「他不喜歡的事情你跟他說一百遍他也不會去做」；如果不是這麼固執，如果不是那麼專注於自己的想法，那就不是 HM 了啊。看來作為 CERS 這麼重要人，也是經常被 HM 弄得很無奈啊。

三十年來 CERS 就是靠著這麼許多贊助者的信任，才取得現在的成績。三十年來奠下了好基礎，那麼接下來呢？有沒有一個長期的、永續的經營模式能夠讓 CERS 不只是一人發光呢？文化的傳承是很重要的，不僅是在人類社會裡，也同樣可以應用到企業和探險學會這樣的組織裡。「我很期待 HM 下一個三十年會出現新的 business model 喔！」Barry 緩慢但清楚地說出了他對 CERS 的期許。

「那麼，一個像 HM 這樣被選為亞洲英雄的探險家，和，您這樣一個成功的大企業家，現在讓你選，你要當哪一個？」我忍不住地問了林百里先生這個問題。

「我啊，我想當攝影家！」看來 Barry 還是很著迷於這個自己追了五十年的興趣，「攝影需要內在的心境和外在的情境產生共鳴，才能有好的作品……我曾經是台大攝影社的社長呢！」說到這裡，Barry 眼睛裡出現的光芒還真是不一樣，嘴角也泛出了難得一見的微笑，看來攝影，真的讓他熱愛啊。

How Man：
百里屬牛，我也屬同年的牛。他常說他出生在春天，是春牛，較辛苦；我是夏天牛，只管吃草享受，我很同意。但若沒有那春牛支持，我可能也享受不了。

He has indeed accomplished greatly in the last 30 years. Barry started his study in Taiwan in 1966 which marks the fiftieth anniversary this year, he has also achieved what most can only dream of in his personal and work life. 1966 was an important year as Barry arrived in Taiwan; the Cultural Revolution was launched that same year. Even though Barry specialized in Electronics his background does not restrict him from developing interest in other fields. His passion for Arts and Culture is the reason why he recognizes the importance of HM's work on culture conservation.

"He's very proud and has his own prejudice. Nobody can make him do something he doesn't like. Practical science and engineering people would see HM as a romantic person. I've travelled with him to see the Tibetan Mastiff in the Tibetan Plateau, and I know the most important thing in HM's world are the big mountains and great rivers." I absolutely understand when Barry said that nobody can make How Man do anything he doesn't believe in because if he wasn't so strong willed, if he wasn't so focus, he wouldn't be How Man. So it seems that if HM insists on a certain matter, even important persons like Barry would sometimes need to back down.

CERS has gained trust from many sponsors in the last thirty years to achieve what they have today. The Society has built strong foundation in the past thirty years. "Passing down the Society's corporate spirit and culture is important in ensuring it will stay strong and healthy. I am also looking forward to seeing HM brings his Society to a new height in the next thirty years, " said Barry as he expressed his expectation of CERS.

他身體不好時曾在我家休養，我心情不佳時也找他開解。那年他願當董事長幫我忙，他身體才剛恢復，我帶點擔心，感謝他。也提到之前兩屆董事長皆屬牛，常有點牛角碰撞，不知第三個牛董是否那樣。百里忙說：「不用擔心，你在前面拉，我在後面幫你推，就可以了。」我聽此擔心全掃，之後合作愉快。

"If you could choose between being HM – a named Asian hero explorer, or yourself - an outstanding business man which would you choose?" I couldn't help but put forward the question to Mr. Barry Lam.

"Me? I would rather be a photographer." It seems like Barry is still very much into a hobby that lasted fifty years. "To produce a good photograph, the inside world need to resonant with the outside view. I used to be the captain of the photography club at National Taiwan University." Barry talks about it with a twinkle in his eye and a faint smile, it's easy to see his passion in Photography.

How Man:
Barry is an Ox in Chinese Astrology. I'm also an Ox born in the same year as Barry. He often says that he was born in Spring, which makes him a Spring Ox that has to work hard unlike me whom is a Summer Ox that only grazes on the grass leisurely all day. I agree with this but I also know that it would not have been possible if it weren't for the support of the Spring Ox.

He stayed in my house at one time – at that time he was ill. And then shortly after he recovered, he showed his support for me by taking up the job of the Chairman which I really appreciated. When I mentioned to him about the conflicts I've had locking horns with two previous chairman, both are oxen, he told me not t   o worry. He assured me that all I need to do is pull from the front and he will pull from the back and that has put me at complete ease and we work seamlessly together.

李娜

2004 年四月進入學會至今。現為昆明中心行政主管。

「每次朋友看見我手機裡那些大山大水的壯麗照片，都會讚嘆並且羨慕著我的工作，只是，他們是不會知道藏在這些照面背後的，其實是無比的艱辛……」總是把自己打扮得漂漂亮亮的李娜已經在探險學會工作十幾年了，有點難以想像，因為大多數學會裡的女性員工皮膚都難可以保持的柔嫩細緻的。原本在交通廣播電台工作的李娜，因為不喜歡那種類型的工作環境，經過了張帆老師的面試後，加入了探險學會。回想那個面試，李娜最記得的就是張帆老師問她是否可以出差。李娜當時單身，自由自在地，想也沒想的就回答了：當然可以。

李娜是張帆老師的助理，她的工作也就剛好可以用「出差」和「不出差」來劃分。不出差的李娜主要是負責昆明辦公室的工作，文書處理外也負責跟學會的客人、來訪者、學生以及中甸中心的聯繫。出差時，李娜會配合 Berry 負責後勤的工作。她會依照行程計畫裡的需要去規劃所需的裝備、物資、食物等等，以確保所有人員一路順暢平安以及不挨餓。如果你曾經跟著 CERS 到過野外，你就會知道這樣的角色有多麼的重要了。

這十幾年來，李娜說，每次到野外就會想著趕快回家，因為外面的條件真的很不好很辛苦，有時遇到天氣不好，思念家裡的那種心情就特別強烈。但是，每次在家裡待久了，又會很懷念到野外工作的日子，想念那種自然風光還有大隊人馬一起做事的那種感覺。

值得一提的是，保護海南島黎族傳統屋舍的那個項目，李娜也參與了「出差」與「不出差」以外的工作內容。李娜跟著王健等人一起執行了收購村屋、建立臨時工作站等第一線的工作，這讓李娜不只

Li Na

Join CERS in 2004, presently Kunming office manager

"When friends see the scenic pictures in my phone they all envy what I do, but they don't know behind those beautiful pictures are hard works" says Li Na. She always dresses pretty and has been with CERS for over a decade. It's hard to believe after working with CERS for so long, she still keeps her skin fair and beautiful. She was working in a traffic radio station but didn't like the working environment, after being interviewed by Zhang Fan, she joined CERS. At the interview Zhang asked if she can travel. She was single then, free as a bird, so she said "yes, of course".

Li Na works as Zhang's assistant. Her work comprises field work and office work. When she's not performing field work, she manages the Kunming office, does administration works, receives CERS guests, visitors, students and liaises with Zhongdian Center. Her field work includes arranging logistics with Berry. They would plan according to the needs of the expedition, preparing equipment, supplies, food, ensuring that everyone on the road would be safe etc.

When she's out in the field, she often would feel homesick, particularly if the weather was bad. But when she's home for a while, she would start missing her days in the field, where she could see beautiful scenery and many wildlife.

Li Na had worked on Hainan Li tribe's traditional house preservation project. Along with Wang Jian and others, they negotiated with villagers for the purchase of a house to build a work station. Li Na

是一名助理，更學習與見識到了探險學會更多元的工作內容與不同的挑戰。讓員工有機會嘗試不同的工作內容，一直是 HM 獨特的用人方法，從這點就可以看出 HM 一定不會被規矩綁住的這種個性。

說到這十幾年裡最難忘的一次探險，李娜跟好幾位成員一樣，都想起了怒江源頭那次：「我是留守在大本營的其中一人，因為有好幾個人都出現了高山反應了，我也必需在這裡確保後勤的補給是正常的。那天說好了 HM 以及考察人員到源頭只是一天的行程，天黑前就可以回到大本營，但是沒想到，天黑了、入夜了都不見他們回來。那晚大本營也在暴風雪中，我們有幾個人也試著到營地附近巡守，但就是沒有任何探險隊回來的跡象。那裏沒訊號、海拔高、暴風雪，大本營裡的每個人都憂心忡忡心情糟透了，完全無法休息入睡。直到第二天的中午，遠遠看到馬隊的歸來，我們才開始放下心來，每個探險隊員看來都疲憊極了，但至少平安歸來，真的很感謝老天⋯⋯」。

加入探險學會的李娜，這十幾年來也同時也探索著自己的人生，她從一個漂亮年輕的女孩，變成了漂亮有型的媽媽。有了小孩之後的她，當然也想過辭去學會的工作好把時間更完整的給先生和孩子。但是 CERS 的環境，從黃先生到每個同事都讓李娜有家人一樣的感情，所以她捨不得辭去這份工作。「雖然黃先生有時候會發脾氣，像個老小孩，但我還是捨不得～～」李娜說著，大大的眼睛裡散發出母性卻又調皮的光芒。

How Man：
李娜說話特別快，可能是當交通廣播員的後遺症，令我經常聽不清楚她帶雲南口音的國語。她的駕駛水平也特快，在城市或公路上穿插超車過線，若非我這種身經百戰的越野經驗，可能會不寒而慄，而我對她駕輕就熟的水平，卻十分欣賞，大可當我的備用駕駛員。

wasn't always just an assistant. When opportunity arises, she would be tasked with more responsibilities. This is the way How Man develops his staff.

Speaking of the most unforgettable exploration experience Li Na like others team members recall Nujiang River Source. "I remained at the base camp with others. Some had started showing high altitude sickness. My job was to ensure we have sufficient supplies. How Man and the team planned a one day trip, they should return to the base camp before it gets dark. However they didn't return the whole night. No telephone signals, everyone was worried badly, we couldn't sleep. It was until the next day around noon, I saw the caravan returning. Everyone was exhausted, but thank God they were safe."

Over the decade, she explores her life too. From a pretty young lady, she now is a pretty mother with a child. She thought about quitting and spends more time with her family. But she values the working environment and everybody work like a family. "Though How Man sometimes lose his temper, like a big boy, but I still can't bear the thought of leaving". Li Na says, her big eyes are warm and motherly, and playful.

How Man:

Li Na talks very fast. It might have something to do with being a traffic broadcaster. Often I don't understand her Yunnan accent Mandarin. She drives fast too, in the city on the highway, over taking cars. However I am not afraid. Instead of admire the ease at which she maneuvers the vehicle, she is qualified to be my back up driver.

蒙德揚 David Mong

信興電業集團 集團主席兼行政總裁

Shun Hing Group. Chairman & Group CEO

世界上有很多成功的企業家，他們有財富、有權勢、有地位以及在商場上有遠見。但是能夠同時體認到自己的「社會責任」進而付諸實行的，是值得給予特別尊敬的掌聲。除了 Barry Lam、Billy Yung 以外，David Mong 是另一個值得一提的 CERS 長期贊助者。

見到 David 的第一面不禁讓人猜想，他應該是個熱愛運動的人，否則怎麼有可能把自己的體態保養的如此好；果然，他說他喜歡慢跑，即使是夏天，一個星期都可以跑上 50-60 公里，難怪都沒有一般中年男人的那種發福跡象，可見得應該是個自律甚嚴的企業家。

「HM 不喜歡說他是『代言人』，但其實還真的是幫我們拍了攝錄機的商品廣告我們才認識的。」David 的普通話非常流利，他細數著兩個人是如何認識的，原來已經有二十年了：「我喜歡他那種把歷史用容易了解的方式留存下來，可以讓後代還看得見……」對於每一個長期支持 CERS 的贊助人來說，大家都有著很明確的共同認知與信仰，那就是保存文化的當務之急，特別是對於急速發展經濟的中國來說。

當然，瀕臨絕種的動物也一樣需要關注。緬甸貓復育的這個項目就讓 David 印象深刻。「那時 HM 跟我說，你來看貓吧，我心中有所遲疑，因為我不是那麼喜歡貓的人。後來 HM 說，那是像狗一樣的貓！這就引起我的好奇了……」果然，喜歡黏人、一點都不獨立的緬甸貓，一下子就讓 David 喜歡上了。「能夠花費那麼大的精神在英國、澳洲找到品種好的，然後繁殖，最後再送回去牠們的老家，

David Mong

Shun Hing Group Chairman & Group CEO

There are lots of successful entrepreneurs in the world. They have wealth, power, high social status and a great vision for business. Entrepreneurs who should be applauded are the ones who are aware of their own "social responsibility" and who take actions to help society. Besides Barry Lam and Billy Yung, David Mong also deserves to be mentioned as a long-time supporter of CERS.

When I first met David, I thought he must be a sporty person to keep himself in such great shape. Just as expected, he likes jogging. He jogs 50-60 km a week even in summer. No wonder he has no over weight problem, which most middle-aged people have. Evidently he must be an entrepreneur who exercises strict self-discipline.

"How Man doesn't like to be called a 'spokesperson'. However we wouldn't have met if he hadn't shoot a commercial for one of our products." David is very fluent in Mandarin. He recounts how he met HM in details. It's been twenty years since they met. David stated "I like how HM preserves history in ways that is easy to understand for the future generations." All long-term supporters of CERS share the same belief, that cultural conservation is a pressing matter, especially in China, which changes are taking place so fast.

The endangered animals also deserved much needed attention. David was much impressed with CERS' effort to reintroduce Burmese cats to Myanmar. He said "How Man told me that I can stop by to check

真的是一件很好的事情。」

這次的見面是在 David 的辦公室，這個空間跟 David 一樣，感覺非常實在，然而書架上滿滿的感謝狀卻是最好的裝飾。David 的父親是開創事業的第一代，那時就已經開始關注慈善教育工作了，不僅是香港的大學，北京、上海甚至劍橋都有他們資助興建的校舍或者獎學金。「中國人要偉大，教育一定要做好！」我完全可以感受到 David 的那種信心跟氣勢。David 甚至用一年一塊錢的租金將石澳 1939 那間具有歷史意義的房子交給 CERS 使用。

關於 David 和 HM，其實有個很大的共同點，「事情不好玩，一定做不好」David 說：「HM 是探險家，董事會一定會給他完全的自由去讓他探索。」一定要好玩的這件事，這兩人可真是不謀而合。David 接著興奮的說：「我今年底還要在公司辦一個用筷子的比賽！」「是夾豆子嗎？」我充滿興趣的回問。看來，一定要好玩的這件事不在年紀，而在個性。

說到 CERS 的幾個項目點，David 去過的地方還真不少，除了中甸中心以外，也去了傈僳族和金絲猴的響古箐，還住在傈僳族傳統的房子裡。過去的三十年，CERS 真的有很多成就，所以學會的董事們當然開始關心下一個三十年：「我們其實已經討論了一陣子了，HM 太特別了，也許不是用找接班人這樣的方式來承接學會……總之啊，請他好好照顧自己的身體，還有很多事要做的。」

「喔，對了，在中甸那裏我喝到那種甚麼茶的，鹹鹹的、油油的，還真是難喝啊！」David 認真的補了一句。若是說，引進新商品到市場是一種探險，嘗試沒喝過的酥油茶也是一種探險，那麼，David，你早已經穩穩地走在你的探險之路了。

out the cats. I was a bit skeptical because I am not a cat lover. How Man later told me that the cats behave like dogs and that got me curious……." Just as expected, David fell in love with Burmese cats right away. They are very warm toward people. David added "going all those troubles sourcing the pure bred Burmese cats from the UK and Australia, breed them, and reintroduce them back to Myanmar was indeed a wonderful thing".

I met with David in his office. Numerous letters of appreciation decorates the office. His father started the business, and back then the family was already doing charity works. Universities in UK, Beijing, Shanghai even Cambridge all have received scholarships or funds to building schools from David's family. He said "Chinese can only be great with excellent education!" I could feel that he truly believes that. Another example of David showing his great support to CERS, in his leasing of a historical 1939 building in Shek O to CERS for a nominal rent of one HK dollar a year.

David and How Man share this in common, "if it's not fun, it won't produce good results. "How Man is an explorer. The board gives him the freedom to explore as he wishes." David then told me with great excitement "I am going to hold a chopstick contest for my company at the end of this year!" I asked "Picking beans with chopsticks?" Fun is valued by a person's personality, not but by one's age.

David has been to quite a few CERS' project sites. He's been to Zhongdian center, Lisu village and golden snub-nosed monkey site, even stayed in a Lisu traditional house. CERS has accomplished a lot over the past thirty years. The board members started thinking about

How Man：

所謂大企業老闆，原來開的是小小的非名牌汽車，一次來石澳訪我之後坐巴士離開，去街市逛，再轉地鐵回家。誰知道樂聲牌老闆的私下生活卻是這麼簡單節儉的。這源自家教，早年我曾數次進住蒙老先生上海的家，也聽說不少他的逸事。我榮幸地接受 David 邀請書寫他父親紀念展覽的前言，更從中得知蒙老先生的家居言行，及至影響下一代的人生觀及待人接物等等。David 的做人身段是企業家的榜樣，身體身段也是探險家的榜樣！

the next thirty years for CERS. David said that, "Board members have been discussing for a while. How Man is so unique and outstanding in the exploration field. Maybe we won't find a similarly capable successor for a while......So HM must take good care of himself as there is still so much to do."

Before ending the interview David added, "Oh, by the way, the yak butter tea I had in Zhongdian did not fit my taste". On my way back, I thought "Ah, David, in a sense you are also an explorer, having the courage to drink something you know might taste awful."

How Man:

Despite being the boss of a big corporation, David leads a simple life. The car he drives is small and humble, not one of a prestigious brand. He once visited me in Shek O, he then left by taking the bus, went to visit local market and took subway home. No one would know that he lives such a simple life. He comes from a well-educated family. I have heard many anecdotes when I stayed in his father's place in Shanghai several times in the early years. I had the honor being invited by David to write the foreward for his father's memorial exhibition. So I got to learn more about his father, his philosophy that affected generations to come. Corporations and explorer all have much to learn from the esteem business owner and philanthropist David Mong.

Valerie Ma

暑期實習生，HKIS/Deerfield 2013-2016

對一個像我這樣的學生來說，今「年」是從二零一六的秋天到二零一七年的夏天。尤其是今年，幾個重要的里程碑是我所期待的：高中畢業，我的父母結婚二十周年，CERS 三十周年，CERS 超越我的年紀也超過父母的二十周年。如果說 CERS 是我生命裡很大的一部分，這會是個含蓄的說法。二零一二年，我初次以一個有史以來最年輕的實習生加入 CERS，那年我十三歲，我才讀完七年級，我的嘴裡還帶著牙齒矯正器。戴了幾年牙套之後，要上十二年級時，我回到 CERS，開始在這裡的第五個夏天。

CERS 長期致力於對教育的奉獻，教育年輕世代關於環境保育跟文化的保護。但是他們的教育風格跟範圍是我從未在學校學過的。實際操作，臨場的體驗，讓我在文化豐富的中國跟其他的地方得到第一手的觀點；但收穫最多的，是我對人生哲學的新發現。關於探險的精神，不管它被詮釋成好奇心、發現、創新或是預期你沒有預期的事，這些道理都將引領著我去過我的生活，無論我在哪裡。

今年暑假回到中甸對我來說有特別的感受，距離我上一次來這裡已經有三年了。（在這中間我去了 CERS 其他地方的項目點，包括緬甸的）。小高跟七珠一看到我馬上就跟我說我長高了不少。探險學會鼓勵我們走出去體驗迷路，但是 CERS 裡的人讓我感覺我好像回到家過聖誕節。所以我要感謝 HM 跟 CERS 所有的人幫助我理解到一件事，偏離了一般道路也不是件壞事，有時候需要走這樣的路才可以找到真正的自己。我要恭喜學會三十年的冒險，一語不足道盡 CERS 對社會還有像我這樣的個人所產生的正面影響。

Valerie Ma

Summer intern, HKIS/Deerfield 2013-2016

For a student like me, this "year" really begins in the fall of 2016 and commences in the summer of 2017. In this particular year, I look forward to many significant milestones: the end of my high school career, my parents' 20th year of marriage, and CERS' 30th anniversary, which outlives both the former. To say CERS has been a big part of my life is an understatement. I first joined CERS as the youngest intern ever in 2012 at thirteen years old. I had just finished seventh grade, back when I still had an expander lodged in the roof of my mouth. A few years of braces and retainers later, I found myself returning to CERS for my fifth summer before heading into the twelfth grade.

CERS has made a long commitment to educate the younger generation about environmental conservation and cultural preservation. However, the style and scope of education is unlike anything I had ever learned at school. The hands-on, in-the-moment experiences have certainly given me a first-hand perspective in the rich cultures of China and beyond, yet the greatest lessons I have taken from my internships relates to my newfound life philosophy. The spirit of exploration, whether that is interpreted as curiosity, discovery, innovation, or expecting the unexpected, has guided the way I now live my life, wherever I am.

Returning to Zhongdian this summer was particularly sentimental for me, as it had been three years since I was last there. (In between, I visited other CERS sites including in Myanmar.) Xiao Cao and Qiju, among others, immediately pointed out that I had grown taller. For a

How Man：

很高興看著一個十三歲的青少年在五年間長大成十七歲的小大人，五年的暑假她都跟著 CERS 實習。讓我最驚訝的是她的轉變，她是個很好奇的人，物理跟自然科學比同齡的小孩好很多，突然間她對歷史跟社會科學變得非常感興趣。通常一般人要花上數十年的時間去轉變，Valerie 只花了短短的五年！我迫不及待地想看她未來五年的轉變呢。

society that encourages getting lost, at the same time, it was the people
at CERS who made me feel like I was returning home for Christmas.
So I thank How Man and everyone at CERS for helping me realize that
wandering off the path is not always a bad thing, which was sometimes
the only way to truly find myself. Finally, I give my congratulations
to 30 years of adventure, which doesn't even begin to encapsulate the
positive influence of CERS on communities and individuals like me.

How Man:

**It has been wonderful to see a teenager of 13 turned into a young
adult of 17 in five years, during consecutive summers with CERS.
What surprised me most was her transformation of someone
curious and fully ahead of her age in physical and natural sciences
to suddenly become fully engaged in history and the social
sciences. What usually take decades for us to age and become
has taken Valerie only 5 short years! I can't wait to see her next
transformation in yet another five years.**

Tracy Man

CERS 財務主任

「我跟普通人一樣都是去景點旅遊的，一點都不接近『探險』，但是我讀學會的刊物的時候，就好像跟大家去了探險！」Tracy 很誠實地說著自己的旅行，跟她工作的探險學會好像一點關聯都沒有。2002 年起，Tracy 作為財務主任，在 CERS 負責會計、簿記和財務報告，雖然她經手的每張帳單和收據都很有「泥土味」，但是本人好像卻沒受到甚麼影響。

「隨和」、「一直在工作」是 Tracy 對 HM 的第一印象。當我問她：「那現在呢？跟 HM 的相處中，印象最深刻的是？」「不畏困難，把每個項目旅程都可以完成！」Tracy 回答得很簡潔，不知是因為跟 HM 工作久了的關係，還是所有做財務的人都能夠把話說得簡單清楚。

「那麼，這麼多年來，妳有沒有擔心過 CERS 會沒錢用啊？」畢竟學會是一個非營利組織，必需靠著有識之士的認同並給予贊助支持，才能一步一步地往前走。這個問題，Tracy 一樣回答的很乾脆：「我從來沒有擔心過探險學會的財務，因為每個項目都是有意思的，學會的工作一直以來都得到贊助人的認同和支持。」我完全同意 Tracy 的回答，CERS 能夠在這三十年裡交出這樣一張漂亮的成績單（雖然 HM 說過是非題的零分就是一百分，但是用在這裡並不合適呢），真的是難能可貴。準確地說，沒有好項目就不會有這些贊助，若得到支持卻做不出成績，這些聰明的董事和支持者是不可能這樣一路相挺的。

關於 CERS 的三十年，Tracy 依舊很認真地說，「永不言休，把這30 年的記錄好好地保存，一直留下去。」

Tracy Man

Financial Controller at CERS

I am just like everyone else who goes to the usual tourist destinations, not remotely resembles exploration. When I read the CERS newsletter and saw pictures of my colleagues' expeditions, I was fascinated and wished that some day I can also do a similar expedition. Tracy very honestly tells me about her travels, it feels like she doesn't work at an exploration society. Since 2002, Tracy has assumed the position of financial controller, in charge of accounting, book keeping and finance statement. Though every bill and receipts passes through her hand smells of dirt from the Tibetan Plateau, it seems to have no effect on her.

The first impression Tracy had of HM were "easy going" and "always working". I asked "what about now? What is the most memorable thing working with him?" Her succinct reply was "Fears no challenges, always manages to get things done". I am not sure whether she's been working with HM for a long time, or people in finance always keep their words simple and clear.

"All these years, have you ever worried that CERS would run out of money" I asked. After all it's a non-profit making organization which relies on people's donations to keep running. About this question, she simply answered "I've never worried about the money, because every project is interesting, and we've always gained the recognition and support of our sponsors". I couldn't agree with Tracy more. In thirty years CERS has managed to deliver astonishingly good results. Simply put, if the project isn't good, then there would be no support behind

親愛的 HM，你真的不能退休喔，即使你的人生、事業已經做到這個高度了，大家還是對你多所期待啊！

How Man：
我是馬不停蹄坐不下來的人，從小上課便是這樣，真佩服 Tracy 能十多年如一日，從來坐在那桌子上專心工作，難道是否會計有如另一種數字遊戲？我這些年來唯一最多的對話便是每一、二個月問她一次「近日的進帳跟支出能平衡嗎？剩下的錢能花上多久？」幸運的，每次她的回答總是能令我放心！

it. Tracy also rightly remarked that, if her Society's projects were not good and meaningful, board members and sponsors would not keep on lending support to them.

On the Society reaching its 30th Anniversary, Tracy said 30 years is a long time, but the Society is still very active and vibrant. It is not tired at all. Indeed it is looking forward to achieve new heights in its goal and missions.

Dear HM, you simply just cannot retire. Even with all your achievements in life and in career, everyone still looks up to you.

How Man:

I am a restless person, ever since I was young. I am very impressed with Tracy's perseverance and consistency. She always sits in front of her desk and concentrating on her works. I wonder if accounting is a sort of number game? Those years my conversation with her every other month was "How's our fund situation? Can we balance the income and expenditure? How long can we last with our present fund level?" Fortunately her answers never made me worried.

七珠七林

藏族人。2002--2014 任中甸中心主任。藝術家，曾在政府文化部門任職。現為學會項目，社會企業「美香奶酪廠」經營者之一。

1981 年的夏天，七珠和從《美國地理雜誌》來的黃效文第一次見面，他請這位遠道而來的新朋友喝酥油茶。這次見面之後，七珠和黃效文都受到審問。「怎麼認識從美國來的人，他跟你是甚麼關係？」七珠回答：「我也是現在才知道他是美籍華人啊。」

七珠，是黃效文的第一個藏族朋友。

1985 年，七珠一家去參加「五月賽馬節」，在馬場旁他見到兩頂小帳棚、一輛豐田越野車、一輛摩托車和自行車，七珠在好奇之下走了過去，他看見那位幾年前害他被審問的那位黃效文先生。

1999 年的某一天，七珠受邀參加東竹林尼姑寺宿舍專案竣工儀式，當時他是文化局負責文物工作的領導，他又見到了這位黃效文先生，然後他們兩個就被緣分這條線綁在一起了。

從 2001 年起到現在，探險學會在藏區的項目，七珠都幫了很大的忙，也擔任了探險學會中甸中心的主任十幾年，是他用心看著中甸中心成立的。七珠說：「認識黃效文先生已經三十幾年了，我們的友誼之果都結在了一起做的文化和自然保護項目中了！」

How Man：
2005 年的長江源考察之後，十個主要的學會成員都獲贈一支奧米茄 X33 手錶。這款專為上太空用的手錶限量生產，每個團友都珍藏不捨得用，只有七珠及美國 NASA 專家成員 Martin Ruzek 天天戴用。兩年後手錶電池用光，我們的在香港換一次上千元，七珠嘛，在昆明小店換了才兩百元，繼續天天在用。

Qiju Qilin

Tibetan
Zhongdian Center manager 2002 – 2014
Artist used to work in the department of culture
Currently manages CERS' social enterprise Mei Xiang Yak Cheese
Factory

1981 summer, Qiju first met How Man, back then How Man was still
working for National Geographic. They drank yak better tea together
and then later they were both interrogated by the local policemen. Qiju
were questioned how he came to know that man from America?" Qiju
answered "I didn't know he is American Chinese until now".

Qiju later became How Man's first Tibetan friend : in 1985 when
HM attended a local horse race which Qiju also attended, he saw
HM and immediately recognized him as the man who almost got him
into big trouble in 1981. They then talked about their experience and
subsequently became friends.

One day in 1999, Qiju was invited to the completion ceremony
of the Dongjulin Nunnery dormitories. He was the director of the
department of culture. There the two met again, and started their work
relationship.

Since 2001, Qiju has been helping CERS implement its projects in
Tibet. He also has assumed the position of Zhongdian Center director
for over a decade. Qiju says "I've known HM for over thirty years, we
were brought together as friends by our common interest in culture
and nature protection".

How Man:

After the expedition to the Yangtze River source in 2005, ten key CERS staff members received a Omega X33 wristwatch as gift from the Society. The limited edition watch was designed for the space. Almost everyone found the watch too precious to be an everyday wear. Only Qiju and NASA scientist Martin Ruzek wear it every day. Battery ran out after two years. It costed all of us over a thousand dollar to replace the battery except Qiju, who was so resourceful to have found a shop in Kunming which charged him only 200 yuan for changing the battery. He still wears the watch with pride every day.

JOHN STRICKLAND

前 HSBC 主席

二零零零年我受 CERS 的創辦人黃效文的邀請，擔任 CERS 的董事。
董事會成員們還有董事長 Daniel Ng Yat Chiu，James Chen Yue Jia，
Magnus Bartlett，Barry Lam，Pak Lee。Daniel Ng 在香港建立麥當
勞餐廳，也是 The Octavian Society 的創辦人，他們蒐集了一系列理
察 · 史特勞斯音樂作品的手稿。James Chen 是 Legacy Advisers Ltd
的董事總經理。Magnus Bartlett 是 Odyssey Books，Guides，Maps
的出版者。Barry Lam 是台灣廣達電腦的創辦人，曾經是世界上最
大的個人電腦代工廠。

一九七四年到一九八六年間，HM 在美國《國家地理雜誌》服務，
住在加州但是去中國探險好幾趟，其中包括定位長江源頭。後來他
回到香港成立探險學會，把家人留在加州。

在那個時候因為路況跟通訊很差，所以很少人可以到得了雲南北
部，四川西部跟青藏高原。HM 跟 Land Rover 建立了特別的關係，
這個英國四輪傳動越野車的製造商，多年來讓 CERS 的裝備裡都有
兩台最新款的 Land Rover Defender，毫無疑問這也是在廣告他們產
品的多種功能跟穩固強壯。從 CERS 最早在雲南省首都昆明的基地
出發，這些越野車讓 HM 跟他的團隊進入中國偏遠地區的許多地
方。

藏羚羊生活在海拔五千公尺以上的高度，是地球上數一數二的嚴峻
環境。牠們的絨毛很特別，很輕又很保暖，這樣的絨毛讓牠們可以
在酷寒的高原上生活。藏羚羊是遷徙的動物，從蒙古到西藏，傳統
裡遊牧民族會緊緊的跟著牠們，他們每年也會走這趟旅程。遊牧民
族會獵捕藏羚羊，取牠們的皮，肉，骨頭，角還有羊毛，簡單的來

John Strickland

Retired Chairman HSBC

Contribution to the 30 year history of the China Exploration and Research Society.

In 2000 I was invited by Wong How Man, founder of the China Exploration and Research Society (CERS), to become a Director of the Society. Fellow Directors at the time were Chairman Daniel Ng Yat Chiu, James Chen Yue Jia, Magnus Bartlett, Barry Lam and Pak Lee. Daniel Ng established the chain of Macdonald's restaurants in Hong Kong and was the founder of the Octavian Society, a collection of manuscripts of music composed by Richard Strauss. James Chen is the Managing Director of Legacy Advisers. Magnus Bartlett is publisher of Odyssey Books, Guides and Maps. Barry Lam is the founder of Quanta Computer based in Taiwan and in those days was the largest manufacturer of notebook computers sold under other brand names.

Between 1974 and 1986 How Man worked for National Geographic magazine, based in California but making multiple expeditions to China, one of which located the source of the Yangtze River. He then returned to Hong Kong, leaving his family in California, and established the Society.

In those days northern Yunnan, western Sichuan and the Tibetan plateau were rarely visited due to poor roads and communications. How Man had established a special relationship with Land Rover, the British manufacturer of rugged off road four wheel drive vehicles and they for many years kept CERS equipped with some current

說，遊牧民族取他們所需要的一切來度過高原旅途。沙圖什是這種用藏羚羊絨毛織成的披肩的名字，由北印度克什米爾的手工藝大師織成。沙圖什披肩非常細緻，一件大件的披肩甚至可以穿過一只婚戒，因此非常珍貴。CERS 是第一個組織喚起大眾對關注藏羚羊的組織，當時藏羚羊已經被獵殺到瀕臨絕種了。這個宣傳活動做的很成功，藏羚羊終於被 CITES（瀕危野生動植物種國際貿易公約）列為瀕臨滅絕的物種，這也促使中國官方下令禁止獵捕，並且確實查禁。

我的太太 Anthea 還有我跟隨 HM 去了雲南「探險」三次。二零零一年一月我們飛到昆明之後開車到麗江、虎跳峽、中甸（在納帕海看黑頸鶴）、東竹林寺，以及在奔子蘭由 CERS 修復壁畫的書松尼姑寺。我們也去了迪慶和梅里雪山，然後回到大理。二零零二年八月，是我們第二趟的「探險」，我們飛到中甸巡視 CERS 新的藏式風格中心的進度。二零零三年八月我們又回到中甸，去金絲猴的故鄉，拜訪 CERS 保存跟修復的傈僳族村莊，還有 CERS 蓋的茶室，用來服務前來梅里雪山轉山的信徒。

How Man:
在他背後我們都叫他 Mr. Strictland，這樣說可能都還有點輕描淡寫，他黑白分明，意志堅定。學會在他的監督整頓下變得更好。當董事會有事情要通過的時候，通常都會先跟他討論過；如果他簽名的話，其他人閉著眼睛都可以跟著簽。前 HSBC 的主席來當我們的董事不是為了榮譽或是虛榮，他是真的來鞭策我們的。

model Land Rover Defenders, no doubt as an advertisement for their versatility and robustness. From CERS initial base in Kunming, the capital of Yunnan Province, these vehicles allowed How Man and his team to range widely in these remote parts of China.

The Tibetan antelope or Chiru lives in one of the harshest environments on earth, at an altitude of over 5,000 metres. Their special type of down fur, which is both very light and warm, allows them to survive in the freezing conditions of the plateau where they gather at one point of the year. They are migratory animals - moving around Tibet - and traditionally followed closely by nomads, who also made that journey every year. The nomads would hunt the antelope for all that it provided them - hide, meat, bones, horns and fur pelts - in short, everything that the nomads needed to sustain them through their journey. Shahtoosh is the name of a shawl woven with the down hair of the Chiru by master craftsmen in Kashmir, Northern India. Shahtoosh shawls are so fine that a large shawl can be passed through a wedding ring, making them very precious. CERS was one of the first organisations to draw attention to the fact that Chiru were being hunted to extinction for their fur, a campaign that was eventually successful, with Chiru being listed by CITES as an endangered species, which in turn prompted the Chinese authorities to ban the hunting and to police the ban.

My wife Anthea and I joined How Man on 3 "expeditions" to Yunnan. In January 2001 we flew to Kunming then drove to Lijiang, Tiger Leaping Gorge, Zhongdian, Napa Hai Lake to view the cranes, Dongjulin Monastery, Shu Song Nunnery at Benzilan supported by CERS, Deqen, Mei Li Xue Shan and back to Dali. In August 2002 we

flew to Zhongdian to inspect progress on the new CERS Tibetan style base there. In August 2003 we again flew to Zhongdian and visited the home of Golden Monkeys, Gong Lisu Village, which CERS was helping to restore and preserve and the Yang Za Teahouse which CERS had constructed to serve pilgrims circumambulating Mei Li Xue Shan.

How Man:

Behind his back, we all call him Mr. Strictland, and that maybe an understatement, black and white, and tough as nails. With him overseeing the organization, we straighten things up. When the board need to pass any circular resolution, standard practice was run it by him first. If he signed it, everyone else could sign it blindfolded. Having the HSBC Chairman on our board isn't honorific or for vanity. He came in with a whip!

冼潔貞 Berry Sin

1997 年加入探險學會至今。

如果沒有她像褓姆一樣的照顧，HM 應該哪個地方都去不了。

加入學會的她，把自己曬得黑黑的，一看就很「野外」。

她雖然覺得每次到「野外」的項目都很麻煩，但是最喜歡的也是到
「野外」。

不吃米飯愛喝啤酒的她說：

不記得是哪一年在哪裡了，當年進入藏區除了在野外搭帳篷外，

有時候也會住在小鎮上或車站附近的旅館，那時所有的條件都很差，

吃也吃不好，很辛苦。

記得有一次好像是在車站附近的旅館，

房間其實是只有四塊木板的房子，那天晚上我做了一個夢，

我夢到自己在東方文華酒店裡，

我點了一客龍蝦，點完後我特別跟點餐的人說，

我要整隻的，不要切，我要整隻！

說到老闆 HM，Berry 只是淡淡地說：

不要發脾氣就是好啦！

雖然他管小事，但也是會放手讓員工做的，

他總會吸引那些欣賞他的人，

只是現在已經有年紀了，但又不服氣，

完全不會「slow down」。

廣東話裡有個說法，應該很能代表 HM

「冇敵最寂寞」

How Man：

**不變不如小變、小變不如大變，就如上廁所，難為 Berry 天天看著我
改變計畫，步步跟進快到二十個年頭。但也有永恆不變的，就是我的
那個榴槤笑話，那卻是她最愛吃的水果。**

Berry Sin

Join CERS 1997

If she didn't take care of How Man like a babysitter, he wouldn't be able to go places. Since joining CERS, she got so tanned, giving her a rather wild look. Every expedition involves a great deal of works and logistics, not an easy task; but she enjoys the work.

She doesn't like rice but drinks beer. Berry says "I can't recall which year it was when we were out in the middle of nowhere in Tibet for many days. Life was so harsh sleeping in tent, no good food, no hot water. One night I had a dream which I still remember now. I dreamt that I was in the Mandarin hotel. It was so comfortable and the food was so nice. And then I suddenly woke up and realized it was only a dream. You can image what cruelty I had suffered from the dream."

Speaking of How Man, Berry said "as long as he hasn't lost his temper, he's very nice". She said he sometimes likes to handle trivial matters inappropriate to his position and standing. That however doesn't mean he has no confidence in his staff. On the contrary, he trusts his staff, always finding opportunities to train them up for more responsible duties. Though he is of a senior age now, he is "young at heart".

How Man:

Berry must have gone through some real tough time over her twenty years working for me. That is because I tend to change things so often and so quickly. But I do have something long lasting and unchanged for her, and that is my story about durians, her favorite fruit.

Daw Yin Myo Su

Founder, Inle Heritage Foundation

HM 曾經跟我說「Missu，妳沒有辦法搶救你國家裡每一樣珍貴的文化跟自然遺產，但是妳可以當它們還存在的時候去紀錄它或是精選樣本保存。至少你還會有紀錄跟資料給下一個世代看」。突然間我覺得我好像遇見一個介於我祖母跟我爸爸中間的人，祖母用很多的智慧帶我長大，而我爸爸是個企業家，他喜歡話一說出口事情馬上就可以辦好。

在遇見 HM 之前我對 CERS 了解不多，不知道他們做什麼，也不知道 HM 是誰。但是現在每當有人問我在 Inle Heritage Foundation 跟我的同胞做些什麼事，我一定得先解釋 CERS 是什麼團體還有誰是 HM。我常常簡單的說明：HM 是一個不只打開我的雙眼的人，他也打開我的心，讓我去為我的社會服務。CERS 跟 HM 為我的國家跟人民做的事對我來說是無價的，對未來的世代也是。他又說所做項目不一定要吸睛，但是要觸動人心，這是最重要的。

像緬甸這樣的國家，我們需要比較個人的項目，像 HM 跟 CERS 做給我們看的，去啟發別人，幫助他們重拾自己的根，重建自己。在跟 HM 合作的過程，我跟我的團隊學到很多，我們一起合作將緬甸貓重新帶回緬甸，在茵萊湖蓋了一個水族館，在緬甸河裡的 HM Explorer 探險船，還有好多好多事。我跟我的鄉親感到非常榮耀，透過這些項目，我們可以去延續 CERS 跟 HM 的願景。

How Man:
文化認同對每一個國家跟人民的自尊是非常重要的。你或許窮但是要過的有尊嚴。這是我一直告訴 Misuu 的，她開始把我的話轉化為行動，上個項目還沒結束就接著一個新的。我們在世界各地面臨一

Daw Yin Myo Su

Founder, Inle Heritage Foundation

How Man said to me once, "Misuu, you won't be able to save everything precious, culture and natural heritage in your country, however you can record it or have samples while it is still available." At least you will have documentations and data so that the next generation can know what you had before. I suddenly felt like I met someone between my grandmother who raised me with a lot of wisdom and my father who is an entrepreneur and like to get things done the minute he said it.

I don't know much about what CERS or who How Man was before I met him. However, nowadays, to everyone who asked me about what I am doing at Inle Heritage Foundation with my people, well I must first say what CERS and who How Man is. My usual simple explanation: How Man is the person who opens not only my eyes but my heart to do what I am doing nowadays for my community. CERS and the work that How Man had done so far for my people and my country are priceless to me and for the generation that follows.

Again, as he said project doesn't need to catch eyes but if it touches hearts that's what matter. In a country like Myanmar, we need personal projects like what How Man and CERS do to show and to inspire others, to help them to gain trust in their roots and to rebuild themselves. My team and I had learnt a lot from cooperating with How Man through reintroduction of Burmese Cats, building and running an aquarium project in Inle Lake, HM Explorer boat on Rivers of Myanmar and many more… It is an honour for my people and I to

場競賽，雖然終點沒有奧運的那面金牌。這場競賽裡我們要有短跑的爆發力，也得有跑馬拉松的耐力。

carry on the mission and vision of CERS and How Man through projects that he helped us to build up in our country.

How Man:

Cultural identity is very important for each country and its people's own integrity. You can be poor yet still live with dignity. That's what I keep telling Misuu as she put my words into actions, starting new projects before the last one is finished. That's a race we are all dealing with all over the world, even though there is no Gold Medal like in the Olympics. In this race we run both sprint and marathon.

次仁卓瑪

藏族。畢業於美國杜克大學 2012 年加入探險學會，現為探險學會
中旬中心主任。

卓瑪是個聰明有主見的藏族女性，光是她的學歷就夠讓人吃驚，再
加上做事的條理，也難怪可以快速地接手中旬中心主任的位子。好
奇的問了為什麼藏族女孩有這麼多叫做「卓瑪」的，她露出開朗的
笑容說，卓瑪是度母，是女性的神！雖然加入學會的時間並不長，
但是卓瑪已經完全負起了每年暑期的教育計劃。她不僅規畫所有的
課程，還親自帶著學生們到重點項目基地做實際的考察和解說，每
年的夏天都可以看見她忙碌身影夾雜在不同國籍的學生當中。

由於本身是藏族的關係，卓瑪更能清楚地知道到底學會的項目對於
當地人的影響是甚麼。有時候，很怕只是學會一廂情願的幫助，而
無法讓當地人有正面的反應，這時候，同樣身為藏族的卓瑪就比較
容易出面協調處理了。甚至有些社區的項目雖小，但卻可以有潛移
默化的功能，好比她教村民小朋友英文的時候，就可以把保護動物
的觀念放到其中，讓這些藏族小孩明白這個環境是他們的，世世代
代，若只會取用而不保護，最後嘗苦果的只是自己，或者下一代、
甚至以後的世世代代。

「妳覺得 HM 怎麼樣？在 CERS 能學到些甚麼嗎？」我問卓瑪。

「他呀，非常的聰明，總是比我們想得更快，又那麼有經驗，每次
的對話幾乎都不是以前聽過的，常常都有新的想法，我們都還來不
及做，下一秒又變了⋯⋯但是他可以把教育這部分放手讓我和畢博
士去做，我覺得非常的感謝，當然，我也希望這一切能得到他的肯
定⋯⋯」陽光下的卓瑪口氣中充滿了自信以及身為藏族的驕傲。我
想，她將會是藏族女性裡的好典範，不僅在探險學會裡，也在香格
里拉，甚至未來整個藏族的社會。

Tsering Droma

Duke University graduate
Join CERS in 2012
Zhongdian Center director

Drolma is a smart and assertive Tibetan woman. One would be
impressed by her high educational qualifications. She's very organized
at work, no wonder she could rise up to the director position in such
short time. I was curious and asked her why so many Tibetan girls
named Drolma. She smiled and replied "Drolma is Tara, Goddess".
Though she hasn't been with CERS for a long time, she is now in
charge of planning every summer's educational program. She designs
the course and brings students to the project sites. Every summer she
would be busy in such work.

Being a Tibetan, Drolma understands well CERS' projects and how
these projects might influence others. There are times when the
locals do not understand the benefits of these projects. When this
happens Drolma would come in to help them understand. Education
is invaluable. She teaches village children English and many other
things. She would incorporate conservation education in the teaching
materials, so that children would understand the importance of
protecting the environment.

"What do you think of HM? What have you learnt in CERS", I asked
Drolma.
'He is very smart, thinks fast, faster than any of us. He is experienced.
There is always something new coming out of our conversations,

How Man：

卓瑪這個名字在藏區最普遍不過了，在我們學會工作範圍內至少有四、五個之多，所以大家都比較喜歡稱她較漢化的名字，陳次瑪。她在中旬中心管的全是學會的藏族員工，很不容易。藏族傳統的一些大男人主義要讓一個年輕女子指揮並不簡單。隨著她當上媽媽，升了做人的一級，應有幫助。

something I've never heard of before. But he changes plans a lot,
sometime even just shortly before we are starting. He has put me and
Dr. Bleisch in charge of educational programs. I am confident I am
most suitable for the task but still I am grateful to him for giving
me the opportunity", said Drolma. She speaks with great confidence
and proud of being Tibetan. I think she will be a good role model for
Tibetan women in the future, not only in CERS, but also Shangri-La,
in Tibetan society.

How Man:

**Drolma is a very common name in Tibet, we have met at least 4 or 5
Drolma within CERS. Therefore we like calling her Chinese name,
Chen Ji Ma. Managing staff in the Zhongdian Center is not easy
as all these staff are Tibetans, many of whom are male. In Tibetan
society where male chauvinism still prevails, having a young woman
in charge of male subordinates isn't an easy task. But now she being
a mother, it should help a great deal.**

王健

雲南大學雲南省地理研究所一員，1991年第一次參與探險學會野外考察，2007年正式加入探險學會至今。現為探險學會昆明中心主任。

跟著黃先生在野外跑了這麼許多年，最令他難忘的還是2011年的怒江探源之行，那次因為王健出現了高山反應，因此沒有跟進到最後的溯源，在準備不夠周全，衛星電話也未攜帶的狀況下，王健說：「我當時真的以為他們回不來了，明明說好進去一天的，但一直等不到他們出來，我真的嚇壞了，後來又聽說有隊員在暴風雪中走失……」探險不是冒險，不需要拿生命去做賭注；但是你又無法預期在探險之路上會遇到老天給的甚麼挑戰和試探。

「我真的很感謝黃先生給我一個機會去承擔海南島的項目，我算了一下，總共有七個月，也就是兩百多天是我一個人和一部車單獨在那裏的。我從來不知道自己的潛力能被這樣激發出來，特別是民居的修復改建是我之前從來沒有經驗過的，我謝謝黃先生對我的信任和支持，我也很高興我自己做到了！」王健跟著HM不僅學習到科研的後勤那個部分，更懂得了如何站在前方指導一個項目的完成。

每次看到黃先生對於事物的好奇和熱情，都讓王健自嘆不如，很慶幸自己遇到這樣的一個老師可以跟隨，除了工作，更多是對生命和文化的看法，尤其從1991年那次的探險之後，開啟了王健對於戶外探險的興趣，而「探險」也就成為王健此生的志業了。

How Man：
王健說話總帶點色彩，就是彩虹中的其中一個顏色，男士都喜歡聽，也可開懷一笑。女士都不好意思，有被吃了那軟軟白色的素食東西一樣的感覺。

Wang Jian

Yunnan Institute of Geography, Yunnan University – fellow researcher
1991 joined CERS' expedition for the first time
Join CERS in 2007
Currently CERS Kunming office director

After years with How Man, the most memorable event was the
expedition to Nujiang River source in 2011. On that trip Wang
experienced acute mountain sickness and wasn't able to go to the
source. Without satellite telephone to reach the rest of the team, he
lost contact with them. Wang recalls "I really thought they would
not come back. It was a clear day when they set out to the source. We
waited and waited, there was no sign of them. I was terrified. I also
heard that some members got lost in the snowstorm". Exploration is
hard work, but it doesn't have to risk people's lives, Wang thought.

"I am very grateful to How Man for giving me the opportunity to
handle the Hainan project. I had spent seven months there. In these
two hundred odd days, I was there alone with my car. I had no
experience of restoring traditional houses, I never knew I had this
ability in me until I had the chance to handle the project. I thank
HM for his trust and support and I am glad that I did it!" said Wang.
Wang has learnt from HM about scientific research and logistics,
and also learnt how to work through a project from the beginning to
completion.

Wang admires HM's insatiable curiosity and quest for knowledge. He
considers himself lucky to have How Man as a teacher, in work, in
life. Ever since the expedition in 1991, Wang became interested in

exploration and chooses exploration as his career.

How Man:

Wang Jian likes to crack jokes. These jokes sometimes were those which men like to hear, and which would make ladies blush. However, I suspect the ladies also like these jokes. So keep on your good work. Wang Jian, if making all happy.

王志宏

台灣經典雜誌總編輯

在印度洋上 Gili T 的大雨中，HM 的多年老友王志宏說：「我可以用一句話來形容我所認識的黃效文，他是個患了過動症的藏族牧民，人家一年遷四次家，他要遷四百次家！」

1980 年代中期，王志宏在《國家地理雜誌》中讀到一則中國少數民族的報導，特別是那些照片吸引了他，然後他注意到拍攝者是個華人。華人怎麼可以做到的？特別是當時台灣人要進中國是很不容易的。1990 年四月，王志宏第一次參加了 HM 的探險，接著是 1991 年與 1994 年兩個比較大的探險，之後，兩人便一直維繫著好的友誼，直到現在。

王志宏和黃效文兩個老友有著許多相似的地方，都是個性急躁的人，都有著白髮，只是現在黃效文的腰圍是王志宏的 1.5 倍。王志宏說，誰叫黃效文那麼熱愛可口可樂。「HM 是個非常浪漫的人，他的浪漫不是從平常他所說的話顯現出來，而是他讀的書。HM 讀了很多早期探險家、探險隊的故事，我想那些都給了他很深的影響，所以一定得要進入藏區尋找到一個屬於自己的位置。」

「想想看，十幾億的華人裡，只有他一個在做這樣的事情，他不只是瀕危的稀有動物，甚至是唯一的那個，應該要讓他做得成，所以當時我在《大地》以及現在的《經典》都非常的支持 HM 的這種探險的精神。其實早期的華人社會是有的，就像鄭和、玄奘和更早期的法顯，只是後來的皇帝和儒家把這樣的精神壓制了。不過，探險的因子常常是國度強大的原因，所以應該要被鼓勵。那種對未知的探尋、對千奇百怪困難的克服、然後前進，這是探險裡最好玩的，也是最重要的精神。當然，在這條探險路上 HM 雖然不是每次的抉

Wang Chih-Hong

Editor-in-chief, Rhythms Monthly (Taiwan)

Rain pours heavily down on the Gili Islands in the Indian Ocean, an old friend of How Man, Wang says "I would use one sentence to describe How Man. He is a Tibetan nomad with hyperactivity disorder. Tibet nomads relocate four times a year. He moves four hundred times!"

In mid 1980s, Wang read an article in the <National Geographic> about ethnic minorities in China. He was particularly attracted by the photographs in the article. Then he noticed that the photographer was a Chinese. How did that Chinese do it? It was a time when entering China was not easy for Taiwanese.

In April 1990, Wang joined How Man's exploration for the first time. Then another two major explorations in 1991 and 1994. The two have become good friends ever since.

The two share many things in common, both impatient, sport gray hair. The difference between the two is now HM's waistline has grown 1.5 times as Wang's. Wang blames HM's beloved Coca-Cola for his expanding waistline. "HM is very romantic. But it's not shown by what he says, it is through the books he reads. HM had read many stories of early explorers and the explorations they made. I think those have great impact on him. Therefore he wanted to find a place for himself in Tibet.

擇都是對的，但，對的還是多。只是這條路 HM 也必需妥協並犧牲一些甚麼，也許是家庭或跟下一代的相處。HM 是一個非常有決心，且前後一致的人，他想要做的絕對想盡辦法達成，不管有沒有足夠的幫忙或資源。我也看著他一步步為目標增添基石，這些都不是物質上的報酬，而根本就是一種浪漫主義！」對於老友黃效文，王志宏總是有說不完的觀感。

從 1990 就跟著 HM 一起探險的王志宏，2011 在怒江溯源的那個暴風雪裡差點丟失了生命，每次說起這件事，他總是會演一下：「真沒義氣，大家只顧著各自逃命！ 不過，在那樣的情況下，誰也顧不了別人，所以我也沒有任何抱怨啦，反倒是那些隊友後來一看到我就滿臉愧疚……」不過這個溯源可不是王志宏這些年來印象最深的一次探險，他說 1993 年那次進入西藏無人區，從羌塘到新疆，只有六個人和兩部剛剛空運來的新車，那次該遇到的困難全都遇上了，才真的感受探險的艱難和必須具備的勇氣，也更堅定了和 HM 的革命情感。

關於 CERS 三十周年，王志宏心情愉悅地說：「恭喜 HM，當時沒人可以預期到 CERS 可以做到今天的規模且堅持了這麼久，HM 做了許多很好的項目，也讓下一代的人看到探險家的精神並學習到不同觀念；我也看到 HM 一直在進步中，做事的方法甚至思維上的進步，不管是硬體上的，或是人與人之間的故事，真的很棒！」

How Man：
那個難忘的晚上，累壞了還等著壞消息，晚上十點多派出去搜索的兩個藏人回來報告餘下兩名隊友已在另一牧民家住下，始安下心來入睡。第二天早上牧民領著志宏和 Chris 騎著馬來歸隊，大家都跑出房子外迎接，拍下了難忘的一刻，寒冷的早晨一下子都溫暖了起來。若他那天回不來，這本書也出不來了。

"Think about it. With over a billion of Chinese, he is the only person who is doing this job. How Man, himself is an endangered animal, he might be the only one. Back then I was with <Earth Journal>, and now with <Rhythms Monthly>, I have always been very supportive of him, his exploration spirit. In the early days there were explorers like Zheng He, Xuanzang, or even earlier Faxian. Afterwards, as emperors and Confucianism teaching did not encourage exploration, no more great explorer has emerged. Exploration makes a country great. It should be encouraged. On the path of exploration, How Man hasn't always made the right decision. But his rights outnumber his wrongs. In order to pursuit his passion, he had to make sacrifices, away from family and children. How Man is a very determined person, when he sets out to do something, he would find ways to achieve his goal, regardless whether he has enough resources or support. I've watched him along the way, he is not concerned about material rewards, he just loves what he does, that is romantic!" Wang always has a lot to say when he talks about his friend, How Man.

Speaking of the exploration Wang went with How Man to the source of Nujiang River in 2011, Wang almost lost his life in the snowstorm. Whenever he talks about it, he would jokingly say "NO brotherly loyalty and love, everyone was busying struggling for their lives and absolutely had no spare capacity to look after others. So, I don't blame anybody. But when I rejoined the team after the near disaster, they all had a guilty look on their faces ......" But that was not the most memorable expedition for Wang yet. The most memorable expedition was in 1993 when Wang and the CERS team entered Tibet's no man's land. Travelling from Qiangtang to Xinjiang, only six of them, with

two new cars that were just flown in. On that expedition, they had encountered every kind of challenges one can think of. It is then that he realized the hardship of exploration and the courage one must have. It also solidifies their friendship.

About CERS 30th anniversary, Wang happily says "Congratulations for HM. No one expected CERS would last this long and achieve so much. HM has done many good projects, setting examples for the future generations, the spirit of an explorer. I can also see HM is always making progress, in his ways of dealing with matters and people, or the way he thinks. It is really wonderful!"

How Man:

That unforgettable night we were all exhaustive and waiting for the bad news. About 10pm the two Tibetan set out to search for the missing members returned and informed us that the two were with a nomad family. We were relieved, able to get some sleep. The next morning nomad led Wang and Chris on horseback came back to us. We all rushed out and took pictures to capture the memorable moment. Suddenly the morning chill was gone, it was nice and warm.

翁國基 Billy K. Yung

蜆壳電器控股有限公司 董事長兼行政總裁

Shell Electric Holdings Limited. Chairman & Chief Executive

「他的眼光真的跟我們很不一樣，我們看到的是破敗，他看到的是未來，他就是一個 artist，而且是有 talent 的那種！」在沒有過多裝飾的會議室裡，Billy 用著他一貫斯文的口吻形容著 HM。與來自台灣的 Eric Chen 一樣，Billy 也是在 YPO 的活動中認識 HM 的，那年是 1995 年，HM 剛剛把學會遷到香港。

CERS 位於黃竹坑的辦公室就是 Billy 捐贈的，可見他對於 CERS 的全力支持。「那個時候的我好像突然有個開關被打開了一樣，年輕時完全專注在工作，沒有注意到原來有些瀕臨滅亡的文化和動物是需要去保護的，所以當我遇到 HM，知道他在做的事情的時候……嗯，就是那種感覺，哪裡被 switch on 了……」。

Billy 很忙，我們的見面還不到三十分鐘，他的助理就必需打斷我們，示意 Billy 應該前往下一個地方了，於是我們移到他的座車上繼續談話。車窗外，香港的高樓比飛鳥還多，車窗內是 Billy 關於教育的長遠想法：「這幾年來，我們每年夏天都會贊助十個學生或老師到 CERS 學習，我希望讓他們從小就有保護文化和保育動物的觀念。我一直都覺得，經濟的發展絕對不是國家能夠強盛的唯一原因，最重要的是最根本的文化。若是你不尊重自己的文化，是無法得到世界的尊重的。」聽到 Billy 這麼說，我已經不必再問他為什麼會這麼挺 CERS 了。

如果你曾經參加過 CERS 的晚會，一定會對晚會上播放的動畫印象深刻。而那些正是由 Billy 所贊助的天水圍中學生所製作的。Billy 重視教育、重視青少年對自己的文化有所認知認同，這個學校的學生

Billy K. Yung

Shell Electric Holdings Limited. Chairman & Chief Executive

"He has a vision that is rather different from the rest of us: what we see as a heap of ruin, he often can see the future out of it. He is indeed an artist and a very talented one!" In an unadorned meeting room, Billy gave such an account of HM. Like Eric Chen from Taiwan, Billy met HM at an YPO event. It was 1995, HM had just relocated the society to Hong Kong.

CERS office in Wong Chuk Hang was donated by Billy. "At that time I felt my mind had been switched on. When I was young I spent all my time work hard for my company and had no time to think about meaningful things like nature and heritage conservation. Later, I met HM and came to know the importance of these matters so I decided to support his Society.

Billy was very busy, for in less than half an hour of our meeting his assistant had to interrupt us and remind Billy of his next schedule, so we continued the conversation in his car. Billy's thoughts on education: "The past few years, we've sponsored ten students or teachers to attend conservation seminars at CERS every summer. I want to instill the concepts of culture and wildlife conservation in their minds when they are still young. I always believe economic development is not the sole reason for a nation's prosperity. Because without a strong foundation in culture, economic development cannot occur. If you don't have respect for your own culture, the rest of the world won't respect you either."

在國際上的 animation 競賽中得到世界第一的榮耀，以及在科學上極為傑出的表現，都是給予 Billy 最好的回報。種甚麼因，便會結甚麼果，其實是一件很美好的事情。

Billy 也喜歡戶外活動，喜歡 hiking，只是因為睡眠的問題，所以無法像 HM 一樣可以在世界的任何角落（任何種類的角落）都呼呼大睡。「我也很羨慕他的呀」看著 Billy 略帶欽慕的眼神，我相信 HM 真的成就了很多 Billy 的夢想，這是一個雙贏的支持與贊助，不是嗎？

「如果你想要贏得尊敬，你該炫耀的不是你的財力，而是文化！」仰望著香港中環的壯麗高樓，我記住了 Billy 說的這句話。

How Man：
經常和 Billy 聊天時聽到他說生意艱難，賺錢辛苦，但不知怎的，每次他捐錢卻都那麼輕鬆容易。這讓我想到很多支持學會的企業家都有這麼一個共通點，錢對他們是工具不是目的，這點可能跟其他大量堆積錢財的守財奴是不一樣的。歷史記錄下來的不是甚麼財主或富翁，而是如何利用錢財去為社會服務的人。唐朝的員外富豪並無青史留名，窮書生及畫家卻留名千古。學會的董事及贊助者都十分支持文化和自然的保護。一次我電話上說石澳鄰近的老校舍要維修做村民活動中心，根本不是學會的事情，Billy 加上 David 兩位董事馬上各承擔三分之一經費，加上學會一份，不需求神拜佛，半小時內成事。

If you have been to CERS's gala dinner, it's very likely that you would be impressed by the animations. The animation was created by middle-school students of Tin Shui Wai Government Secondary School. For many year the school has been receiving sponsorship from Billy in order to send their students and teachers to attend the CERS conservation seminars.

Billy values education and cultures. The world champion prize that students of this school have won in an international animation competition and the outstanding scientific achievements they won were what Billy regards as the best rewards for himself. "you sow, so you will reap" said Billy.

Like HM, Billy loves outdoor activities, such as hiking. Unlike HM who can sleep well anywhere. Billy has sleeping disorder and cannot sleep well. "I envy him." Seeing Billy's expression of admiration, I believe that HM had fulfilled many of Billy's dreams.

"If you want to earn respect, you should show your support for protecting nature and culture heritage, not showing your wealth" Billy said.

How Man:

In our chats, Billy often talked about hardships and difficulties in business. But for some reasons, he is always quick and generous in giving us donations. I think of the shared common trait of many of our entrepreneur supporters. To them money is a mean to do greater good. History remembers those who use their wealth to serve the society. The rich from the Tang dynasty were not remembered;

however poor but talented artists and scholars were remembered. Board members and our sponsors were very supportive of culture and nature conservation. One occasion I mentioned on the phone that an old school building in Shek O would be renovated into a community center for villagers, which was not CERS' project; but Billy and David, both board members immediately pitched in one-third of the cost for each, and CERS shared one-third too. It's all done in half an hour. No need to pray for help from the divine.

如果說書寫後記是視為對過往的回顧，那麼有幾位已經不跟我們同在的人應該要被回憶，這些曾經在 CERS 的不同階段扮演關鍵角色的人物。

首先一定要提 Daniel Ng 伍日照先生，他擔任 CERS 董事主席超過十年。你不用假裝你已不在，我知道你還在看著我們，在遙遠的地方，但還是密切的關注我們。

你一直告訴我，甚至帶點威脅的口吻，如果我沒有一個計畫、預算還有問責說明，沒有人會持續支持我的。好，真不知道是怎麼辦到的，但我們已經來到三十周年關口了。現在我們真的有個計畫，只是我可能不會永遠乖乖地遵循計畫。我們確實把問責說明做得更好，因為我們也有了最好的會計師／財務主任。

我一直告訴自己結果將會不言而喻，即使你沒有計畫。我們過往的紀錄比我們說的和我們寫的還更有力量。一個不在規畫之內出生的孩子也仍有可能成為一位有用的人，重要的人。擴展到今天長期的項目時，我相信我們是值得友人跟支持者投資的。

在我們最困難的那幾年，許多友人對我們伸出援手，特別照顧我們。在重大的一九八九年天安門事件後，一夜之間所有跟中國有關的管道跟支援都斷了。李國鼎博士是台灣經濟，工業，科技業奇蹟的舵手，他在我們最需要的時候挺身而出。連續兩年，他指示他主持的基金會提供緊急資金。那兩次我們都是收到資金後才補上我們的計畫書。

蔣彥士博士，擔任過台灣農業與教育部長，以及連續幾任的總統府秘書長，他為我們引薦台灣資深跟年輕的企業家，給予我們莫大的支持。他曾親自帶我去那些會議，鼓吹大家支持，他也會確定他的朋友確實都出錢出力了。那段時期，這兩位紳士陪我們度過艱困的

Epilogue

If writing an epilogue can be considered thoughts remembered in passing, a number of individuals who passed away must be remembered. They were critical to CERS at different stages during our formative years, assisting us in our growth.

I must first mention Daniel Ng, who was CERS Chairman for over ten years. No use pretending he is gone, as I know he is watching, as well as watching out for us, from a distance.

Daniel would often tell me, even in threatening words, that if I didn't have a plan, a budget and accountability ; no one would continue to support me. Somehow we managed to pull through to our 30th year, and now we do have a plan, though I may not always abide to it. We certainly have tightened up accountability, with a first class accountant/controller.

I always tell myself that the result speaks for itself, even if you don't have a plan. It's about thinking, doing, done. Our track record should speak louder than our words, and our writings. A child that is not planned for may still become loved and important. Stretched out into the long-term, somehow I feel we have been equitable and a worthy investment for our friends and supporters.

In our most difficult years, many friends made exceptions for us. After the momentous Tiananmen incident of 1989, literally all channels and support regarding China dried up overnight. Dr. Li Kuo-ting, architect of Taiwan's financial, industrial and IT miracle, rose to the occasion of our needs. Twice, over two consecutive years, he instructed the foundation that he chaired to provide immediate funding. Both times we needed only submit our proposal, after receiving support.

幾年，當時支持我們還算不上政治多敏感的事，而台灣大眾對中國大陸的觀感也還未惡化。

甚至連在香港，一九九七年回歸前社會充滿不確定的氛圍下，我們新認識的 Gordon Wu 胡應湘先生和邵逸夫爵士在跟我們第一次見面時就承諾我們一筆在那時是很大的資金，給予我們完全的信任跟信心。而這兩位見面之前從沒有聽過我是誰。

不久後企業的支持開始湧入，大品牌像是 Shell，可口可樂，IBM，HSBC，Jebsen〈捷成國際洋行〉，國泰航空，Land Rover 還有其他等等。還有許多儘管在金錢上沒有這麼寬裕的朋友，他們也會投入時間提供服務，這對我們來說也是一樣重要的。要列出來的名單實在是族繁不及備載，但是他們都深深的在我的心裡，不管這些人是否已經不在了。

是的，我做事非主流。但是你又怎麼可以去期待一個探險家，牛年出生，去跟隨主流呢。或許我們一般人沒有對外展現探險和富有想像力的潛在精神，也並非總是有實際的探險行動，但是我們每個人的心裡多多少少都有這種精神，雖然可能不像還是孩童時候那樣的強烈。

是的，我越來越老，CERS 也是。但是如果我們持續保有探險的精神，我們永遠都和時代有一定相應，不僅在中國或是這個那個區域裡，而是在世界上。精神是沒有界線的，不管是地理或政治上的。它也不受限於歷史跟時間。我將與 CERS 持續大步向前。

探險家是個很特殊的職業。我很高興許多友人認可我的不同，而給予我莫大的支持。非常感謝一路幫助我們的所有人。

黃效文 二零一六年九月

Dr. Tsiang Yen-si, minister of agriculture and education and subsequently Secretary General of the President's Office in Taiwan, provided unmatched connections to junior and senior businessmen in Taiwan. He would personally escort me to those meetings to drum up support, making sure that his friends would pitch in.

These two gentlemen, both very much respected in Taiwan to this day, saw us through our toughest years. It happened during a brief window before such support would become politically sensitive as Taiwan's public sentiments for the Mainland turned for the worse.

Even in Hong Kong, before the uncertainty of the 1997 handover, two new acquaintances, Mr. Gordon Wu and Sir Run Run Shaw, both committed, at our first meeting, what at the time were relatively large sums in our support, with trust and confidence. Neither had ever heard my name before.

Soon, other corporate support began pouring in; big names like Shell, Coca-Cola, IBM, HSBC, UBS, Jebsen, Omega, Panasonic, Cathay Pacific, Land Rover, and more. In time we would receive far more private and personal support, which was more stable, and gradually be able to move away from corporate donations. Many friends, despite less financial means, would nonetheless pour out time and services, which were just as important. They are too numerous to list here, but please know that I have them in my heart, be they gone or still alive.

I don't do many things the mainstream way, but then what can you expect from an explorer, and a stubborn explorer born in the Year of the Ox ? While most of us may not exhibit that exploration and imaginative spirit on the outside, nor act upon it, we all have a bit of

that within us, though no longer as intense as when we were children. Somehow I managed to not grow out of it.

Yes, I am getting older, and so is CERS, but if we stay with that exploration spirit, we will always be relevant, not just for China or the region, but universally. Spirits know no boundaries, be they geographic or political. They won't even be confined by history and time. I shall march on with CERS.

Being an explorer is an exceptional career. And I have enjoyed exceptional support through many friends who recognized me as an exception. I thank all of them for helping us get so far. I could never have achieved this on my own.

Wong How Man, September 2016

黃效文與探險學會 大事記

Wong How Man		
1949	· 出生於香港	
1961	· 進入香港九龍華仁書院	
1969 - 1973	· 進入美國威斯康辛大學河城校區	
1974	· 第一次進入中國	
1986	· 離開可以坐頭等艙旅行的美國《國家地理雜誌》	· 在美國帕薩迪納的山中小屋成立 · 出版第一期通訊,影印紙八頁 · 昆明為探險旅程的起點 · 考察布達拉宮、貴州
1987	· 認識畢蔚林博士	· 帶畢蔚林博士進入雲南 · 決定以保護「自然」、「文化」為使命 · 共有會員 87 名,入會費美金 25 元

Wong How Man	
1988	• 懂得了唸誦六字箴言「嗡嘛呢叭咪吽」	• 考察南疆少數民族節慶 • 紀錄滿州鄂溫克族 • 西藏東側考察 • 第一次見到黑頸鶴
1989	• 於中印邊境被拘留十天 • 出版《Exploring the Yangtze》	• 支持一夕蒸發 • 發表繼續在中國境內工作的聲明 • 於西藏印度邊界考察登人 • 探索薩爾溫江上游
1990	• 於英國出版《Islamic Frontiers of China》	• 得台灣李國鼎、蔣彥士等人支持 • 與雲南地理研究所展開合作
1991		• 考察四川西部18座寺廟 • 進入阿爾金山保護區
1992	• 多次於新加坡及香港演講 • 試用美國友人 Conny Klimenko 特製的太陽能浴缸 • 長達二十九天沒洗澡	• 與張帆探查黃河源頭 • 來自亞洲的贊助快速增加
1993	• 獲頒勞力士獎（對於西藏高原寺廟所做的保護）	• 首次於中國使用路虎越野車衛士號 • 進入塔克拉瑪干沙漠 • 重訪帕米爾高原 • 於香港註冊為非營利機構

Wong How Man		
1994		· 開始修復四川白雅、八蚌兩所寺廟 · 展開保護黑頸鶴的計畫
1995		· 長江源頭第二次探源 · 出版《西藏》DVD · 於敦煌成立辦公室
1996		· CNN 報導 CERS · 中國中央電視台《東方之子》欄目介紹
1997		· Discovery Channel 節目報導 · 遷入黃竹坑辦公室 · 首次年度晚會
1998	· 出版《From Manchuria to Tibet》	· 發現藏羚羊產羔地
1999		· 發現懸棺遭盜墓者洗劫，製作紀錄片 · 考察喜馬拉雅山脈邊境 · 開始與瑞士聯合銀行合作 · 開始台灣年度晚宴
2000		· 開始東竹林尼姑寺項目 · 支助多項雲南新疆之研究計畫 · 確認懸棺年代為唐代

	Wong How Man	
2001	• 被金絲猴飛踢	• 再次回到藏羚羊產羔地 • 開始學生參與項目計畫
2002	• 《時代》雜誌選為 25 個亞洲英雄之一：探險中國的今人中，成就第一 • 獲威斯康辛大學河城校區頒贈傑出校友獎，這是百年來首次頒給在國外出生的畢業生。	• 岡仁波切轉山 • 中甸中心啟用
2003		• 建造茶屋與診所於卡瓦卡博轉山必經之處 • 藏獒基地建立 • 陪同沙智勇神父回到藏區教堂
2004	• Discovery 節目介紹	• 中甸中心啟用 • 響古箐傈傈族項目完成 • 開始研究駝峰歷史 • 開始製作氂牛奶酪
2005	• 雞足山轉山	• 三探長江源 • 協助復原七世達賴之出生地
2006	• 愛上緬甸	• 藏獒犬舍完工 • 學會獒犬 Chili 圖像上了中國發行的郵票
2007	• 到美國陪同 Bill 最後一次飛行	• 開始海南洪水村黎族項目 • 湄公河探源 • 緬甸貓項目開始

Wong How Man	
2008	· 黃河探源
2009	· 為黑頸鶴配戴衛星追蹤器
2010	
2011	· 怒江探源
2012	· 陳文寬踏上緬甸 · 再訪瑪麗亞索
2013	· 獲星雲真善美新聞傳播獎 「終身成就獎」 · 沙智勇神父離世 · HM Explorer 緬甸下水
2014	· 邀何秋蘭參加石澳粵劇節
2015	· 拔了兩顆牙齒 · HM Explorer 2 在巴拉望下水
2016	· 達摩祖師洞閉關室完成 · 中甸中心博物館完成

CHRONICLE

	Wong How Man	
1949	• Born in Hong Kong	
1961	• Entered Kowloon Wah Yan College	
1969 - 1973	• Enrolled University of Wisconsin, River Falls	
1974	• First entered China	
1986	• Left First-class travel with National Geographic	• Established CERS in Angeles National Forest cabin in Pasadena • Published 1st newsletter, 8 page photocopies • Using Kunming as operation base • Expedition covering Guizhou and Tibet's Potala Palace
1987	• First introduced to Dr. Bill Bleisch	• HM & Bill embarked on Yunnan Decided protecting "Nature" and "Culture" as CERS' mission • 87 members in total, USD 25 for membership fee

Wong How Man	
1988 • Learned the mantra "om mani padme hum"	• Southern Xinjiang expedition to observe minority ethnic group's festival • Manchurian expedition to study and film reindeer herding Ewenki • Eastern Tibet expedition • First encountered with Black-necked Crane
1989 • Detained ten days after visiting Teng people at Zayu in southeastern Tibet • Published 《Exploring the Yangtze》	• After the Tiananmen incident of 1989, literally all channels and support regarding China dried up overnight • Issued statement that CERS would continue working inside China • Studied Deng people in Tibet and India • Upper Salween expedition
1990 • Published 《Islamic Frontiers of China》 in UK	• Dr. Li Kuo-ting, Dr. Tsiang Yen-si from Taiwan supported CERS • Collaboration with Yunnan Institute of Geographic
1991	• Surveyed 18 surviving Tibetan monasteries in Kham of western Sichuan. • Arjin Mountain expedition

Wong How Man	
1992	• Gave multiple speeches in Singapore and Hong Kong • Tested the custom-made solar bath tub built by American friend Conny Klimenko • Went without taking shower for 29 consecutive days	• Yellow River headwater expedition • Sponsorship from Asia grew rapidly
1993	• Won the Rolex Awards for Enterprise (restoring Tibetan monasteries and murals)	• First introduction of two Land Rover Defenders into China • Entered Taklimakan Desert • Expedition to Pamirs • Set up of CERS in HK as an NGO
1994		• Started restoring Baiya and Bapoun temple in Sichuan • Started Black-necked Crane conservation program
1995		• Second expedition to Yangtze source • Released 《Tibet》 DVD • Established office in Dunhuang
1996		• CERS reported by CNN • Featured on CCTV program 《Son of the East》

Wong How Man		CERS EXPLORER
1997		• Featured on Discovery Channel • Moved office to Wong Chuk Hang • Held the 1st annual gala dinner
1998	• Published 《From Manchuria to Tibet》	• First discovery of an Antelope Calving Ground
1999		• Discovered hanging coffin raiders and made documentary about it • Expedition to Himalayan border • Started cooperation with United Bank of Switzerland • Started hosting annual gala dinner in Taiwan
2000		• Began Dongjulin Tibetan nunnery restoration project • Supported Yunnan & Xinjiang research projects • Confirmed the hanging coffins dated back to Dang dynasty

	Wong How Man	CERS EXPLORER
2001	• Got kicked by a snub-nosed monkey	• Returned to antelope calving ground • Students started participated in project planning
2002	• Time Magazine chose Wong as one of its 25 Asian Heroes, calling Wong "China's most accomplished living explorer." • Wong named University of Wisconsin River Falls Distinguished Alumnus. It was the first time the prestigious awarded graduated student born outside of USA	• Circumambulation of the Kailash • Launched Zhongdian Center
2003		• Built tea house and clinic to serve pilgrims to perform circumambulation on Khawakarpo • Established Tibetan Mastiff breeding center • Accompanied Father Savioz revisited churches in Tibet
2004	• Featured on Discovery Channel	• Lisu Hill Tribe conservation project • Began research The Hump history • Started producing yak cheese

	Wong How Man		
2005	• Kora of Mt. Jizus		• Third expedition to the source of Yangtze river • Restored the 7th Dalai Lama's birth house
2006			• Tibetan Mastiff kennel constructed • Flagship Tibetan Mastiff Chili featured on China's stamp
2007	• Accompanied Bill Maher's on his last flight in USA		• Began Hainan Hongshui village conservation project • Expedition to Mekong river source • Began Burmese cats breeding program
2008			• Expedition to the Yellow river source
2009			• Installed satellite tracking device on Black-necked cranes
2010			

Wong How Man		
2011		• Expedition to Salween river source
2012		• Brought Moon Chin back to Myanmar • Revisited Ewenki Mariasol
2013	• Lifetime Achievement Award from Monk Hsing Yun	• Father Savioz passed away • Launched HM Explorer in Myanmar
2014	• Featured on Discovery Channel	• Invited Cuban Cantonese opera singer to perform in Shek O festival
2015	• Pulled two tooth	• Launched HM Explorer II in Palawan
2016		• Damo cave meditation cave constructed • Zhongdian Center exhibition hall furnished

410

作者 ———————————— 劉鋆
攝影 ———————————— 黃效文
譯者 ———————————— 翁瑞麟
發行人 ——————————— 劉鋆
美術設計 —————————— 胡發祥
責任編輯 —————————— 王思晴
出版者——依揚想亮人文事業有限公司
經銷商———聯合發行股份有限公司
新北市新店區寶橋路235巷6弄2樓
電話 ———————— 02-29178022
印刷 ———— 禹利電子分色有限公司
初版一刷———— 2016年11月／精裝
定價 ———————————— 1200元
ISBN

國家圖書館出版品預行編目(CIP)資料
山/海/經：黃效文與探險學會
/ 劉鋆著；黃效文攝影
-- 初版. --
[新北市]：依揚想亮人文, 2016.11
面；21x28 公分
ISBN 978-986-93841-2-4(精裝)

855   105019553